DUMPLIN'

DUMPLIN'

JULIE MURPHY

THORNDIKE PRESS
A part of Gale, a Cengage Company

Farmington Hills, Mich • San Francisco • New York • Waterville, Maine
Meriden, Conn • Mason, Ohio • Chicago

GALE
A Cengage Company

Recommended for Young Adult Readers.
Copyright © 2015 by Julie Murphy.
Dumplin' Series.
Thorndike Press, a part of Gale, a Cengage Company.

ALL RIGHTS RESERVED
Thorndike Press® Large Print The Literacy Bridge.
The text of this Large Print edition is unabridged.
Other aspects of the book may vary from the original edition.
Set in 16 pt. Plantin.

LIBRARY OF CONGRESS CIP DATA ON FILE.
CATALOGUING IN PUBLICATION FOR THIS BOOK
IS AVAILABLE FROM THE LIBRARY OF CONGRESS

ISBN-13: 978-1-4328-6535-1 (hardcover alk. paper)

Published in 2019 by arrangement with HarperCollins Children's Books,
a division of HarperCollins Publishers

Printed in Mexico
1 2 3 4 5 6 7 23 22 21 20 19

For all the fat bottomed girls

Find out who you are
and do it on purpose.

— Dolly Parton

ONE

All the best things in my life have started with a Dolly Parton song. Including my friendship with Ellen Dryver.

The song that sealed the deal was "Dumb Blonde" from her 1967 debut album, *Hello, I'm Dolly.* During the summer before first grade, my aunt Lucy bonded with Mrs. Dryver over their mutual devotion to Dolly. While they sipped sweet tea in the dining room, Ellen and I would sit on the couch watching cartoons, unsure of what to make of each other. But then one afternoon that song came on over Mrs. Dryver's stereo. Ellen tapped her foot as I hummed along, and before Dolly had even hit the chorus, we were spinning in circles and singing at the top of our lungs. Thankfully, our love for each other and Dolly

9

ended up running deeper than one song.

I wait for Ellen in front of her boyfriend's Jeep as the sun pushes my feet further into the hot blacktop of the school parking lot. Trying not to cringe, I watch as she skips through the exit, weaving in and out of after-school traffic.

El is everything I am not. Tall, blond, and with this impossible goofy yet sexy paradox going on that only seems to exist in romantic comedies. She's always been at home in her own skin.

I can't see Tim, her boyfriend, but I have no doubt that he's a few steps behind her with his nose in his cell phone as he catches up on all the games he's missed during school.

The first thing I ever noticed about Tim was that he was at least three inches shorter than El, but she never gave a shit. When I mentioned their vertical differential, she smiled, the blush in her cheeks spreading to her neck, and said, "It's kinda cute, isn't it?"

El skids to a stop in front of me, panting. "You're working tonight, right?"

I clear my throat. "Yeah."

"It's never too late to find a summer job working at the mall, Will." She leans against the Jeep, and nudges me with her shoulder. "With me."

I shake my head. "I like it at Harpy's."

A huge truck on lifts speeds down the lane in front of us toward the exit.

"Tim!" yells Ellen.

He stops in his tracks and waves at us as the truck brushes right past him, only inches from flattening him into roadkill.

"I swear to God!" says El, only loud enough for me to hear.

I think they were made for each other.

"Thanks for the heads-up," he calls.

We could be in the midst of an alien invasion and Tim would be like, "Cool."

After he's made it across the parking lot, he drops his phone into his back pocket and kisses her. It's not some gross open-mouth kiss, but more like a hello-I-missed-you-you're-as-pretty-as-you-were-on-our-first-date kiss.

A slow sigh slips from me. If I could avert my eyes from all the kissing people ever, I'm positive that my life would be at least 2 percent more fulfilling.

It's not that I'm jealous of Ellen and Tim or that Tim steals Ellen away from me or even that I want Tim for myself. But I want what they have. I want a person to kiss hello.

I squint past them to the track surrounding the football field. "What are all those girls doing out there?" Trotting around the track are a handful of girls in pink shorts and matching tank tops.

"Pageant boot camp," says Ellen. "It lasts all summer. One of the girls from work is doing it."

I don't even try not to roll my eyes. Clover City isn't known for much. Every few years our football team is decent enough for play-offs and every once in a while someone even makes it out of here and does the kind of thing worth recognizing. But the one thing that puts our little town on the map is that we're home of the oldest beauty pageant in Texas. The Miss Teen Blue Bonnet Pageant started back in the 1930s and has only gotten bigger and more ridiculous with every passing year. I should know since my mom has led the planning committee for the last fifteen years.

Ellen slides Tim's keys from the front pocket of his shorts before pulling me in for a side hug. "Have a good day at work. Don't let the grease splash you or whatever." She goes to unlock the driver's-side door and calls over to Tim on the other side, "Tim, tell Will to have a good day." He pops his head up for a brief moment and I see that smile

Ellen loves so much. "Will." Tim may have his face in his phone most the time, but when he does actually talk — well, it's the kind of thing that makes a girl like El stick around. "I hope you have a good day." He bows at the waist.

El rolls her eyes, settles in behind the wheel, and pops a fresh piece of gum in her mouth.

I wave good-bye and am almost halfway to my car when the two speed past me as Ellen yells good-bye once more over Dolly Parton's "Why'd You Come in Here Lookin' Like That" blasting through the speakers.

As I'm digging through my bag, looking for my keys, I notice Millie Michalchuk waddling down the sidewalk and through the parking lot.

I see it before it even happens. Leaning against her parents' minivan is Patrick Thomas, who is maybe the biggest douche of all time. He has this super ability to give someone a nickname and make it stick. Sometimes they're cool nicknames, but more often they're things like *Haaaaaaaa-nah,* pronounced like a neighing horse because the girl's mouth looks like it's full of . . . well, horse teeth. Clever, I know.

Millie is that girl, the one I am ashamed to admit that I've spent my whole life looking at and thinking, *Things could be worse.* I'm fat, but Millie's the type of fat that requires elastic waist pants because they don't make pants with buttons and zippers in her size. Her eyes are too close together and her nose pinches up at the end. She wears shirts with puppies and kittens and not in an ironic way.

Patrick blocks the driver's-side door, him and his rowdy group of friends already oinking like pigs. Millie started driving a few weeks ago, and the way she zips around in that minivan, you'd think it was a Camaro.

She's about to turn the corner and find all these jerks piled up around her van, when I yell, "Millie! Over here!"

Pulling down on the straps of her backpack, she changes her course of direction and heads straight for me with her smile pushing her rosy cheeks so high they almost touch the tops of her eyelids. "Hiya, Will!"

I smile. "Hey." I hadn't actually thought about what I might say to her once she was here, standing in front of me. "Congratulations on getting your license," I say.

"Oh, thanks." She smiles again. "That's really sweet of you."

I watch Patrick Thomas from over her shoulder as he pushes his finger to his nose to make it look like a pig's snout.

I listen as Millie tells me all about changing her mom's radio presets and pumping gas for the first time. Patrick zeroes in on me. He's the kind of guy you hope never notices you, but there's really no use in me trying to be invisible to him. There's no hiding an elephant.

Millie talks for a few minutes before

Patrick and his friends give up and walk off. She waves her hands around, motioning at the van behind her. "I mean, they don't teach you how to pump gas in driver's ed and they really —"

"Hey," I tell her. "I'm so sorry, but I'm going to be late for work."

She nods.

"But congratulations again."

I watch as she walks to her car. She adjusts all of her mirrors before reversing out of her parking space in the middle of the near-empty lot.

I park behind Harpy's Burgers & Dogs, cut across the drive-thru, and ring the freight doorbell. When no one answers, I ring again. The Texas sun pounds down on the crown of my head.

I wait as a creepy-looking man wearing a fishing hat and a dirty undershirt rolls through the drive-thru and recites his painfully specific order down to the exact number of pickles he'd like on his burger. The voice on the speaker gives him his total. The man eyes me, tilting down his orange-tinted sunglasses, and says, "Hey

16

there, sweetcheeks."

I whirl around, holding my dress tight around my thighs and punch the doorbell four times. My stomach is squirming with discomfort.

I don't *have to* wear a dress to work. There's a pants option, too. But the elastic waist on the polyester pants wasn't quite elastic enough to fit over my hips. I say the pants are to blame. I don't like to think of my hips as a nuisance, but more of an asset. I mean, if this were, like, 1642, my wide birthing hips would be worth many cows or something.

The door cracks open and all I hear is Bo's voice. "I heard you the first three times."

My bones tingle. I don't see him until he opens the door a little wider to let me in. Natural light grazes his face. New stubble peppers his chin and cheeks. A sign of freedom. Bo's school — his fancy Catholic school with its strict dress code — let out earlier this week.

The car behind me at the drive-thru backfires, and I rush inside. My eyes take a second to adjust to the dim light. "Sorry I'm late, Bo," I say. Bo. The syllable bounces around in my chest and I like it. I like the finality of a name so short. It's the type of name that says, *Yes, I'm sure.*

A heat burns inside of me as it rises all the way up through my cheeks. I run my fingers along the line of my jaw as my feet sink into the concrete like quicksand.

The Truth: I've had this hideous crush on Bo since the first time we met. His unstyled brown hair swirls into a perfect mess at the top of his head. And he looks ridiculous in his red and white uniform. Like a bear in a tutu. Polyester sleeves strain over his arms, and I think maybe his biceps and my hips have a lot in common. Except the ability to bench-press. A thin silver chain peeks out from the collar of his undershirt and his lips are red with artificial dye, thanks to his endless supply of red suckers.

He stretches an arm out toward me, like he might hug me.

I drag in a deep breath.

And then exhale as he stretches past me to flip the lock on the delivery door. "Ron's out sick, so it's just me, you, Marcus, and Lydia. I guess she got stuck working a double today, so ya know, heads up."

"Thanks. School's out for you, I guess?"

"Yep. No more classes," he says.

"I like that you say classes and not school. It's like you're in college and only go to class a couple times a day in between sleeping on couches or" — I catch myself — "I'm gonna go put my stuff up."

He presses his lips together, holding them in an almost smile. "Sure."

I split off into the break room and stuff my purse in my locker.

It's not like I've ever been extra eloquent or anything, but what comes out of my mouth in front of Bo Larson doesn't even qualify as verbal diarrhea. It's more like the verbal runs, which is gross.

The first time we met, when he was still a new hire, I held my hand out and introduced myself. "Willowdean," I said. "Cashier, Dolly Parton enthusiast, and resident fat girl." I waited for his response, but he said nothing. "I mean, I am other things, too. But —"

"Bo." His voice was dry, but his lips curled into a smile. "My name's Bo." He took my hand and a flash of memories I'd never made jolted through my head. Us holding hands in a movie. Or walking down the street. Or in a car.

Then he let go.

That night when I replayed our introductions over and over in my head, I realized that he didn't flinch when I called myself fat.

And I liked that.

The word *fat* makes people uncomfortable. But when you see me, the first thing you notice is my body. And my body is fat. It's like how I notice some girls have big boobs or shiny hair or knobby knees. Those things are okay to say. But the word *fat,* the one that best describes me, makes lips frown and cheeks lose their color.

But that's me. I'm fat. It's not a cuss word. It's not an insult. At least it's not when I say it. So I always figure why not get it out of the way?

TWO

I'm scrubbing down the counter as two guys and a girl walk in. Work is so slow that I've damn near wiped the enamel off. "What can I get y'all?" I ask, without looking up.

"Bo! Starting point guard for the Holy Cross Bulldogs!" yells the guy on the right in an announcer's voice with his hands cupped around his mouth.

When Bo doesn't immediately appear, both boys bark his first name over and over again. "Bo! Bo! Bo!"

The girl situated between them rolls her eyes.

"Bo!" yells Marcus. "Get out here so your friends will shut up."

Bo rounds the corner as he stuffs his visor into the back pocket of his pants. He crosses his arms over his puffed-out chest. "Hey, Collin." He nods to the girl. "Amber. Rory." He leans back against the counter behind us, widening the space between him and his friends. "What're y'all doing on this side of town?"

"Field trip," says Collin.

Bo clears his throat, but says nothing. The tension between them vibrates.

The other guy, Rory, I think, studies the menu on the counter. "Hey," he says to me. "Could I get two dogs? Mustard and relish only."

"Uh, yeah." I punch his order into the computer as I try not to let my eyes wander.

"Been a long time," says Amber.

How is that even possible? There are maybe thirty people in each graduating class at Holy Cross.

Collin drapes his arm over Amber's shoulder. "Been missin' you at the gym. Where you been lately?"

"Around," says Bo.

"Do you want a drink with that?" I ask.

"Yeah," says Rory, and holds a fifty-dollar bill in front of my face.

"I can't break anything bigger than a twenty." I point to the small handwritten sign taped to the front of my register.

"Bo," says Collin, "all I've got on me is plastic. You think you could do Rory a solid and make some change?"

For a moment, there's this dead silence that sinks. "I don't have my wallet on me."

Collin smirks.

Amber, the Amazing Eye-Rolling Girl, reaches into her pocket and drops a ten on the counter.

I make change and tell Rory, "Your order will be out soon."

Collin tilts his head toward me. "What's your name?"

I open my mouth to answer, but —

"Willowdean. Her name's Willowdean," says Bo. "I gotta get back to work." Bo heads for the kitchen and doesn't bother turning around as his friends call for him to come back.

"I like the facial hair," says Amber. "It suits you." But he's already gone.

She stares me down, and all I can do is shrug.

At home, I walk around to the back and let myself in through the sliding glass door. The front door's been jammed for years. Mom always says we need a man to come over and fix it, but my aunt Lucy always said it was the perfect excuse to not have to answer the front door. And I tended to agree with her.

My mom is sitting at the kitchen table, still in her scrubs and with her blond hair piled high on top of her head, watching the news on her portable TV. For as long as I can remember, she's always watched her shows in here because Lucy was almost always on the couch in the living room. But it's been six months now since Lucy's funeral, and she's still watching her shows in the kitchen on her portable television.

Mom's shaking her head at the news anchors when she says, "Hey, Dumplin'. Dinner's in the fridge."

I drop my purse on the table and grab the plastic-wrapped plate. The last few days of school mark the start of pageant prep season, which means my mom is on a diet. And when my mom is on a diet, so is everyone else. Which means dinner is grilled chicken salad.

It could be worse. It has been worse.

She clicks her tongue. "You've got a little breakout there on your forehead. You're not eatin' that greasy food you're selling, are you?"

"You know I don't even like burgers and hot dogs that much." I don't sigh. I want to, but my mom will hear. It doesn't matter how loud the TV is. It could be two years from now and I could be away at college in some other town, hundreds of miles away, and my mom would hear me sigh all the way from home and call me to say, "Now, Dumplin', you know I hate when you sigh. There is nothing less attractive than a discontent young woman."

There are, I think, lots of things wrong with that sentiment.

I sit down to eat and liberally spread salad dressing across my plate, because on the eighth day God created ranch dressing.

My mom crosses her legs and points

her toes, examining her chipped pedicure. "How was work?"

"It was fine. There was some old guy catcallin' from the drive-thru. Called me sweetcheeks."

"Awww," she says. "Well, that's kind of flattering if you think about it."

"Mama, come on. No, that's gross."

She flips the dial on her TV, turning it off. "Baby, trust me when I say that the man market narrows as you age. No matter how well maintained you are."

This is not a conversation I want to have. "Ron was out sick."

"Bless his heart." She laughs. "You know he had the biggest crush on me in high school."

At least once a week since I took the job, she brings this up. When I first applied during Thanksgiving break, Lucy told me she always suspected that it had been the other way around. But the way my mom tells it, every guy in town had a thing for her. "Everyone wanted a piece of Clover City's Miss Teen Blue Bonnet," she slurred one night after a few glasses of wine.

The pageant is my mother's single greatest accomplishment. She still fits into her dress — a fact she won't let anyone forget, which is why as head of the pageant committee and the official hostess, she takes it upon herself to squeeze into the dress as a yearly encore for all of her adoring fans.

I feel the weight of Lucy's cat, Riot, settle in on top of my feet. I tap my toes and he purrs. "I saw a bunch of girls doing some kind of pageant boot camp after school."

She grins. "I tell you what. The competition gets stiffer every year."

"What about you? How was the home?"

"Oh, you know, just one of those days." She flips through her checkbook and massages her temples. "We lost Eunice today."

"Oh no," I say. "I'm so sorry, Mom."

Once a year, like Cinderella, my mom's life is glamorous. It's the life she expected to live. But for the rest of the year, she works as an orderly at the Buena Vista Ranch Retirement Home, where she does exotic things like dole out daily prescriptions, feed the elderly, and wipe their asses. Eunice was one of my mom's favorites. She always confused her for one of her sisters and whispered childhood secrets in her ear every time my mom bent down to help her up.

"She had her after-lunch ambrosia and closed her eyes." She shakes her head. "I let her sit there for a minute because I thought she was napping." She stands and kisses the top of my head. "I'm going to bed, Dumplin'."

"Night."

I wait for the sound of her door clicking shut before I bury my dinner in the trash can beneath one of those free newspapers. I grab a fistful of pretzels and a soda before running upstairs. As I pass Lucy's closed door, I linger for a moment, letting the tips of my fingers brush the knob.

THREE

"I think I want to have sex with Tim this summer," says Ellen as she plucks a cube of cheese from her lunch spread and pops it into her mouth. El has been "considering" having sex with Tim every Friday for the last year. Seriously, before the start of every weekend we debate the pros and cons of Ellen and Tim finally doing it.

"That's weird." I don't look up from my notes. I'm not a bad friend. But we've had this conversation so many times. Plus, it's the last day of school and I have one final left. I'm trying to cram and El is not because she's done with all of her finals.

With her mouth full of candied pecans, she asks, "Why is it weird?"

"Quiz me on this." I pop a few grapes

29

in my mouth and hold out a study sheet dissecting the branches of the government. "Because it's not like a wedding. It's not like, 'Ohh, I like summer colors. I'm gonna do it over the summer so that I can properly coordinate my lingerie with my most preferred season.' You should do it because you want to."

She rolls her eyes. "But summer's like a time of transition. I could come back to school a *woman,*" she says, sparing no dramatics.

I roll my eyes back at her. I hate talking to talk. If El was actually going to go through with it, I'd have crawled over the table to have a nose-to-nose conversation with her about every detail. But she never goes through with it. I don't get how she can talk about the *possibility* of sex so much.

When she sees that I haven't taken the bait, she glances down at the paper. "The three branches of government."

"Executive, legislative, and judicial." I decide to give her a crumb. "Plus, having sex doesn't make you a woman. That is so freaking cliché. If you want to have sex, have sex, but don't make it this huge thing that carries all this weight. You're setting yourself up for disappointment."

Her shoulders sink and her eyebrows pinch together. "How many senators and representatives serve in Congress?"

"Four hundred and thirty-five and one hundred."

"No, but yes. You got it backward."

"Okay." I repeat the numbers under my breath. "And it doesn't matter what time of year it is as long as it feels right. Right? I mean, winter is cool, too, because you're all like, 'Oh my God, it's so cold. Body heat.' "

She laughs. "Yeah, yeah. You're right."

I don't want to be right. I don't want El to have sex before me. Maybe it's selfish, but I don't really know how to handle her doing something I haven't. I guess I'm scared I won't know how to be her friend. I mean, sex is serious business, and how can I navigate her to places I've never been?

I want to tell her that she should wait. But she and Tim have been dating for almost a year and a half and she still blushes every time she talks about him. I don't know how to measure love, but that seems like a good place to start. And I don't know that I'd be asking her to wait for any other reason than me.

As I look over my review, Millie walks down our aisle of tables with a trayful of food and her best friend, Amanda Lumbard, not far behind. Millie and Amanda together are basically one giant moving target that says MAKE FUN OF US.

Amanda's legs are uneven, so she wears these thick corrective shoes that make her look like Frankenstein. (At least according to Patrick Thomas.) When we were kids and she didn't have her shoes yet, Amanda just limped around, her hips swiveling up and down with each step. She never seemed bothered, but that didn't stop people from staring. The nickname thing is pretty lame if you think about it. Frankenstein was the doctor, not the monster.

Millie waves, and I quickly lift my hand as she walks past us.

El smirks. "New friend?"

I shrug. "I feel bad for her sometimes."

"She seems happy to me." El asks me a

few more study questions as we finish our lunch. "What system is in place so that no part of the government becomes too powerful?"

"Checks and balances."

"So, hey, how was work last night? How's Private School Boy?"

I twist the loose wire from the spine of my notebook around my finger. "It was good." I glance down at my cafeteria lunch. "He's good."

I want to tell her about his shitty friends and his new facial hair, but I'm not sure how to bring it up without sounding like I'm a total nut who saves his nail clippings in a jar underneath my bed. Last night I had to recount my register three times because he kept walking by.

"I like Sweet 16 and all, but I'm kinda jealous that you work with guys, too." She drops her half-eaten carrot into her plastic bag and seals the zipper. "I still can't believe we're not working together."

El would never let me forget that I'd ruined our after-school job plans by taking the position at Harpy's. But if she didn't intuitively get that I didn't really want to work at a store where I couldn't even fit into the clothes, then I didn't want to bother explaining it to her. "Why do you care about working with other guys? You're the one who just told me you wanted to do it with Tim."

She shrugs me off. "It'd be fun is all."

We finish lunch, and I take my government final. And that's it. Tenth grade is over. The parking lot is all primal cheers and tires screeching. But I don't have it, that sense of progress. Instead, I feel stuck, waiting for my own life to happen.

FOUR

My mom's car is in the driveway when I get home from my last day of school. As I slide my car into park and pull the e-brake, I lean my head against the headrest. I love my car. Her name is Jolene and she is a 1998 cherry-red Pontiac Grand Prix, given to me by Lucy.

Inside I follow the sound of rustling upstairs to Lucy's room, where my mom's teal ass is wiggling in the air. Teal because she's been wearing the same designer tracksuit that an ex-boyfriend gave her six years ago. She calls it her "loungewear" and, second only to her Miss Teen Blue Bonnet crown, it is her most prized possession.

"I'm home," I say, panic creeping into my voice. "What are you doing in here?"

She stands upright and exhales, pushing hair off her forehead. Her face is red with heat and the blond wisps around her forehead have curled into ringlets. "The funeral home finally got that urn we ordered, so I called it a half day. Thought I'd come home and get a head start on all this."

I drop my backpack in the hallway and take a few steps into the bedroom. "A head start on what?"

Mom plops down on the bed next to a stack of housedresses, all starched and hung on Lucy's yarn-covered hangers. "Oh, you know, clearing Luce's stuff out. God, she was a pack rat. You can barely open her drawers. You know, I found your grandmother's wedding veil. I've been looking for that thing for ages."

My lips twitch into a smile. "Oh yeah?"

Mom claimed ownership of my grandmother's wedding gown while she was in hospice. It never would have fit Lucy, so there was never really any argument. Except for the veil. The veil could fit anyone. They fought over it for months until Lucy's nerves had worn so thin that she gave up. Then a few years ago, the thing went missing.

36

It was my mom who was always harping on her, but this sort of feels like maybe Lucy got the last word.

It wasn't like that all the time. The two of them weren't always at odds with each other, but those moments stand out more in my memory than the Friday nights I would come home and find them both giggling on the couch over their favorite old movies.

"So what are you going to do with all this stuff?" I ask.

"Well, I guess I'll be donating it. You know how hard it is for women of size to find clothing, so I'm sure someone will greatly appreciate it."

"What if I want some of it? Not to wear. Just to keep."

"Oh, Dumplin', you don't want these old muumuus. And all that's in the dressers are underwear, slips, and newspaper clippings."

I know I should be over Lucy being gone. It's been six months now. And yet I keep expecting to see her on the couch with Riot in her lap or doing her crossword puzzles in the kitchen. But she's not. She's gone. And we don't even have any pictures of her. The reality of her body wasn't something she liked having reflected back at her in the form of a photograph.

It scares me. Like, if I can't hear her or see her, I will somehow forget her.

At the age of thirty-six, weighing in at four hundred and ninety-eight pounds, Lucy died. She died alone of a massive heart attack, while sitting on the couch, watching one of her shows. No one saw her die. But then again, no one outside of this house really saw her live. And now there's no one here to remember her. Not in the way she'd want to be remembered. Because when my mom thinks of Lucy, she only remembers how she died.

That's why the idea of my mom disassembling her room like a traveling exhibit takes this echo of pain and turns it into something new and fresh.

Mom pulls open the drawer on the nightstand and begins to sort papers into different stacks. I can see her mind working. Keep, toss, maybe. Some days I wonder which pile I fall into.

"Can you just not?" I ask. "This is her room."

My mom turns to me with this incredulous look on her face. "Dumplin', this is an entire room that we're allowing to collect dust. And pageant season is here. I'm going to be hard at work all summer. It'd be nice to have a room to sew costumes and create set pieces without the whole house being overrun."

"A craft room?" The words are bitter on my tongue. "You're wanting to turn Lucy's room into a craft room?"

She opens her mouth, but I don't stick around long enough for her to respond.

At Harpy's, Bo is at work behind the grill with his earbuds in. I lift my hand to wave at him as I walk by. "Happy summer, Willowdean," he says a little too loud. His lips are sticky and red and something I would very much like to taste.

Kissing Bo. The thought embarrasses me. I want to melt into a puddle to be washed down the kitchen drain.

Up front, Marcus is already at his register.

"You beat me here," I say.

"Tiff's been dropping me off early because of practice."

Marcus and I have always sort of been extras in each other's lives. He's a year ahead of me, and we've gone to school together since we were kids. I know him in the same way you know your best friend's cousin: by name and face. When I started at Harpy's, it was nice to work with someone I at least recognized, and now I guess we're friends. He and Tiffanie, the captain of the softball team, started dating at the beginning of the year and in a matter of weeks their lives had fused together like a set of suction cups.

"How'd you do on your finals?" Marcus asks.

I shrug and glance back to catch Bo watching us from behind the heat lamps. He doesn't look away. My stomach turns. "I was there," I say. "That should count for something. What about you?"

"Good. Studied with Tiff. She's visiting colleges this summer."

I understand that life after high school

40

is probably something I should be thinking about, but I can't picture me in college and I don't know how to plan for something I can't imagine. "What about you? Are you going to look at schools, too?"

He twists his visor to the side and nods thoughtfully. "I guess." The bell above the front door rings back and forth as a few guys from school file in. As we're waiting for them to look over the menu, Marcus gazes past them and out the front window, and says, "My girl's gettin' out of this town and all I know is I'm going with her."

Clover City is the type of place you leave. It's love that either sucks you in or pushes you away. There are only a few who really make it out and stay out, while the rest of us drink, procreate, and go to church, and that seems to be enough to keep us afloat.

Since we close late on Fridays and Saturdays, my mom is asleep by the time I get home. Once I've turned off all the lights and have locked the back door, I tiptoe down the upstairs hallway and double-check that she is asleep. Light snores curl out from beneath her door as I let myself into Lucy's room, careful to avoid any creaking floorboards, and begin to search through my mother's piles.

There is plenty of junk and stacks of newspaper clippings about people and places I will never understand. I hate that there are things — trivial things, like why she needed a newspaper clipping about a cookbook author who'd be visiting the library — that I never knew to ask Lucy about.

Her funeral was the worst. And not just for the obvious reasons. Half of Clover City showed up because what the hell else is there to do? I guess they all expected to see her folded into a casket like some kind of cautionary tale. But the sad truth was that we couldn't afford the more expensive wide casket. So, despite my mother having a total melt-down over her inability to give her older sister a "proper funeral," Lucy was cre-mated.

But I don't like to remember her fu-neral. I like to remember things like the time she took me to my first dance class when I was in third grade. My leotard barely stretched over my protruding belly and my thighs touched no matter how hard I begged them not to. I was too fat. I was too tall. I didn't look like all the other girls waiting to go into class.

Since I refused to get out of the car, Lucy came to sit in the backseat with me. "Will." Her voice was smooth like warm honey. She tucked a loose hair behind my ear and handed me a tissue from the front pocket of her housedress. "I've wasted a lot of time in my life. I've thought too much about what people will say or what they're gonna think. And sometimes it's over silly things like going to the grocery store or going to the post office. But there have been times when I really stopped myself from doing something special. All because I was scared someone might look at me and decide I wasn't good enough. But you don't have to bother with that nonsense. I wasted all that time so you don't have to. If you go in there and you decide that this isn't for you, then you never have to go back. But you owe yourself the chance, you hear me?"

I only stuck with it for the fall, but that didn't seem to be the point.

In Lucy's sock drawer, I find a small box of cassette tapes — all Dolly Parton. I choose one at random and put it in the stereo on her nightstand. I lie back on her bed and listen with the volume turned down so low it sounds like a murmur. Lucy loved Dolly probably more than anything. And I guess Ellen and I do, too.

Mrs. Dryver is maybe the best-known Dolly Parton impersonator in this part of Texas. She's got the petite physique and voice to match. Since Lucy was the vice president of a regional Dolly Parton fan club until a few years ago, their paths crossed on a regular basis. It's hard for me not to believe that my friendship with Ellen wasn't somehow fated long before we were born, back when Dolly was still a poor nobody in Tennessee. Like El was some kind of gift that Lucy had always meant for me.

It wasn't just the look of Dolly that drew us in. It was the attitude that came with knowing how ridiculous people thought she looked, but never changing a

thing because she felt good about herself.
To us, she is . . . invincible.

FIVE

Summer vacation doesn't have the same effect it had on me when I was a kid. When El and I were in elementary school, Lucy would take us to Avalanche Snocones. With syrup dripping down our hands, we'd sit in the dim living room with the ceiling fan whirring on high while Lucy flipped through channels until landing on the trashy talk shows that my mother would never let us watch.

But the first weekend of summer passes like it's nothing special. On Monday morning I wake to find my phone blinking.

ELLEN: SWIMMING. NOW. SUMMER. SO. HOT.
ELLEN: NOW.
ELLEN: NOW.

I can't help but smile when I see her text. Ellen lives in a non-gated community with a poorly maintained neighborhood pool. But during the summer, the place is an oasis.

I know that fat girls are supposed to be allergic to pools or whatever, but I love swimming. I mean, I'm not stupid. I know people stare, but they can't blame me for wanting to cool off. And why should it even matter? What about having huge, bumpy thighs means that I need to apologize?

When I pull into El's driveway, I find her sitting on her porch in her bikini with a towel wrapped around her waist.

Our flip-flops smack against the sidewalk as we walk the three blocks to the pool, and even though it's only ten in the morning, we are dripping (or as my mother says: *glittering*) with sweat.

"Oh God," El says as we're waiting in line. "There are a shit ton of people here." She crosses her arms over her stomach.

I loop my arm through hers. "Come on."

Because of the crowd we're only able

to stake out one lawn chair. El unwinds the towel from her waist and rushes off to the pool. I yank my dress over my head, kick my shoes away, and speed walk on my toes.

El sinks down to her shoulders as the water laps against my waist and the cool relief of it makes my eyes roll to the back of my head. Ahh, now it's summer.

We float around on our backs like starfish and it reminds me of when we were kids and we'd go under water with our goggles on and scream secrets to each other. Except that there were no secrets between us then and it was mostly things we already knew. "CHASE AN-DERSON IS SO CUTE!" El would say. "I STOLE TEN DOLLARS FROM MY MOM'S WALLET!" I would scream.

I let myself float until my shoulder brushes up against the side of the pool and I feel a shadow hanging over me. Opening my eyes a sliver, I see a little boy squatting at the edge of the pool. His lips make the shape of words.

I stand and noise bleeds into my ears, almost giving me a brain freeze. I squeeze my eyes shut for a quick second. My head feels like it's been shrink-wrapped. "What?"

The boy's red swimming trunks are dripping wet, leaving a pool of water beneath him. "I thought you were dead," he says. "And you're all red." He stands and, without ceremony, walks away.

I touch my cheeks and the water from my fingers drips down my face like drops of rain against a dry, cracked earth. I have no idea how long I'd been floating for. Looking around for El, I find her sitting on our lawn chair, talking to a girl and a guy. I take my time moving to the shallow end in the hope that they'll leave, but after a few minutes of stalling, they haven't budged.

Bracing myself, I race out of the pool. El sits at the foot of our lawn chair while a girl I've never met sits at the other end with a boy behind her, like they're riding a motorcycle and she's the one driving.

"Hey," I say.

There's this split second where El says nothing and this other girl stares at me with this how-can-I-help-you-do-you-need-something-you-can-leave-now face.

"Guys, this is my best friend, Will." El

turns to me. "This is Callie. And her boyfriend . . ." Her voice drags for a second and she snaps her fingers.

"Bryce," says Callie. Bryce nods from behind her. He's got those total douche glasses on, the ones that coaches wear that almost look like *Star Trek* glasses. His hands grip Callie's shoulders and I can tell they're the type who is always touching.

"Nice to meet y'all," I mumble.

El glares at me.

It's not that I don't like new people. It's just that, in general, I do not like new people. And this is maybe the thing El dislikes most about me. For as long as I can remember, she's tried to drag a third wheel into our perfect little mix. Maybe it makes me a total grouch, but I don't need another best friend. And I especially don't need this girl who can't seem to stop staring at me like I'm some kind of car wreck.

El scoots over for me to sit next to her, but I stay where I am. "So, Callie's entering the pageant."

Bryce squeezes Callie's shoulders and

she lets out a shrill giggle. "Yeah," she says. "My sister was a runner-up a few years ago. Guess you could say it's in my genes."

"Good for you." My voice is thick and bitter even though I really don't mean for it to be.

El forces a smile. "Callie's actually doing that pageant boot camp we saw after school last week."

I actually don't know what she expects me to say to that. This whole conversation is a flashing sign that reads DEAD END.

"Uh, Callie," says Ellen. "You know Will's mom runs the pageant."

Football players are gods in the South. And cheerleaders aren't too bad off either, but down here, the females who reign supreme are beauty queens. Unfortunately, though, being the tubby daughter of Clover City's most cherished beauty queen doesn't win me much street cred.

Callie uses her hand to block out the sun as she looks up at me. "Wait, that's your mom?"

"Yeah." If I could change only one thing about my mom, it would be the pageant. In fact, I'm sure that my whole life would fall together like a set of dominoes if I could delete that one annual event from my existence.

Callie laughs. "You're not entering, though, are you?"

I wait for a second. Two. Three. Four. Ellen says nothing.

"Why wouldn't I?" Obviously, I would never enter that depraved popularity contest. But still. What kind of shithead makes that assumption?

"It seems like you're not that type of girl. Like, not in a bad way."

I am suddenly reminded of how small my bathing suit is. The leg holes cut into my hips and the straps dig into my shoulders. Anxiety creeps through me like twisting vines.

"But," Callie says, "Bekah Cotter is going to be some serious competition. Girl is as all-American as they come."

The need to escape pulls at my feet.

And, of course, Callie is using my dress as a beach towel so that her precious skin doesn't touch the hot plastic seat.

I turn to Ellen. "I'm going to run back to your house to use the bathroom." I slide my feet into my flip-flops and grab the first towel I see before walking off as fast as I can.

"Is something wrong?" I hear Callie ask in the kind of way that says, *What's her problem?*

"But they have bathrooms here!" El calls over the crowd.

The towel barely fits around my waist. I don't care. I keep on walking.

A car of boys passes by me and honks.

"Oh, fuck off!" yells El from behind me.

I turn. In nothing but her swimsuit, she jogs down the sidewalk with my dress and bag in her arms.

"I've been trying to catch up to you!" she says.

I open my mouth to speak, but remember that I'm mad at her. I keep walking. We don't fight. I know that best friends are supposed to fight, but El and I never get into it. Sure, we argue over dumb stuff like TV shows and which Dolly look is the best, but never anything real. Yet I'm so mad that she left me out there to dry with that Callie girl. She said nothing.

Maybe I'm making a bigger deal of this than it is. Maybe it's the type of thing only I noticed. Like, how when you have a pimple and you think it's the only thing anyone else sees when they see you.

But then there was the way Callie looked me up and down. Like I was some kind of abomination. The truth is that I'm mad I felt uncomfortable to begin with, because why should I? Why should I feel bad about wanting to get into a pool or standing around in my swimsuit? Why should I feel like I need to run in and out of the water so that no one has to see the atrocity that are my thighs?

"Will! Freaking wait! Jesus Christ."

Not bothering to stop, I say, "I need to head home."

"Can you tell me what happened back there? You turned into a total psycho. What was that?"

I stop because I've reached El's house and now that my feet have nowhere else to go, it's like I can't stop my mouth from talking. "What was that?" I yell back at her. "That was you leaving me out in the pool by myself. You abandoned me out there. And who the hell was that twiggy bitch?" As soon as it's out of my mouth I regret it. All my life I've had a body worth commenting on and if living in my skin has taught me anything it's that if it's not your body, it's not yours to comment on. Fat. Skinny. Short. Tall. It doesn't matter.

But El only says, "You looked so relaxed! How does leaving you in the pool by yourself make me a shit friend? You're sixteen years old and you're mad at me for leaving you in the pool by yourself?"

I've seen El and Tim argue enough times to know that this is her specialty. She simplifies the situation to the point that whoever's sitting across from her is left feeling foolish. She's the type of person you want arguing for you. Not against you.

I shake my head at her because I don't want to say it out loud. I don't want to say that I'm mad because I was left without my security blanket: her. Or that she should have stood up for me back there.

"And that 'twiggy bitch,' " she says, "is my coworker. You don't have to be her friend, but you could at least be nice to her."

I throw up my hands. "Whatever. It's done. I don't want to argue."

She drops my bag and dress on the trunk of my car. "Fine."

I slip the dress over my head and hand her the towel from around my waist before digging my keys out of my purse. "I'll talk to you later." I walk to the driver's-side door, but she's still standing there.

"Wait," she says. "Come inside."

I sigh through my nose.

"Oh, quit your sighin'. I need your help."

In Ellen's room, I sit down on the floor with my legs crossed. "Lemme hold Jake."

She locks her bedroom door and walks straight to her closet. "Next time. He's shedding."

Like any other sane person, I'd always had a healthy fear of snakes, but then, when we were eleven, El's parents separated for a little bit, and she absolutely lost her shit. To appease her, Mr. Dryver promised her a pet. What he did not expect was for his daughter to ask for a snake.

When she first got Jake, an albino corn snake, he was no longer than a pencil, but I still refused to come over to her house. I couldn't even bear the thought of being under the same roof as him. But then El had her twelfth birthday, and I couldn't miss it. Lucy took me to the pet store so I could see the snakes and she even arranged for me to hold one. When I chickened out, she held the snake instead. I could see her hands shaking, but it still calmed me.

Now I can sit for hours while we watch movies, with Jake weaving in and out of our hands like he's stitching us together.

Ellen pulls a Sweet 16 shopping bag from the depths of her closet. "I need your help deciding."

I pop up on my knees as she empties

lace bras and matching panties all over her bed.

"For Tim." She plops down on the edge of her mattress. "I want to look good."

I hold up a sheer pair of purple underwear by my pinkie. "You bought all this stuff at work?"

"Callie helped me pick out some of it, but I need you to narrow it down so I can return the rest."

"Oh." I want to ask her if she told Callie that this was for her first time. We sift through the pile. Pink, white, black, red. Even green. Of course she told her. I know I'm making this into something more than it is. I don't have the monopoly on Ellen-Tim sex conversations, but it feels like a betrayal.

"Okay," I say, "white is out. You're a virgin, which is cool. I mean it wouldn't be uncool if you weren't, but what I'm saying is you don't need to look like something that shouldn't be defiled. I mean, the whole point is to get defiled, right?"

"Right." Her voice is definitive as she plucks out the white bra and pantie.

"Should I have gotten, like, legit lingerie?"

I shake my head. "I think this is definitely the way to go. It says, 'I'm ready to have sex' without putting too much pressure on Tim."

"I would die without you. Just straight up cease to exist."

A smile grows on my face. "The black is too intimidating. I mean, it's super fucking hot, but maybe save it for later."

She stuffs it into the bottom drawer of her nightstand.

"I like the green, but it's not quite right." I bypass nude, red, purple, and blue. "This." I swipe my hand across her bed, pushing aside every other set except for a tan-and-blush-striped set. "It says 'summertime virgin, but not for long.' "

El smacks my arm and then reaches for it. The whole thing is trimmed in lace with little pearl buttons as accents. She holds the set close to her chest and slides down on the floor next to me. I turn around and sink to the ground.

She rests her head on my shoulder. I love how we smell after the pool. Like chlorine and sweat. The scent of summer. "Tonight. We're gonna do it tonight," she says.

Six

After leaving Ellen's, I am drained and the idea of taking fast-food orders all night feels impossible.

I tiredly pull my Harpy's cap on over my head and tug my ponytail through the back as I take my place on the register.

"Hey, hey, Will," calls Marcus from the condiment bar. "Lookin' kinda toasty. You get some sun?"

"I guess."

"You're a little on the late side."

I check my rolls of coins to see if I need to run to the office for change.

"Hey, I'm thinking of pulling together a betting pool for the pageant. You think you could get me some inside intel when the time comes?"

I shake my head and slam my register shut.

"What?" Marcus asks. "You don't talk anymore? Strong and Silent back there rubbing off on you," he says, referring to his self-given name for Bo.

I take one deep breath as I check the to-go bag supply underneath the register. "It's been a long day. Need some space."

Marcus mumbles something about PMS and to my surprise, from the kitchen, Bo says, "Why can't she just be having a shitty day? You don't need to make up some bullshit reason why."

Ron lets out a low whistle from his office.

Marcus laughs. "Damn."

"Maybe she saw your face," says Bo, "and she knew the day was a lost cause."

He winks at me from the service window. I whip my head around and smile.

I keep my hands busy in between customers, stocking and restocking napkins and condiments. Bo listens to his music, but with only one earbud in instead of two. Marcus is on his phone all night and, from what I gather, is arguing with

Tiffanie via text.

Bekah Cotter, with her long, golden hair and compact curves, comes in with a huge group of friends and they sort of camp out with fries and fountain drinks. Callie's right. Bekah will enter the pageant, and she'll probably win. She's one of those pretty girls you try so hard to hate. But she's nice and kind of talented. Well, if you count baton twirling as a talent.

Bo's on dining room duty, and when he makes the rounds with the cordless vacuum, Bekah is quick to pick up some spare trash from the surrounding tables. She says something to him. Nothing I can hear. But he smiles, and it's hard not to feel like I've swallowed a handful of rocks. I don't get why we call it a crush when it feels more like a curse.

The bell above the door rings, and in walk Millie and her friend Amanda with the corrective Frankenstein shoes. Millie wears a light yellow T-shirt and shorts set with little heart-shaped gems glued to the collar of her top. I wish there was a way for me to tell her all the ways she makes her life harder than it needs to be without me coming off as a bitch.

Her forehead is damp with sweat, but her smile is unflinching. "Oh, hey, Will! I didn't know you worked here."

Amanda nods, appearing to be quite impressed. She wears soccer shorts and a T-shirt with a picture of her little brother in his Little League uniform silk-screened to the chest. Like the type of shirt you see parents wear to their kids' big games.

"I bet you get tons of free food," Amanda says, and hikes her thumb back toward where Bo stands in the dining room. "And the sights aren't so bad either."

I shake my head, trying not to laugh. "Uh, yeah. I do all right."

They take their order to go, and Amanda hangs back for a little too long to check out Bo as he walks to the kitchen.

I take my break after Marcus and Bo. When I open my locker to grab my lip balm, I find a red sucker. It's one of those fancy ones that sits in the wooden stand at the grocery store checkout. I twist my lips back and forth for a moment before sliding it into my pocket, trying hard to play it cool in case he's somehow watching.

When I was a kid, we used to decorate shoe boxes at school and use them as Valentine's Day mailboxes. We'd leave them on our desks all day. I never liked for anyone to see me check my box. It wasn't that I was scared of not getting any valentines. Everyone gave each other cards. It was required. But it was that I always hoped for more. I wanted to be the girl with a special card signed *Your Secret Admirer.*

It may not be a note in a shoe box, but it still makes my heart feel like it's made of springs.

As I unwrap the sucker, I think about texting Ellen, but turn my phone facedown when I can't decide what to say. I slump down in my chair and savor my candy. She could be having sex *right now.* She could be an official non-virgin and I wouldn't even know it.

I wonder if she talked to Callie after I left. She's probably done it. She'd know what to say to El. After I finish my sucker, I chuck the stick and the wrapper in the trash can. I stuff my phone in my bra and as I'm passing through the kitchen, my boobs buzz. I stop right there to check my phone before I go up front.

ELLEN: kinda nervous. will call you later.

ELLEN: like, after.

ME: you're going to be a total sex kitten. meoooooow.

ELLEN: you're the best. maybe I can stay over tonight at your house and talk. xo

My sticky lips break into a faint grin. I look up to see Bo staring at me as I put my phone back in my bra, only to realize two seconds too late how awkward it might look to be stuffing your hand down your shirt in front of the guy you like.

I've been stared at a lot in my life. Enough to know that when someone gets caught staring, instinct says to look away. But Bo keeps on lookin', like he's got nothing to be ashamed of.

Color floods my cheeks. I wipe the back of my hand across my lips and start my closing duties up front.

Ron lets Marcus leave a few minutes early at the end of the night because Tiffanie is waiting and she's pissed about something. Sitting in his office, Ron finishes the end of the night paperwork while Bo mops up the kitchen and I scrub down all the countertops.

"Watch out," he says. "I just mopped behind you."

I step lightly, careful not to slip, and wash the grease from my hands using the big industrial sink.

All my jobs are done, but I find myself keeping busy while Bo finishes the floors. I fill the sink for him so that the mop can soak overnight, how Lydia likes it.

"You two head on home," calls Ron. "I'll see y'all later."

I rush to my locker to grab my things, like I'm scared Bo might leave without me or something. I follow him out the back and he holds the door open for me so that I have to duck beneath his arm. Which doesn't even smell bad, by the way. How can he spend the night flipping burgers and not smell like a fast-food menu?

As we walk to our cars in silence, his

hand accidentally brushes mine and I wonder what it might feel like if he caught it, letting our fingers entwine.

Standing at my car, I look over the hood and say, "Thanks for the sucker."

He doesn't turn, but tilts his head up to the sky. "Good night, Willowdean."

SEVEN

Without me even having to ask, El gives me every gory detail of losing her virginity. They did it in Tim's bedroom because his mom was out of town visiting his grandma, and his dad, a police officer, was working the late shift.

We lay nose to nose in my bed with the lights off. "How did it feel?" I ask. "Not it, but like, how did it make you feel?"

She closes her eyes for a second. "I felt . . . in control. Like, of my life." She opens her eyes. "And loved. But I feel funny, too."

"How do you mean?"

"We did this grown-up thing. This really adult thing. But we were still ourselves. We still laughed and made jokes. I expected to feel like this whole new person, but really it was me — plain old me — making this decision that I can never unmake."

I nod. I nod with fervor because pared down to those terms, I understand.

With the tips of her fingers, El touches my cheeks and, for the first time, I notice the sparse tears rolling down my face. She touches her forehead to mine and I don't know who falls asleep first.

Despite pageant supplies swallowing my house, the next few weeks are pretty okay. I work mostly with Ron, but sometimes Lydia. Mondays and Wednesdays are always pie, but it's Fridays and Saturdays that can be killer. Mom hates that we're open until midnight, but there's not much I can do about that.

One Friday night as we're shutting down, Ron walks into the dining room carrying plastic-wrapped towers of cups. "Got new cups," he says, and drops them all on the counter.

"What's wrong with the ones we have now?" I ask.

He tears the plastic from one of the towers and hands me a red cup. Our logo is there, but beneath that in italicized letters it says: *Official Sponsor of Clover City's Miss Teen Blue Bonnet Pageant.* Sometimes I think the pageant is like Christmas, and we just keep trying to celebrate it earlier and earlier until it turns into a year-round event.

"One of those girls on your mom's committee came by, and well, my mama won back in '77. I couldn't pass up an opportunity to support the crown jewel of Clover City."

I feel myself frowning. "So we're just going to chuck all the perfectly fine cups we already have in favor of these?"

He shrugs. "Restock the dispensers before we head out, would ya?"

I always forget how horrible the second half of the year leading up to the pageant is. The thing crowds in around my life, leaving barely enough room for air.

After we're done closing up, Marcus and Ron are in their cars and reversing out of their parking spots before Bo and I are even to our cars.

As I'm unlocking my door — I don't have one of those fancy clicker things —

71

Bo says, "There's a meteor shower to-night. It's a small one."

I throw my bag onto the passenger seat. "How do you know?"

"My stepmom. She's big into stars and astrology."

I know very little about astrology except that my mom's church calls it witchcraft. Without deciding to, I close my car door. "I've never seen a meteor shower."

He nods toward the bed of his truck as the parking lot lights flicker off. "Let's wait for it."

I suck in a breath. This is what it feels like when your life starts happening, I think.

"You got anything for us to sit on back there?"

He turns on his radio and grabs a Holy Cross letter jacket from the cab of his truck. "Use this."

Bo makes a show of closing his eyes as I hoist myself onto his truck. I'm hoping his eyes are actually closed because the word *hoisting* and my polyester work dress do not belong in the same sentence. He offers me his hand, and I'm not ashamed to admit that I pretend to need it.

I'm surprised to know that his fingers are calloused with wear. I like how they contrast against my own skin. Once I'm settled, it's hard to let go.

He winces a little as he pulls himself up.

"Are you okay?"

"Bum knee." He sits next to me, holding his leg straight as he does.

"What's wrong with it? Is it an injury or has it always been like that?"

"A little of both."

"But you're okay?"

He coughs into his fist. "Yeah."

The last lights on the street flicker off. We might live inside the city limits, but every night when this town shuts down, it's hard to forget how secluded we are. We're not off a highway or any major route, so it's the type of place that can only be found by those who want to find it.

Bo glances at the clock on his cell phone. "Should be dark enough to see them."

73

I can easily make out the shape of constellations. "You said your stepmom's into astrology?"

He rubs his knuckles across his chin. "Yeah."

"Your parents are divorced?"

He shakes his head, but says nothing.

"I — I'm sorry for asking. I have the manners of a cat in a box of bubble wrap. Like, it's a problem."

"No," he says. "It's not that. I don't mind talking to you. So don't apologize for it, okay? I just don't do much talking. It takes getting used to."

I lean my head against the rear window of his cab and cross my legs at the ankle. "I, on the other hand, talk like the world will only continue to spin if it can revolve around me."

"I like listening to you talk." He laughs. "It's kinda like Stockholm syndrome. At first it was a little terrifying, but now it's sorta comforting. Like, the world could be ending, but I could come to work and you'd be talking like it's your duty."

"I'm sorry," I say, "but was that some sort of backhanded way of saying that

I'm captivating?"

"Very punny," he says.

I smack his arm. He grabs my hand, not giving it back. The radio behind us crackles out "Creepin' In" — that Norah Jones and Dolly Parton song. And everything in this little town is dark, but I can feel Bo's eyes connecting with mine. "It's starting," he whispers, and finally lets go of my hand.

I let out a shuddering breath I didn't know I was holding in.

"It's a small meteor shower," he whispers. "Sorry it's not more impressive."

I'm still completely taken with it all. Faraway streaks of light split through the sky, leaving traces like a bruise. I shake my head. "No. I've never seen one. I think that makes it special enough, right?"

We both tilt our heads even further to the sky. It's a few minutes before he says, "The first meteor shower I saw was huge. I never wanted it to end."

"Well," I say. "You can't have stuff this good all the time. It would turn you rotten."

He nods. And we sit there for a long time, like this is all some good song on the radio that we can't pause.

"Don't you sort of feel like we're the only people in the world who are seeing this?" I say after a little while, almost scared of ruining the moment.

"I don't know." Bo's voice is a quiet rumble. "My mom died. Five years ago. And I guess I like to think that wherever she is, her sky has meteor showers, too." Each word is a naked patch of him, and I want so badly to add up all the bread crumbs I have and make sense of him.

I wait for some kind of disclaimer from him about his theory being dumb or that he's sorry for being a downer. Because that's what I would say. But there's no apology from Bo. And I like that. I like that he has nothing to be sorry for. I want to tell him that I feel bad about his mom or that I like thinking of Lucy that way, too, but instead I say, "I guess it's an awfully big sky not to share."

EIGHT

The next morning when my mom asks me what time I got home, I lie and say the place was an even bigger mess than normal. My lips twitch the whole time with the memory of sitting in the bed of Bo's truck.

I should call Ellen, I know, and tell her every detail. But I don't want to share this yet. I like the idea of keeping my world in these little compartments where there is no risk of collision.

The Saturday night crowd is pretty brutal. It's always dead from 10:30 to 11:30 and then, as we're getting ready to close, we get one last rush.

Ron's in the back helping with the food and I'm taking orders. Marcus is on drive-thru for the night. The headset barely fits around his bush of hair. Between drive-thru orders, he runs over to help me assemble trays of food, but still the line is consistently ten deep.

I've stopped even bothering to look up from my register until I hear, "Oh my God. I totally forgot that Ellen said you worked here."

My shoulders slump as I recognize the voice.

Callie leans across the counter and says, "I am so sorry, but those uniforms are the worst."

"Welcome to Harpy's Burgers & Dogs. How can I help you?" I ask.

Her boyfriend, Camdon or Brandon or whatever his name is, tosses Callie his wallet and says, "Gotta take a leak."

They exchange a kiss — which, I mean, why? Is he going to drown in the toilet? — and Callie looks back at me with a sympathetic smile. "Okay, so could we get a number one with a Dr Pepper. No tomato and extra grilled onions. Swap those fries for tater tots, too, if you don't mind. And I'll have a burger. No cheese. And a kids' fry." Her smile turns conspiratorial. "Cheating on my pageant diet already. Boys are such a bad influence."

"Ten dollars and seventy-four cents is your total."

"This is probably weird of me to ask, but maybe one day me and El-bell could come over? I would love to, like, just talk to your mom about the pageant and the year she won. Like, in a casual way."

I don't even know this girl and she's elbowing her way through my life like everything is hers for the taking. "I've been really busy," I say, my voice dead-pan.

She squints her eyes at me for a second before smiling and thumbing through her boyfriend's wallet for a twenty. "Holy shit. Did you completely die when" — she lowers her voice — "Ellen told you about her and Tim's *oral* mishap?"

"What?" I *knew* El was talking to Callie and not me about this stuff. I shake the surprise off my face. "Oh yeah. Totally nuts," I say. "Your order will be out soon."

I'm so mad. I knew this would happen. I knew that sex would create a rift be-tween me and Ellen. But more than anything I feel inadequate.

Ron comes out from the kitchen and says, "We're closing up, folks. You either take your food to go or you don't take it at all." I stuff Callie's food in a bag and hand it to her as her boyfriend walks out of the bathroom.

After we've locked the lobby doors and have closed the register, I head to the kitchen to gather up some trash. "I'm taking this stuff out back."

"Give me a few minutes," Bo says. "I'll help."

When he's done and Marcus has turned off the drive-thru lights, Bo follows me out the back door, each of us carrying several bags of dripping trash. As the door is about to swing shut behind us, Bo kicks a rock in between the door and the frame. He drops his trash to the ground and takes mine from me and tosses it over his head and into the Dumpster. He does the same with his bags.

"Thanks." I turn to go back inside.

"Wait." His fingers brush my elbow, and I suck in a breath. "Last night. I liked hanging out with you."

"I know," I say. "I mean, me too." I reach for the doorknob.

"Willowdean." His voice startles me. He's so close I can smell his skin, thick with sweat.

I part my lips to respond, but he leans in, pauses for a second, and pushes my words away when his mouth meets mine. I don't have time to think about his tongue in my mouth and how my tongue is answering his. Not sure what to do with them, I hold my hands at my sides, my fingers balled into a fist. He tastes like artificial cherry and toothpaste. I want to kiss him until my lips fall off.

He pulls away.

My first kiss. It's the fastest thing that lasts forever.

The midnight air is hot and dry, but that doesn't stop me from wrapping my arms around myself. I wait for the words — either his or mine — but nothing comes. The shock I feel is etched into his expression. I run my thumb along my bottom lip and walk back inside. He doesn't stop me.

■ ■ ■ ■

Closing takes forever. The dining room is a mess and so is the kitchen, but I barely notice because my thoughts are absorbed with Bo and my first kiss. My first kiss, which took place behind Harpy's Burgers & Dogs and next to a Dumpster full of day-old trash.

Yet, it was perfect. Every bone in my body aches, like I've been in a car accident and there's nothing physically wrong with me, but still I can feel the impact of it everywhere.

At the end of the night, I'm in my car and pulling out of the exit before Ron's even locked the door behind him.

I roll to a stop at the light on the corner and scrub my hands up and down my face as I try to process all that happened tonight.

A car horn honks and I glance up at the light, but it's still red. I hear a muffled yell to my right.

Bo sits in the neighboring lane, waving his arms, pointing at my window. This isn't even how he goes home. We always turn in the opposite direction. Him, east. Me, west.

The minute I roll down my window, he starts talking. "I'm sorry," he says. "I shouldn't have just" — *kissed you,* my head fills in — "done that. I just —" He glances up, and I watch as he notices the light for the intersecting street turning yellow. "Follow me. Please."

I glance at the clock. It's already 1:35 in the morning.

The car behind him honks. "Please." He drives off and changes lanes so that he's in front of me.

I probably shouldn't follow a guy I only kind of know down a dark road in the middle of the night. Because he could, like, kill me, and then it wouldn't matter if I was fat or if my first kiss had been next to a Dumpster, because I'd be super screwed.

When the road splits and it's me who should be heading right, I veer left and follow a strange boy down a dark road, the sky above us in a deep sleep.

NINE

We drive all the way to the edge of town to the old elementary school that caught on fire a few years ago and has since been condemned.

This is probably one of those red flags. I think maybe I'm missing some kind of self-preservation alarm in my head because this has cautionary tale written all over it.

When we park, I wait for him to get out of his car first. If El were here, she'd tell me to grab a tire iron or to heat up the car lighter, but she's not. I search my front seat for a weapon, but all I've got is an empty jar of peanut butter, a buck thirty-two in change, and some junk mail I forgot to take in the house a few weeks ago. I weigh my keys in my hand for a moment.

Aha! I take my three keys on my ring (car, house, El's) and hold my hand in a fist so that each of the keys is peeking out from between my fingers. I remember seeing this on a self-defense special of *Maury.* Television saves lives.

I feel ridiculous, but whatever.

Bo leans against the hood of his old truck. Along the side is the shadow of lettering, like he bought the truck off someone who'd owned a business.

"So this is creepy," I say, motioning to the school with my non-key-shiv hand. The whole place is singed, but you can still see the definitive structure of a school, except for straight down the center, which is entirely gone. The elements have not done the exposed structure any favors. From here I can see the outline of the playground, entirely dark except for the highlights of the moon. On the entire lot there is only one lone streetlight. We are far outside of its glow.

"Sorry." He's taken off his work shirt — I can see it draped over the bench seat inside his truck — and is wearing his crewneck undershirt. The chain I always notice peeking out from beneath his work shirt carries a patron saint pendant. "I used to go here. Before it burned down. It's the only place on this side of town that I could think to go to at this time of night."

"Oh." I want to ask him what happened with his mom and who his favorite teacher was and if he took the bus or if his parents gave him rides every morning. But I don't. I want. I want. I want.

He starts laughing, and not some quiet chuckle. He's gasping for air. "You come prepared," he says, pointing to my fist.

I hold my self-defense hand up. "Um, you led me to an abandoned elementary school. That has 'I want to kill you and play dress up with your dead body' written all over it."

His laughter subsides for a moment, and he says, "Okay. That's fair. Good on you."

I drop the keys in the pocket of my dress, and kick a few pieces of gravel around. "Just don't kill me."

A smile flickers for a moment before he says, "I shouldn't have kissed you like that. Without asking."

"So. Why. Did. You?" Each word comes out like a drop in an empty bucket.

"You know how when you're a kid and you're having a great day? You like your teacher. Your friends are okay. You don't suck at school. But then you do something that you would never be able to stop even if you saw it coming?"

He sees the confusion on my face.

"Like — like calling your teacher Mom."

I can't hide my horrified expression. "Wait. What? I'm sorry, but did you compare kissing me to calling your teacher Mom?"

He pushes his hands through his hair and groans. "No. Well, yes. But it was like this reaction I had. Like this thing I couldn't control."

"And now you're embarrassed?"

"No, no!" He throws his hands out, like they could wash away his words. "I meant that it felt like I couldn't help it. I'm only embarrassed that I didn't even take the time to read you. That I just did it. And I'm sorry if that's not something you wanted me to do."

"It's okay," I say, mostly because he normally doesn't talk so much and I'm a little mesmerized by it.

He steps forward. "Is it okay as in, 'don't let it happen again,' or . . . was it okay?"

I shrug because the rest of my body is frozen.

He takes another step forward. It's quiet for a moment. This is my chance to step back and stop whatever this is from happening. I feel my self-control slipping.

"Because I think you kissed me back."

My cheeks flood with heat. He's got me there. "It didn't suck. It just wasn't, like, explosions," I lie.

"So, mediocre?"

I bite down on my lips, making them disappear. I take three steps, closing the distance between us.

He props his elbows up against his truck and tilts his head back.

I do the same, and for a moment, we share the sky until I break the silence. "So you kissed me on an impulse?" The tension winding through my muscles eases as I find myself getting more comfortable with him. "But why?" There's still that hum, though. That vibration of adrenaline.

Drizzles of rain splash down on top of us, making the air feel instantly thicker with humidity. Bo glances up, like he might somehow figure out how to make it stop.

"Let's get in the truck." He opens the passenger door for me and I hop inside while he jogs around the front and lets himself in.

We just miss the onslaught of rain. Drops slap angrily at his windshield. It's so loud he almost has to yell. "On a scale of one to ten," he says. "How was it?"

"You're really not going to let this go, are you?"

"I'm kind of an egomaniac."

I feel brave. I am brave. "Maybe you should go for a do-over. Best out of two."

He clears his throat, and my eyes are all on him. "Well, I usually prefer to get it right on the first try, but I'd hate to deprive you." He scoots past his steering wheel, traveling to me. His hand cradles my cheek in his palm. Nodding his head down, his lips nearly meet mine. "You're sure?"

Surprising even myself, I don't answer. I kiss him. I kiss Bo Larson. And when he parts his lips with mine, I don't think about it. Because for the first time in my life, I fit. I fit without any question.

He braces my cheeks with both hands and pulls me even closer to him.

If El even feels one-tenth of this with Tim, then I don't know how she waited so long to have sex, because when Bo's lips move against mine, I can think of nothing outside of us.

His hands travel down to my neck and along my shoulders. His touch sends waves of emotion through me. Excitement. Terror. Glee. Everything all at once. But then his fingers trace down my back and to my waist. I gasp. I feel it like a knife in the back. My mind betrays my body. The reality of him touching me. Of him touching my back fat and my overflowing waistline, it makes me want to gag. I see myself in comparison to every other girl he's likely touched. With their smooth backs and trim waists.

"I'm sorry." His breath is hot and short.

"No," I say. "Don't. Don't be sorry." I'm not that girl. I don't spend hours staring in the mirror, thinking of all the ways I could be better. Me shrinking away from his touch embarrasses me in a way I don't entirely understand.

He shakes his head. "No, I mean, I shouldn't have — I don't think — I shouldn't be dating anyone right now."

I guess what's funny is that until he mentioned it, the thought — the possibility — of us together hadn't even crossed my mind. "Oh." It comes out like a sigh.

"I have a lot of shit going on. And I shouldn't. Or at least I haven't for a while."

I nod.

If any other girl had told me that she'd been told this by a guy, I'd tell her to back it up. To put the brakes on. Because he sounds like a jerk. I just can't think that about Bo. But I guess this is how every girl in the history of the sexes has been played. Because the rules apply to every situation except your own.

I open the door to his truck. "I better

get home." Rain splatters inside the interior.

"It's late." That's it. That's all he has to say.

"I'll see you at work."

It takes 2.5 seconds for the rain to soak through my clothes. My dignity has left the building. I get in my car and speed off out of the parking lot. I turn the volume on the radio up all the way in the hope that it might drown out everything rattling inside of me. Lucy, my mom, Ellen, Bo. Little versions of each of them seem to live inside of me, one louder than the next. The only voice that isn't there — the one I need the most — is my own.

TEN

It is officially too hot to go swimming. Even for Ellen. Jake slithers in and out of our hands as we watch a daytime talk show about a woman who is in love with her brother, but didn't know he was her brother because they didn't grow up together.

"They have got to be lying," I say.

El shakes her head. "No, no, they're weird, but I think they're telling the truth. Plus, why would they lie?"

"Um, because they're gross and because they know it. They probably got caught and needed an excuse or something."

"God," she huffs. "You are such a skeptic. Would it hurt you to believe that not everyone has shitty intentions?"

Jake coils around my wrist. His scales

are smooth from having just shed. "I'm not always a skeptic, but the odds of them telling the truth are practically non-existent. I mean, that's like saying Tim could be your brother."

She's so engrossed in the show that she doesn't answer.

This would be a good time to tell her about what happened with Bo. My mom was already asleep when I got home, but she said she heard me come in after two and that next time that happened she would call my boss. *An unladylike hour,* she called it. It sort of killed me that she automatically assumed I came straight from work. *I WAS MAKING OUT WITH A BOY IN AN ABANDONED PARKING LOT,* I wanted to scream. But that sounds pretty unbelievable. Even to me. And I was there.

I don't know how to form the words to explain to El that not only did I get my first kiss, but it ended up being a full-on make-out session. She'd already be pissed at me for not telling her about my feelings for him in the first place. And even though neither of us said that what happened last night was a secret, it feels like one.

It's stupid, I guess, because El would never think this, but I feel like last night was so completely unfathomable. A boy — a totally hot boy who girls stare at — kissed me, like *really* kissed me. It was the type of kiss that leaves you short of breath. I don't know how to talk about that with my best friend. Not to mention that if I told her about last night, I'd also have to tell her how the night ended. With Bo promising that this would never happen again and with me mortified by the thought of his hands touching my body.

I don't want to tell her any of that, though. As foolish as it is, I want to preserve her good impression of him because I guess a little part of me thinks that despite how last night ended, he and I might somehow still stand a chance.

But a chance at what? At being boyfriend and girlfriend? The idea is so ridiculous to me that I can't even imagine what it might feel like to hold someone's hand in public.

It's not that I feel unworthy. I deserve

my happy ending. But what if, for me, Bo is a high point and, for him, I'm a lapse in judgment?

I need Lucy.

The credits on the talk show begin to roll and El wipes a few stray tears from her cheek. "Oh my God," she says. "Oh my God. That was so sad. They love each other so much and they can't help it. And society will never understand."

"Are you on the rag or something?"

"You're a real shithead sometimes, you know that?" She stands with Jake. "I'm putting him up. You want to hang out for lunch?"

I smile. "I better go home. I want to dig through some of Lucy's stuff before my mom gets home. She started cleaning her room out a few weeks ago."

I follow El to her room as she lowers Jake into his cage. He nestles himself beneath his heat lamp. The light clings to his scales, and he revels in it.

After a few minutes, El says, "Will?"
"Yeah."

"Luce used to wear this bee brooch

when we were kids. Do you remember that? The one she'd wear on her winter coat when she picked us up from school?"

My mouth goes dry. I nod. She wore it on the collar of her winter coat. This was before she was at her largest, but still pretty big. The coat was black and drab and obviously purchased for the sake of utility without any thought of fashion. It's the type of sacrifice you make when you're a bigger person. Her brooch, though, was like the sun peeking through dark clouds. She'd call us her bee-utiful girls and take us for hot chocolate on Mondays, because Fridays didn't deserve all the attention.

It was funny. I used to think of myself as a Monday and Ellen as a Friday. But Mondays and Fridays were just twenty-four-hour stretches of time with different names.

"If you see that brooch — and only if you don't want it — would you mind keeping it for me? Not that I'm, like, owed it or anything, but I always really loved it."

"Yeah," I say. "I'll be sure to look for it."

Since the day she died, I've felt that Lucy was only mine to memorialize and that if I faltered, I'd be letting her down in the worst kind of way. The realization that she wasn't just mine comes as a painful relief.

ELEVEN

I will not kiss Bo Larson. I will not think about Bo Larson. I will not kiss Bo Larson. I will not think about Bo Larson. It's a mantra that repeats over and over again in my head, and whenever I'm by myself, I even say it out loud.

A few hours before I leave for work on Monday afternoon, my mom asks me to fill a prescription for her, because she's scared the pharmacy will be closed when she gets off work.

I drive downtown to Luther & Sons Pharmaceuticals. Because parking is limited, I have to take a spot in front of All That Shines, a jewelry store nearly as old as Clover City, which has been the sole distributor of Miss Blue Bonnet crowns for the entire state of Texas.

The heat clings to my shoulders as I'm

locking my door. "Shit," I mumble. In front of my parking spot and anchored to a bucketful of cement is a sign that reads: CUSTOMERS ONLY.

I double-check, but see no parking, so I take a second to run inside.

Behind the dusty glass case, sitting on a creaking wooden stool, is Donna Lufkin. The Lufkins have such family pride that not even conservative tradition can sway a Lufkin woman into changing her last name when she gets married. Donna, though, never did get married.

Donna is round with a sturdy build. Her cargo shorts are frayed at the edges, and her gardening clogs smell like they've been doing exactly what they were made for. She is the opposite of what you might expect from a person who sells pageant crowns. Sure, she sells other stuff, but it's the crowns that make this place a landmark.

"Willowdean Dickson," she says. "I haven't seen you since —" She stops herself.

"Lucy's funeral," I finish.

She nods, but doesn't try to smile,

which I appreciate more than she will ever know. "Did your mama send you in for something? I just got the new crowns in."

"No, ma'am. Just not a whole lot of parking out there and I was wondering if I could leave my car while I run inside the pharmacy?"

She waves me off. "Hell, those signs don't do a bit of good anyway."

"Thanks," I tell her with one hand on the door.

"You wanna see 'em?"

"See what?"

She grins. "The crowns, of course."

Now this might seem like no big deal, but the cubic zirconia pageant crowns are guarded more safely than the bank across the street. No matter how much I despise this pageant, it's not something I can just say no to.

Donna locks the front door and I follow her through the curtain leading to the stockroom. We have to walk through two offices before she unlocks a tiny closet lined in boxes. Each box is marked with the names of towns from all over the state, but front and center are three labeled CLOVER CITY.

"Wait," I say. "Why do we have three?"

She counts them out on her fingers. "One: the original. Sometimes it goes on display at city hall. Two: the one given to the winner. Three: held in reserve in case crown number two goes missing."

She takes all three boxes and lines them up on her desk. The one given to the winner and the backup are almost identical, but the original . . . well, it looks like the type of thing you'd find in your grandmother's jewelry box. The rhinestones are foggy and the metal tarnished with age, but there's still something so regal about it. I like that it's not too shiny or too prissy like the newer crowns, and yet, it has a presence.

Donna catches me looking at the original. "I like her best, too."

For a moment, the pageant makes sense, and I get why my mom devotes half of her life to it and why most of the girls in this city dream of gowns and spotlights when the sky is heavy with stars. "Do you ever try them on?"

Her cheeks turn the lightest shade of

pink. "Between you, me, and these four walls: once in a while." With great care, she reaches into the box holding the original. "Try it on."

"Are you sure?" With my luck, I would be the person to break the original crown.

She looks directly at me. "You think I look like the type of woman who isn't sure?"

I shake my head.

She situates me in front of the mirror on the back of her door. I hold my breath as she places the crown on top of my head. I know it's just costume jewelry and that none of this is real, but that doesn't stop me from feeling the weight of the crown like a responsibility. I wish Lucy or Ellen or even my mom were here to see me in my red and white Harpy's uniform with Clover City's prized possession resting atop my head.

"Truth be told, I don't think your mama's even tried it on. Best not to tell anyone about this."

I say yes with my eyes, because I'm scared to even nod. "Why are you letting me try it on?"

She shrugs. "Maybe 'cause you don't always have to win a pageant to wear a crown."

I will not kiss Bo Larson. I will not think about Bo Larson.

Marcus called in sick, like he could somehow smell how awkward tonight was guaranteed to be.

The shine of the crown has worn off, and we are slammed. Bo ends up having to come out of his kitchen cave to help me on register. From what I can tell, the only phrases in his vocabulary are: "Dine in or take out?" and "That'll be [insert total]."

Every now and again, our hands brush or we bump into each other. And every touch sends electricity through my veins. But when he gets into an argument with a customer over pickles, Ron tells him to go back to the kitchen.

At the end of the night, Ron sends us all home early and promises to come in tomorrow morning to do the closing checklist. I would protest because my mother taught me that a southern lady always puts up a fight when anyone else volunteers to do the cleaning, but I'm all too ready to be home.

I try to be quick and beat Bo out the door, but with every step I take, he's on my heels.

I have got to find a new job.

My hand is on the door of my car and I'm nearly home free.

"Willowdean."

I turn.

He moves toward me so quickly that I feel like I'm moving, too.

Our noses brush and his lips stop short of mine. My mind's eye has yet to catch up and process that he is here, in my bubble, redefining everything I thought I knew of myself. My discretion. My pride. They're both gone and it's like I've got horse blinders on.

I am kissing Bo Larson. I am thinking of Bo Larson.

For the first time in my life, I feel tiny. I feel small. And not in the shrinking flower kind of way. This feeling: it empowers me.

"I want to kiss you," he says, and with

each word, his lips brush against mine.

I lose all words and, instead, lace my fingers through his hair and pull his lips to meet mine.

■ ■ ■ ■

Two Months Later

■ ■ ■ ■

TWELVE

Standing on my tiptoes to reach the top shelf, I feel my apron fall loose, the tie at my waist coming undone. I glance behind me to my right and then to my left to see Bo grinning.

He winks.

Bo has become the best and worst part of my day.

The watch on my wrist tells me it's 6:02 p.m. Time for my break. I shove the last bag of buns onto the shelf, carelessly crushing them no doubt, and turn to follow him. My feet carry me without my mind having any say. Behind me noise fades and all I hear are the echoes of Harpy's. Orders shouted out. Customers complaining. Marcus whistling. Meat sizzling. It all fades to zero.

Until earlier this summer I'd never

known anything like this. It's the moment right before I grab the bag of trash piled on top of the crates in the back and kick the already ajar back door open.

It's the second before I drop the leaking plastic bag next to the Dumpster as Bo Larson crushes me up against the metal door and nothing but his lips touch me. It's that millisecond of no hands. Just lips.

Then, like a dam releasing water, his hands roam and the moment is gone. And I remember how uncomfortable his touch on my soft body makes me feel.

When it hits, my mind turns back on like it's on a timer. Every moment feels rehearsed because as things between us progressed, I spent more and more energy trying to predict what he might do next. And now I know. I know that when he inches me toward the short Dumpster with the lid and holds his hand around my waist that he wants to lift me up. So I always reach back and hoist myself up, because the thought of him trying to lift me and failing makes me cringe every time. When his fingers trail down my chest and across my stomach, I suck in.

Which is stupid because it never makes any difference in pictures and I doubt it does now.

It's in those moments that I'm a shadow of the person I was. The woman Lucy had meant for me to be.

But when he says my name, it's always a surprise. "Willowdean," he says, and each letter tickles all the way down to my toes.

Every night, when Ron sends us home, we walk to our cars, a few feet separating us. When we've slipped into the darkness outside the red glow of Harpy's, Bo brushes his fingers against mine before walking around to his driver's-side door. "Follow me."

I don't even bother nodding because I will and he knows it.

He starts his car and I start mine. This thing between us is a roller coaster. The brakes might be out and the tracks might be on fire, but I can't make myself get off the ride.

THIRTEEN

I've learned so much about Bo. And yet he's still a mystery. Like the thing with red suckers. He used to have anger issues as a kid, so his mom would give him a red sucker and say, *If you're still angry after you've licked this lollipop gone, you can scream and kick and shout all you want.* But then there were things like his necklace, which he always tucked back into his undershirt every time it fell out. If I ever asked about it, he'd shrug it off and tell me it was some saint pendant from Holy Cross.

The old elementary school has become what I guess could be called "our spot." I was such a wreck that first time we came here. But this old, half burned down elementary school has become our sanctuary.

I park beside him, pulling my keys from the ignition and opening my door all at once. He reaches over and pushes the door open for me.

I hop up into his truck.

He kisses my nose. Reaching beneath his seat, he pulls out a red gift bag creased with use and drops it onto the dashboard. "Happy birthday."

My birthday was three days ago. I didn't tell anyone at work. Not because I didn't want people to know, but because telling people (mainly Bo) meant that there was pressure for them to do something for me. And that's not how Bo and I have worked. There are no strings. No responsibilities. "How'd you find out?"

He shrugged. "Heard Ron tell you happy birthday."

"Can I open it?"

"No," he says. "That's your gift. That bag is all you get."

Rolling my eyes, I yank the bag from the dash. My stomach is in a hissy fit of nerves. The weight of the bag sinks into my lap. One small bag to fit an entire summer history.

He clears his throat. "I didn't have any tissue paper."

His stare heats my skin. I close my eyes and pull a random item from the bag.

"A Magic 8 Ball," he says.

A smile spreads across my face. I feel silly. "Well, I'll never feel the burden of decision again."

"Keep going," he says.

So I do. A metal Slinky, Silly Putty poppers, and a bag of saltwater taffy.

Bo blows bubbles into the Silly Putty and uses it to strip the ink from his owner's manual while I weigh the Slinky, letting it slide back and forth in my hands, like Jake.

"Thank you," I say. "You totally didn't have to get me anything."

He shrugs and scans the spread of items between us. "You forgot something." He reaches for the bag. "Close your eyes."

I do.

I feel his hands against my cheek as he slides a pair of glasses over my nose. My hair catches in a hinge, but he's careful to be sure the glasses are tucked over my ears.

"Okay," he says. "Open."

He slaps the rearview mirror in my direction and I see a bright red pair of heart-shaped glasses. The lenses are dark and tinted and it takes a moment for my eyes to recognize myself. I pull my hair from where it's caught.

They're supposed to be funny. I get that. But I love them. They're transformative. In the mirror, I see a girl I don't think I've ever met. "They're great," I say and immediately feel silly. They're cheap dollar-store glasses. Something he probably threw into his basket as an afterthought.

His body leans into me as he presses his lips against mine. My entire body softens against his weight.

"You should go home," he whispers between kisses.

I nod. We keep on kissing.

I stay in the parking lot with Bo for far too long, but am lucky to find that my mom is dead asleep with her door closed when I get home. All summer I've made up reasons and excuses for why I've had to "work" later than normal. She's not too pleased by any of it, but never questions me. Plus, she's been sewing banners, interviewing new judges, and finding sponsors for the pageant, which means she's checked out of parenthood completely for a few months.

Lucy's door is closed, like it has been for the last two months. I brush the door handle as I walk by, but don't open it. Ever since that day my mom started cleaning out her room, and we got into an argument, she's let it sit, like she's forgotten about it. I don't ever bring it up for fear that she'll pick up right where she left off.

As I'm falling asleep, my phone buzzes.

ELLEN: liar

Shit. She knows. I mean, it's not like she hasn't been keeping secrets from me, too. I can't hear her talk about Tim without remembering what Callie said that night in Harpy's about their "oral mishap." I know it was something small and that in the long run, it's nothing, but

I can't help but wonder what else she's not telling me. Now, I'm her virgin friend who doesn't get it.

ELLEN: you freaking liar. you were supposed to come to tim's after work.

Oh, thank baby Jesus. I'd completely forgotten about Tim's party, but she'll let that go much easier than she would if she'd found out about me and Bo.

My phone buzzes again.

ELLEN: you missed some real D-R-A-M-A

I flip over on my side and send a quick reply to say sorry and that we'll catch up in the morning before scrolling down to my next message.

BO: night

I sigh. I don't even care that I do.

FOURTEEN

I wake up to the doorbell.

Before rolling out of bed, I stop to check my phone.

ELLEN: outside lemme in

I pull on an old pair of gym shorts and trip down the stairs to answer the back door. I find Ellen's face pressed to the glass as she makes fart noises with her mouth.

This whole summer has been this bizarre, new territory for us. We've always been opposites. Lucy always said that the greatest friends have nothing and everything in common all at once. *Y'all girls are different versions of the same story,* she would say. But these last two months, I feel like we're being pulled in different directions, and I'm the only one who seems to notice.

I slide the door open and for a second, El lets her face slide with it. She stumbles through the door and into a chair at the kitchen table. "Jesucristo, Will. I was melting out there."

I check the time on the microwave. "It's early," I mutter, slumping into a chair. I don't add that I was out until two in the morning with Private School Bo.

"It's payday for me. It is never too early to get paid." She stands and opens a few cabinets, trolling around for some junk food. "And it's eleven. So not early. Your mom would shit her panties if she knew you slept in this late."

"Whatever." Crossing my arms on the table, I bury my head. "You're happy. Why are you so happy?"

"I don't know. I'm alive. Life doesn't suck. Schools starts in a week." She slams a cabinet door shut and whirls around. "And maybe I am not so sucky at having sex anymore?"

"There can't be much to it, right?" But really the entire thought of THAT is terrifying.

"You'll see someday." She bobs her head.

Nope, I think. *Virgin for life. Team hymen here to stay.*

"Get dressed. Time to get paid!"

"There are some chips in the pantry," I say, and head for the stairs. "Give me forty-five minutes."

"You're lucky I've got trash TV on your DVR to catch up on," she yells after me.

I take a quick shower and towel dry my hair before twisting it into a sloppy bun. I glance through my closet, and decide it's too hot to try and instead opt for gym shorts and an old T-shirt from one of my mom's pageants.

"All right," I say, jogging down the stairs. "I gotta fill up Riot's dry food —"

"Already did," replies Ellen.

I loop around to the kitchen to find her stowing away a half-eaten bag of chips.

"My mom's going to think I ate all of those," I tell her. She wouldn't ever say anything, but she wouldn't need to.

"Your mom needs to get laid." Riot hops up onto the kitchen counter and

Ellen indulges him with a solid behind-the-ear scratch. "Took my mom's car and I basically drove here on fumes. Can we take your car?"

"Yeah. Sure." El follows me out the back door and as I'm locking the gate behind us, I ask, "And what does getting laid have anything to do with my mom and chips?"

She shrugs and pulls on the door handle, waiting for me to unlock the car. Ever since Ellen lost her virginity, she thinks she's Dr. Ruth — that old lady sex doctor — and the cure to everything is more sexy times. It drives me crazy. I'm a virgin. I'm not stupid.

I unlock the car doors and slide in behind the wheel, both our lips whistling involuntarily as we're saturated with stale heat.

"Oh God," says El, "roll down the mother flippin' windows."

What I've always found ironic about Sweet 16 is that they don't go above a size twelve. I mentioned this to Ellen once, but I think she pretended not to hear.

The first time I went into Sweet 16 with El, I made a pointed effort to not be a total jerk about how uncomfortable I felt. But after coming in with her every Thursday to pick up her paycheck, I can say with confidence that I have enough evidence to form a scientific opinion of this place.

My Scientific Opinion: This place is a shithole and all the girls who work here are vapid skanks who treat me like El's charity case friend.

The walls of Sweet 16 are covered with mirrors and mannequins with jutting hipbones, low slung jeans, and tiny T-shirts that say things like, *I'm too pretty to do homework.* I follow Ellen through the crammed racks, careful not to knock over the whole goddamn store with my hips.

"El-bell!" squeals Callie, who I've decided is my sworn enemy. "Mo-mo," she calls behind her with one hand cupped around her lips, "El-ephant is here to pick up her moolah!" She reaches into a box below the register and hands El a pristine white envelope. "Hi, Willow!" Leaning toward me, she adds, "Oh my God. Pageant boot camp has been a miracle. I almost have a six-pack. But, like, I don't want to get too muscle-y. That'd be gross."

"It's Willowdean," I mutter, but she doesn't hear me because Morgan, the too-old-to-be-in-college-too-young-to-be-your-mom store manager, floats out from the break room. She's tall and willowy, all the things El is on her way to becoming. "Oh my gosh, we got all this super cute stock and I am capital D dying over here. Seriously, my paycheck is, like, gone. Bills who?"

El laughs. Which pisses me off, because how was that funny?

"El," she continues, using *my* nickname for *my* best friend, "you've got to come back and try this stuff on."

El turns around and glances back at me.

I nod her on despite myself.

She claps her hands together. "Okay, but I have to be quick!" She turns back again. "I promise this'll be fast. I bet none of it'll fit me anyway."

I smile with my lips closed. Following

her to the back, I stop, frozen in place by the raise of Morgan's brow. "Sorry," she says, her lips twitching into a smile. The kind of smile that says you're not really sorry. "Employees only."

"You okay out here?" asks El, her eyes catching mine.

"Yeah. Just hurry."

She skips to the back behind Morgan as Callie stations herself behind the counter, swaying her hips to the beat of the poppy music playing on the speakers as she pretends to read some kind of sales report.

Squeezing between the racks, I think about how miserable this place must be on a Saturday. Callie turns the music up when the song changes to a hyper-techno beat and I take that as my cue to sneak into one of the fitting rooms. Each stall is made of a wall of curtains and consists of one little stool. The only mirror is the communal mirror outside. That's got to be a pain in the ass — to have to leave your room every time you want to see how something looks on you.

On the other side of the curtain, hangers scrape against metal. "Where'd El's friend go?" asks Morgan.

"I don't know," says Callie. "I didn't see her leave, but she'd be pretty hard to miss."

"Aw, be nice," says Morgan. And it seems like it should be a kind thing to say, but her voice is laughing.

"Did El-bell find anything?"

"She's trying on some dresses in the break room."

More hangers-against-metal scratching. "It's really sweet of El to hang out with that girl, but all she does is follow El around like a puppy dog. I mean, get your own life, right? It's sad."

That's all it takes for my whole body to tense with anger. I yank the curtain aside and trip over the fabric as I do.

Their four eyes follow me to the bench outside of Sweet 16, where I slouch down as low as I can so that I can't see the two of them anymore.

If I could unzip my skin and step outside of myself, I would.

All the display windows in the mall are packed with formals for homecoming

125

and pageant season. Across from Sweet 16 is a store called Frills with a glittering baby blue gown on display. Written across the window, in shoe polish, it says, *Clover City can only have one Miss Teen Blue Bonnet. Make it you. Check out our one-of-a-kind dresses!*

I hate how much I despise the pageant, but it feels like a disease. And the whole town is sick.

"Hey."

I twist around to find Bo sitting down on the back side of the bench.

"What are you doing here?" I ask, like an accusation.

"Shopping with my stepmom and brother." He points to the shoe store next to Sweet 16. "I saw you sit down on the bench. My little brother's been trying on basketball shoes for forty-five minutes." He smiles and dips his chin down into his chest. "What are you doing here, Willowdean?"

I want to touch him. I want to reach over and kiss his face hello. But I don't. Because we're not pressed into darkness behind Harpy's or huddled together in the cab of his truck and because even though neither of us has ever said so, we are a secret.

"Here with my friend. She's picking up her paycheck."

"Ellen?"

I nod. I've talked about El with Bo, but in a past tense kind of way. I don't know how to explain the strange gap that has formed between us, so it was easier to talk about her in the same way I talked about Lucy. Like she was a thing from a life before him.

I notice that he's wearing an old basketball tournament T-shirt and a pair of basketball shorts. "It's weird seeing you without your uniform on. I almost didn't recognize you."

"Oh, I recognized you." He stretches his legs out along his side of the bench. And his legs. I've never seen his bare legs. "So where does your friend work?"

I point back to Sweet 16.

His mouth opens and I know that I will forever judge him based on how he reacts to this information, but a voice interrupts him.

127

"Bo," calls a tall, thin woman with shiny chestnut-brown hair cut into long layers. She's too young to be his mom and too old to be his sister.

Bo glances over his shoulder and then back at me. "My stepmom," he whispers.

My face falls slack. I've been dreading the moment when our worlds collide.

Behind Bo's stepmom is his brother. He's as tall as Bo, but his round cheeks tell me he's at least a year younger.

"I let the time slip on by, didn't I?" she says. "Sammy's got basketball at one. Time to hop to it." Her eyes travel to me, sitting there on the other side of the bench. "And who is this?"

"Ma'am." I stand and hold my hand out to her because I'm southern and even if my mom says otherwise, I do have manners.

"This is Willowdean," says Bo. There he goes, saying my full name again. "We work together."

"Willowdean. Well, isn't that a mouthful?"

I half smile, about to say thank you — for what, I have no idea — when Ellen appears next to me and says, "But you can call her Will."

I swallow and nod.

Bo's stepmom's head anchors to one side, like she's just seen the most adorable thing. "And you are?"

"This is Ellen," I answer for her. "My best friend." I take a deep breath. "Ellen, this is Bo. We work together."

Bo gives Ellen a short wave, but she touches his arm and says, "So nice to meet you."

His stepmom smiles. "Aren't you precious?"

I know that Ellen loves Tim. And yet jealousy creeps up my spine, paralyzing me. Over the course of the summer, I have given myself plenty of reasons why I shouldn't tell Ellen about what's been going on with Bo. But no matter how I spin it, I know that, to Ellen, my not telling her is as good as any lie. Actually, this might be worse.

"I guess y'all must go to Clover City High?"

We nod in unison.

"How wonderful that Bo will have

some familiar faces on his first day!"

"Excuse me?" I blurt. There are many things wrong with the relationship between Bo and me. But the one thing that's right is that outside of work, our worlds do not intersect. And for as long as that's the case, it's easy to pretend that I am a normal girl, making out with a normal boy.

"Yeah, Bo and Sammy won't be back at Holy Cross this year." She frowns a little. "It'll be good. Change is good, right, boys?"

Neither respond. Bo's lips press together in a thin line and I know that he knew this whole summer and didn't tell me. "Loraine," he says to his stepmom, "we better get going. Sam's got practice." He scoops up their bags and his stepmom leads the way, her hips swaying from side to side. And that's it. Not even a gaze or a shrug. Nothing that might promise me an explanation.

Anger boils all the way up from my toes to my cheeks.

"Seriously!" screeches El. "He is even hotter than you let on."

"Let's go." I storm ahead of her, toward

the parking garage.

"Did you notice that, like, sexy bed-head thing he had going on? And that stubble?"

I noticed. Of course I noticed. But it doesn't matter. Because this is going to have to end. My illusions of our after-school romance are dissolving like vapor.

I had a vision in my head of how I would survive the school year. We would both come to work and leave our real lives at the door. There would be no questions, only us. But there's a reason why Bo didn't tell me he was changing schools. There has to be. And even if there's not, he and I have to be done because I can't let this bleed over into real life.

I won't be ridiculed. I won't be one-half of the couple who everyone stares at and asks, *How did she get him?*

FIFTEEN

All summer I have spent every free evening at home, holed up in my room with my laptop and my summer reading looming on my shelves. But tonight my mother is dead set on me watching television with her while she crafts props for the pageant's opening dance number.

I sit on the coach, opposite where Lucy always sat, with my laptop nestled on top of a pillow. My mom has moved her crown, which sits in a glass case, from the center of the mantel to make room for Lucy's urn. It's a small thing, but it's enough to remind me that my mom is more than the pageant.

She uses wax paper to iron some kind of patches onto denim tablecloths, for the pageant luncheon, I'm sure. "Now, I saw a commercial for this special the other day."

She flips through channels until she lands on MTV.

The camera follows a girl from behind, walking down the street of a snow-covered neighborhood. She's wide and her stomach hangs over her jeans. I immediately know where this is going.

I hate seeing fat girls on TV or in movies, because the only way the world seems to be okay with putting a fat person on camera is if they're miserable with themselves or if they're the jolly best friend. Well, I'm neither of those things.

A voice-over kicks in atop footage of the girl doing perfectly normal human things, like, walking and eating. "Sixteen-year-old Priscilla of Bridgeport, Connecticut, may have a sweet tooth, but that doesn't mean that sixteen has been so sweet. Teased and ridiculed her entire life, Priscilla is done carrying the extra weight. She doesn't know it yet, but we here at MTV have heard her plea." The camera zooms in on her ass, which is the kind of butt that tapers down at the bottom and always makes you look like you have a wedgie. Then the camera cuts away to a purple screen with the title of the show stamped across it like a rejection stamp. **TRANSFORM ME: I HATE MY FAT BODY.**

I glance over at my mom, but she trains her eyes down on her project. I want to get up and lock myself in my room, but I sort of want to know Pathetic Priscilla's fate, so I decide to stick around. Maybe Priscilla's life is an even bigger mess than mine and I'll walk away feeling like I've at least got it better than this poor girl.

This isn't new territory for my mom and me. She had me on more fad diets than I can list before I even turned eleven. It was always a sore point between her and Lucy. I'd hear the two of them downstairs, arguing back and forth about it long after I should have been asleep.

"She's a child," Lucy would say.

"I want her to be healthy," my mom would retort. "Surely you understand where I'm coming from, Luce? I just don't want her to grow up to be . . ."

"Like me? Just say it, Rosie. You don't want her to grow up to be like your big sister. She sees me every day for Christ's sake. I think my existence is deterrent enough."

"You know what it was like for us when we were kids. You remember."

My mom never talked about her life before high school. She was big. Like me. And it wasn't something she was proud of. But the summer before ninth grade, Mom shed her baby fat like dead skin. Lucy was in eleventh grade by then and she hadn't been so lucky. The dieting eventually stopped when I hit middle school. I don't know exactly what it was, but it could've only been Lucy.

On the TV, Priscilla is ambushed at school by a tiny yet aggressive woman who turns out to be her personal trainer. Despite signing up for the show herself, Priscilla goes into freak-out mode, locking herself in a bathroom stall and crying herself silly. Eventually the trainer comes in and shows her soft side while giving the ultimate pep talk. I mean, seriously, it even got me feeling a little fired up. Over what, I have no idea.

I don't have to look at my mom to know that her eyes are watering. The this-is-your-life-stop-standing-in-the-way-of-your-thinnest-self moment is my mom's favorite part of any weight-loss show.

I zone out for most of the hour, but I can't look away when during a morning workout at the school track, Priscilla's trainer pushes her so hard that she throws up all over the bleachers — just in time for the entire boys' soccer team to bear witness.

After that, Priscilla's trainer moves things to a local gym. But the girl refuses to go inside. The trainer loses it, calling her all kinds of names. "I'll feel so alone," Priscilla says between sobs. "Have you ever walked into a building that is dedicated to being everything you're not? I want to be healthy, but I also want to be happy."

In the end Priscilla loses twelve pounds. Her trainer claps for her at her final weigh in, but you can see the disappointment in her eyes. The credits roll and as they do, the captions tell us that six months later, Priscilla is still committed to a healthy lifestyle but has come to terms with the fact that her weight will be a lifelong struggle for her.

If El were here we'd talk about how ridiculous it was that this was even considered entertainment.

"Well," says Mom, "that was inspiring."

I have nothing to say that she would want to hear. "I'm going upstairs. Are you done down here?"

She takes the remote and switches over to the evening news. "No, no. I've got piles of things to do before tomorrow's pageant board meeting."

"I'm going to bed."

"Night, Dumplin'."

Upstairs, I stand in front of Lucy's door for a moment too long before going to my bedroom. I unplug my phone from the charger and find that I have zero messages from Bo. Plopping down on my bed, I hold the Magic 8 Ball he gave me in both hands. I have too many questions to ask only one, but I shake the ball three times and check for an answer. *Outlook not so good.*

My phone buzzes.

ELLEN: Just got off work. You okay? You were weird after the mall.

I settle for a lie because I've already

told too many to stop now.

ME: I'm fine. Just the pageant taking over my house. Boobs up! Ass out! So annoying.

ELLEN: Gross. Want me to come over?

ME: I think I want to sleep.

ELLEN: Cool. Tim bought massage oils. Is that trashy?

I think about this for a second.

ME: Not unless they smell like cotton candy. Y'all are disgusting. Night.

Sixteen

Yesterday's pulsing anger is now just a sad frustration. I have no reason to think Bo owes me anything.

Kisses behind a Dumpster and in the parking lot of a condemned school don't amount to anything. If that's all that we are — those shadow moments and a bag of gag gifts — then how foolish of me to think I deserved anything of him.

This is the conversation I have with myself on my drive to work.

I drop my stuff in my locker and weave through the kitchen as fast as I can. I take orders as quickly and efficiently as possible, not even bothering to glance up at customers. Bo stares holes into my forehead as he sets sandwiches beneath the heat lamps or covers sandwich wrappers in unnecessary stickers, something that always wins a smile from me. But I stay diligent, with my eyes narrowed on anything but him.

I can feel the change between us, thick and palpable, but Marcus and Ron treat us no differently, because, to them, nothing visible is out of place. My little summer world is caving in on me and I am the only witness. *This is what happens,* I think, *when a secret turns into a lie.*

After the dinner rush, the entire kitchen is a mess, like there was some kind of take-no-prisoners food fights. When Ron asks for a volunteer to restock the condiment bar, I gladly offer.

I wait for the door of the supply room to shut behind me, but when it doesn't, I know why.

"Hey," says Bo.

I don't turn around.

Pulling from different shelves, I begin to assemble a stack of supplies to take out front.

"Hey, listen," he says. "I was going to tell you."

I hear him take a few steps and his breath is on my neck. He covers my hand with his and his skin is dry from the plastic gloves he wears in the kitchen, but still, he absorbs me.

"It never came up." He nuzzles the nape of my neck. His nose presses through the wisps of hair fallen from my ponytail. "Don't be mad."

"I — I can't talk about this right now." I don't even know how to talk to him. Not without our lips pressed together.

He kisses my neck, the soft patch of skin south of my ear.

"Please. Please stop." I yank my hand free and press the boxes of napkins, utensils, and condiments close to my chest and brush past him.

"Willowdean."

I want to take back my name. I want to erase that moment when we first kissed and he took it and made it his.

"Come on," he says, a little too quietly, like he's resigned himself to losing a fight that hasn't even begun.

At the end of the night, I start refilling the salt and pepper shakers. The bell above the door dings, so I let Marcus take it. "Hey," he calls. "Bo, your boy is here."

I peer around the corner to see Collin, the same guy who visited Bo at the beginning of the summer.

"What do you want, man?" asks Bo. He looks exhausted, with dark circles weighing under his eyes.

Collin grins. "Checking in on my old buddy. It won't be the same at Holy Cross without you."

"You'll survive," says Bo.

"Speaking of, Amber says hi. She's doing a lot better. Some distance did her good." Collin shrugs. "A few distractions didn't hurt."

"Good for her," Bo says through his teeth.

"You should come by the courts one night. Hang out on the sidelines or something."

Something tickles my hand. I look down to see I've poured salt all over the table. "Shit."

Both of them turn to me.

Collin smiles. "Ah, I remember you.

142

What was your name again?"

I open my mouth to answer, but —

"Will. Her name's Will," says Bo.

It cuts so deep to hear him call me anything but Willowdean. I leave the salt and pepper there on the counter, and head back through the kitchen to grab the trash. Footsteps follow me.

"Please talk to me," Bo says.

I push through the back door without answering him. Reaching up for the tall Dumpster, I try flipping the lid one, two, three times. He reaches over me and opens the thing on one try.

"We need to talk." He takes the bags from my clenched fists and vaults them over the top.

I drag my sweating palms down my thighs. "About what? How about that girl? Huh? What was I? Your summer rebound?"

He takes a step toward me and I nearly take a step back to restore the balance, but I'm not willing to show any ounce of weakness.

"You weren't a rebound, okay? That's

not what this was. Is. What this is." His voice drops an octave. "But it's not like our relationship is based on communication."

"You could have at least told me you weren't going back to Holy Cross."

He's quiet for a minute, and I take his silence as a concession.

"Why wouldn't you tell me that, Bo? What? Were you hoping I wouldn't notice?"

"No, it's just —"

"It doesn't matter." I sigh. "What are we even arguing over? We make out behind the Dumpster and in an old parking lot. That doesn't really seem like anything worth arguing for."

And then there's the way everything in me turns to shit every time he puts his hands on me. Like, I'm not good enough. Not pretty enough. Not thin enough.

"I used to think that you were misunderstood. That people didn't get you. But I was wrong. You're a real jerk, Bo Larson." I take a step back now, loosening the line between us that's held us taut all

144

summer. I wish I could tell Ellen about this. "And I'm done being your secret."

SEVENTEEN

I barely even glance at my schedule before the first day of school.

I wait outside of second period for El. It's the only class we have in common this semester. The second bell rings, and I'm about to go inside without her when I see her sprinting down the hallway toward me with Tim at her heels.

"So sorry!" she breathes. Tim squeezes her hand as he runs past her and on to his next class.

"What were you even doing?"

Her eyebrows pop up and down as she shrugs.

I shake my head and follow her inside.

There are only two desks left. One behind Callie, El's coworker, who is waving her to come over. And the other is at

146

the long table at the back of the room next to Mitch Lewis.

El turns to me and whispers, "I'm sorry, Will. We'll get here early next class. I promise."

I shuffle to the back of the room to sit next to Mitch.

As I sit down, Mitch pulls his backpack in, so that I've got more space at my end of the table. Mitch is big. He's got a bit of a belly and shoulders wider than most door frames, but people don't look at him and think fat. They think athletic. Which makes sense seeing as he's a defensive tackle for the CCHS Rams.

"Hey," he whispers. His accent is the type of southern accent you hear Hollywood actors use. It's almost charming. "Will, right?"

With my eyes on Mr. Krispin, I nod, like I can't bear to be torn away from his riveting roll call.

"Well, I'd be willing to bet we haven't shared a classroom since the sixth grade."

"Mrs. Salisbury." I smile, surprised that he even remembers. She was the best teacher I've ever had. I remember Mitch because he would ask the silliest questions, like, "Why can't we see air?" and while everyone would snigger underneath their breath, she would answer his question. And her answer would be so smart that you'd start to realize maybe his question wasn't so dumb in the first place.

Mr. Krispin goes through the first day motions and as the bell is buzzing, he says, "I hope none of you struggle with commitment issues. Where you sat today will be your assigned seat for the semester."

As the rest of the class is pushing for the door, El fights the tide to get to me. "I am so sorry," she says.

"It's our only class together," I say. "And we don't even get to sit next to each other."

Callie slips through the crowd and interrupts us. "El-bell, you're heading to C-hall, right?" She turns to me. "Hi, Willow."

I fake smile as wide as my face will stretch.

Ellen squeezes my hand. "I'll catch up with you later, okay?" She's three steps in the opposite direction before she turns and adds, "And hey, I'll talk to Krispin about the seating chart."

I see no evidence of Bo all day long except for his little brother when I pass the freshman hall. Even though I'll see Bo at work tonight, I feel sweet relief as I head for the parking lot in search of Tim's Jeep.

"Will!" I glance up. Mitch's head bobs far above the crowd. "Walk with me!"

I find myself smiling as he catches up to me.

He falls in step with me and says, "So, what do you, like, do?"

I almost laugh, but then I feel Mrs. Salisbury like a little bird on my shoulder. "Besides school?"

"Yeah."

"Well, I work." My shoulders hunch up in a question. "I watch TV?"

"Where do you work?"

"Harpy's. Why?"

He steps in front of me and holds the door leading outside open for me. "Well,

I want to know where I should take you on our date, and I figure I should find out a little more about you before I decide on a destination."

"Our date?" I wait as he holds the door for a stampede of freshman girls.

Manners. Sweet Jesus. He has manners.

"Yeah. The date I'm about to ask you on. So, you'll do me the honor of allowing me to take you on a date?"

"I — Why?"

"Why did I ask you out?"

I nod.

"Well, you're cute. And you remember me from sixth grade."

"Okay." I'm not thrilled by the sound of cute, but it's better than some other names I've been called. "Have you ever asked a girl out before?"

"A few."

"Have any ever said yes?" I stop and turn to him, my hands thrown up in the air. "Wait. No. You know what?" That image of Bo in the storeroom flashes through my memory. I hear him say my name and the thought feels like nothing more than a dead end. "Yes. Yes. I will go on a date with you."

He holds his hand out for a shake and I take it. I expect his palm to be sweaty, but it's not. Like Goldilocks and her third bed. It's just right.

Mitch taps my phone number into his phone and promises to text me so that I can save his. He veers off toward the locker rooms outside of the stadium.

I think this might be a bad idea, but I think a lot of things. And I need to forget Bo. This seems like a good start.

"Will!" snaps Ellen. She speed walks through rows of junior parking, her hips swishing back and forth like those people who do Olympic speed walking. "What. Was. That?"

I shrug.

"You fucker. You gave him your number."

Tim comes up behind her, his phone dangling from one hand. "Wait," he says. "Was that Mitch Lewis?"

Ellen answers before I can think of the words. "Oh, it so was. And this little hooker gave him her number."

"That guy's a beast. I heard scouts have been all over him."

That's the story with every decent football player in Clover City. Every once in a while it turns into more than a story. The only thing that comes close to football is the pageant. The both of them make up the lifeblood of this place. I don't even mean it in a bad way. The pageant and football pull this little town out of itself and turn it into something more. Because when those stadium lights are on or when that curtain parts, we are the best versions of ourselves.

"Doesn't matter how good he is," says Ellen. "He's friends with Patrick Thomas."

"Oh Christ. Not that asshole." I can still see him glaring back at me after school that day when I diverted Millie.

Tim nods. "It's true. They've been friends since we were kids."

We walk toward my car, with Tim trailing behind, buried deep in his phone again.

"So, maybe the seating arrangement in Krispin's class won't be so miserable after all," says El. If she knew about all that had happened with me and Bo, she would be my conscience and tell me that it's too soon. That I need to get over Bo first.

I reach around to the front pocket of my backpack and fish out my keys. "Yeah, I guess, but I'd still rather sit with you," I tell El.

"You guys aren't sitting with each other for second period?"

"No," I say. "Thanks to this one" — I point to El — "we were too late."

"I'm sorry," she says again. "Have I said I'm sorry?"

"Well, at least you have Callie," I tell her.

"Oh, come on. Don't be like that."

"But really, babe," says Tim. "You know she's the most annoying person ever?"

"Y'all need to back off my shit. She's my friend, okay?"

"But we're your only friends," says Tim, a smile curling at his lips. "You don't get to have any other friends." He kisses her cheek.

"Yeah," I pipe in. "Just us." And I almost mean it.

El knocks her shoulder against mine. "I missed you today."

"Me too." Even though she's standing right here next to me, she feels far. Further than I can see.

EIGHTEEN

That night, at work, my phone rings. I leave Marcus at the front, and answer it as I'm walking to the break room. "Hello?"

"Hi. Hey. It's Mitch." The line is dead for a second. "I was calling about that date?" He doesn't sound nearly as confident on the phone. It's kind of endearing, and also sort of like false advertising. But I guess it was pretty sweet of him to do more than text.

"Oh. Right. Of course."

"How about this Saturday?" he asks. "Our first game is on Friday."

"Yeah, that'll work."

"Sure." I can hear him smiling. "Cool."

"Okay, so Saturday. But I'll see you at school before then," I remind him.

"Right. Yes, I'll see you before then. Because of school. And because that would be weird if I avoided you until then."

I laugh. "Right. Yes. Weird."

After I hang up, I walk back out through the kitchen where Bo is leaning up against the cooker with his arms crossed. He chews on his bottom lip, his gaze following me until I turn the corner.

I feel good. It makes me feel good. To be wanted, but not had.

At the end of the night, I walk out with Bo and Marcus since Ron is still doing payroll. Marcus is in his girlfriend's car and gone in a matter of seconds.

Bo says nothing, but waits to pull out as I turn my car on and reverse out of my parking spot.

My car goes over the hump at the exit and my lights flash over the windows of the Chili Bowl across the street. Framed by the window is a huge NOW HIRING sign. Chili may be a southern specialty, but the Official Willowdean Opinion is: looks like dog food, smells like dog food, must be dog food. There is a very long list of things I would do before working there.

Bo passes me. I hold my eyes steady. Straight ahead.

Here I am, waiting to talk to the manager at the Chili Bowl.

The whole place has been built to look like a Lincoln Logs cabin. The walls are covered in mismatched frames holding pictures of Clover City locals from the last sixty years doing all kinds of things like tailgating, drinking beer on the porch, or sprawling out on the grass for the Fourth of July parade.

I slide into a booth to wait for a manager with Harpy's sitting across the street, taunting me.

This is Bo's fault. Everything was fine until fifth period. My day was great. Work had been okay the night before and maybe I was a little too pleased with myself. An okay first day of school. A first date on the books. And an amicable-ish working relationship with Bo.

But then fifteen minutes into World History and in came Bo with a yellow folded piece of paper. A transfer slip.

"Class," said Miss Rubio. "Welcome Bo Larson. He'll be joining us for the remainder of the year."

Millie's best friend, Amanda, who I sit next to, lets out a low whistle.

He sat one row over and two desks ahead of me. As he settled into his seat, he looked over his shoulder and winked right at me.

"Isn't that the guy you work with?" she whispered.

"Yeah." The sinking pit of dread in my stomach left me nauseous.

"How do you get any work done? His butt looks like a peach."

"What?"

"Like the bottom of a peach," she said. "Peachbutt."

After school, I was on a mission. I didn't even stop to wait for El and Tim. I got in my car, slammed the gearshift into drive, and sped out of the parking lot as fast as I could. Miraculously, I did not take down any pedestrians on the way.

So that's what brought me here to the

Chili Bowl.

"You here for the job?" A guy no older than twenty-five with floppy black hair plops down in front of me. "I'm Alejandro."

I nod. "Yeah."

"Pay is shit."

"I need a job."

"Okay." He leans in closer, like someone might hear even though the place is empty. I think he's the anxious type of guy that might work in such a quiet place on purpose. "So here's the deal: Have you been arrested?"

"No."

"You've worked with food before?"

"Kind of. I ran the register at Harpy's."

"Close enough. And, lastly, were you fired from your last job?"

"Nope."

He twiddles his thumbs and takes a few measured breaths. "When can you start?"

And that's my interview.

I lean back in the booth. Outside of Harpy's, Ron sits on the curb, taking a smoke break. I feel like a jerk leaving them like this without any notice, but I can't face Bo four nights a week. "Now," I say.

Ron's door is open. He's sitting there behind his desk in khaki shorts and a CCHS athletics booster club polo.

"Will."

"I — Can we talk?" I push the door open a little further; the hinges creak.

"What's going on, kid?"

I suck in a breath and exhale. "I need to quit."

He presses his lips together as his thick brows furrow. I see the questions on his face, but all he says is, "Did something happen?"

I shake my head. "I'll return my uniform after I wash it."

He nods. "It's no rush."

And just like with Bo, I find myself wishing that he'd put up more of a fight.

Neither of us says anything.

"But thank you," I add, breaking the silence. "For the opportunity."

"Well, I'll miss seeing your face around

here," he says.

I drive the whole way home in silence with the windows rolled down, my thoughts swallowed up by the wind.

NINETEEN

After school on Friday, I head over to El's. We sit at the dining room table, sharing a bag of chips while her mom unpacks scrapbooking supplies. Sprawled out on the table in front of us are snapshots of Mrs. Dryver dressed as all different incarnations of Dolly Parton. After wiping my fingers on my jeans, I study one picture of her in a suede coat with fringe hanging from the sleeves and a long, fitted denim skirt. Her hair is smooth and round like Dolly in the early years.

"I like this one," I tell her.

She rests her hand on my shoulder. "Oh, me too. I think that's my favorite hair. A drag queen out in Odessa styled that wig for me. Took him a week to get it just right."

El picks up a photo of her mom in a

floor-length red sequin gown. "Nice perm, Mom. So chic."

"Ellen Sadie Rose, you wouldn't know chic if it bit you on the asset." She tickles the back of El's neck with her long nails.

Where Ellen is long and lean, her mom is compact and curvy. But you see their connection in the way they twirl their hair or chew on their bottom lips or how they whistle through their straws before each sip.

"Here," says Mrs. D. "You take this one to keep." She hands me a picture of her and Lucy from years ago. They stand in front of a neon sign that reads the hide-away. Behind them is a large, smoke-filled crowd. Looks like some kind of bar or club, but whatever it is, it's somewhere Lucy never would have gone on her own. Mrs. Dryver wears fitted overalls with a tight red shirt underneath while Lucy's in one of her signature sack dresses, but with a touch of blue eye shadow. I'd never seen her wear makeup before. Mrs. D brought out the bravest parts of Lucy. I know Lucy was important to Mrs. D, but for Lucy, Mrs. D was a lifeline.

I slide the picture into the front pocket

of my backpack. I love the photo so much, but it hurts, too. Mrs. Dryver is the perfect Dolly, and it was impossible for Lucy with her thick, pale legs and flat hair not to look sad in comparison. Her smear of blue eye shadow is an unheard call to the person she always wanted to be. No matter how high she held her chin, I can't unsee what she isn't. I feel like a traitor.

"Mom," says El. "How come you never entered the pageant?"

It's something I've always wondered, too. Mrs. D's whole life is basically a pageant on steroids. She would have killed the competition.

She shrugs. "I thought about it. I think every girl in this town does. But I wasn't the same person I am today. I didn't have it in me back then to pretend I felt good enough about myself to enter a beauty pageant."

Her words sink in. I wonder if that's why the pageant has bothered me more this year than in the past. The girls who enter have got to be proud enough of themselves to say they *deserve* to compete. That kind of unflinching confidence makes me uneasy in a way it never has before.

Ellen shoves a handful of chips into her face. "Let's go upstairs."

I take the bowl of chips and follow her to her room. On her bed, we lie in opposite directions with her head at the foot of the bed and mine on her pile of pillows.

"So you quit Harpy's? Out of nowhere?" she asks with her mouth full.

"The Chili Bowl was hiring."

"The Chili Bowl is always hiring," she retorts.

I reach for some chips. "I don't know. I was tired of the uniform."

I guess that's a good enough reason for El because she's quick to change the topic to something much juicier. "So when's your date?"

"Tomorrow."

"You nervous?"

"I guess? But not really."

"Mitch. I never would have guessed," she says. "You really like him?"

"Yeah. I mean, I guess I needed something new." I pull one of her pillows over my head, muffling my words. "I wouldn't have said yes if I didn't like him."

"New? You've never even been kissed." She ties my shoelaces together in a sloppy knot. "He doesn't seem like your type."

My insides are swimming in guilt. I can't tell her about Bo now. It's too late, and there's nothing left to tell. "I don't have a type."

"Not yet you don't."

Later, when I pull up to my house, the first thing I notice is the glowing square that is Lucy's room.

I should sit here for a moment and prepare myself for whatever it is my mom is doing to that room, but I don't. Instead, I tear my keys from the ignition and storm up the walkway to the back door. Riot is rubbing the length of his body against the sliding glass door. The first thing I hear is Olivia Newton-John blaring from the second floor.

I drop my purse on the counter and

Riot runs up the stairs, a few steps ahead of me.

I don't know what I expect to find, but it's not the sight of my mother seated behind a card table with all of Aunt Lucy's furniture pushed up against the walls.

"What are you doing?" I spit at her. The framed Dolly Parton records that had lined these walls for my entire life are stacked at the end of the dresser, and sitting on top of Aunt Lucy's pastel-pink record player is my mom's iPod.

This is the worst-case scenario.

"Well," says Mom, squinting over her sewing machine as she runs a seam. "I've always needed a craft room. We've talked about this. And my bedroom isn't cutting it anymore."

"Your bedroom? You have the whole house."

She pushes her reading glasses up the bridge of her nose. "I know you're upset, Dumplin'. I do. But we can't let this room sit here like a tomb. We've got to move forward. Luce would understand."

I don't understand. "But you moved

everything. Can't you work in here without changing everything? You even took down her records. Why would you do that?"

"Oh, baby, those records are so old. We're going to have to take down this wallpaper because of the squares those things left on the walls."

I pick up as many records as I can carry and take them across the hallway to my room. If I had any free hands, I'd be slamming doors, too. After leaving the records on my bed, I go back for more.

"Dumplin' —"

I whirl around, the musty records pressed against my chest. "It's like you're trying to get rid of her."

"You know that's not true," she mumbles, holding a needle between her teeth.

"What are you even working on?"

"Backdrops. This year's theme is Texas: Ain't She Grand?" She marks the red satin with a pencil. "And aren't you supposed to be at work?"

"I quit."

"You quit?" Her voice is higher than

normal.

She straightens a long piece of satin through her sewing machine with her foot hovering over the pedal.

All my life, the pageant has invaded every facet of my world, except for this room. Because in the world I lived in with Lucy, no one cared about crowns or sashes. "It feels disrespectful for you to be up here making your dumb costumes. I mean, what could be so hard about a Lady Liberty costume? Just throw some fabric over your shoulder." My voice is breaking. I hold my eyes open wide, scared that if I blink a whole river of tears will come splashin' down my cheeks.

The sewing machine thumps a methodic beat, never ceasing, but only getting stronger and stronger with each stitch. The ever-constant needle taps against my head, waiting for me to crack.

"Dumplin'," she calls over the sewing machine, not even acknowledging what I just said. "Why don't you take yourself downstairs for a tall glass of ice water?"

Desperation swells in my chest and I think I might do anything to get her out of this room.

I march over to the dresser and yank the top drawer free. Without hesitation, I fill the detached drawer with everything I can reach — mostly records.

"Willowdean Dickson, you better hope that you did not ruin the track on that drawer."

"It's like her being dead isn't good enough!" I yell. "You won't be happy until every bit of her is gone and you've filled this room with all the things she wasn't."

Finally, the sewing machine stops. Mom stands, but says nothing.

I take the drawer and slam my bedroom door behind me. Dust swirls through the air and tickles my nostril. I sneeze loudly into the albums.

"Bless you," my mother says from the hallway. She's so quiet, I almost don't hear her.

TWENTY

Getting ready for my date with Mitch is like a freaking makeover montage in my bedroom. El makes me try on everything from my eighth-grade graduation dress to this formless, chiffon floral tunic my mom bought me last Christmas. "It makes you look so mature," my mom had said.

I didn't take it as a compliment.

We settle on jeans and a black-and-white-striped shirt with my dark blond hair spread out across my shoulders.

I told Mitch to pick me up at five because my mom had a pageant board meeting until six and I didn't really feel like getting the how-to-be-a-lady/what-boys-want-in-a-girl talk from her. And, of course, there's the fact that I'm pissed at her.

After locking the back door behind me, I sit on the curb next to our mailbox. I can both hear and smell it from around the corner. He drives an old maroon Suburban that probably hasn't passed inspection for the last five years. He parks in front of me and hops out the minute the engine whines to a stop.

"Was I late?" He pulls me up by one hand, and I mean really pulls me up.

"No. No, not at all."

"I figured because you were sitting out here, and I guess guys normally go to the front door to pick up their dates."

"Oh," I say, hiking my thumb back to our front porch. "We don't use the front door. It's been broken for years."

His heads cocks to the side. "Well, you look real nice."

"You too." He really does. He's wearing a too-long-even-for-him button-down shirt and starched jeans, like with a crease and everything. And boots. Not those pointy-toed cowboy boots you see in movies, but round-toed work boots. Gram used to say that you should never trust a man in clean boots.

The front seat of Mitch's car is clean-ish with dust and lint deeply embedded in every crevice. But the back half is drowning in a sea of clothes — lots of camo and boots — and fast-food cups.

He takes me to a Chinese restaurant called Mr. Chang's Chinese Palace, a local favorite in an old shopping center with fast cash loan offices, insurance storefronts, and one of those tax places that make their employees dress like the Statue of Liberty.

The hostess seats us at an iridescent booth that looks like one of those giant clamshells from *The Little Mermaid* that Ariel and her sisters hang out in. To my surprise, Mitch slides in next to me rather than across from me and I can't stop the "oh" that slips from my lips.

The waitress comes for our drink order and Mitch asks, "Hey, you know those little crispy things? Could we get some of those and that orange sauce?"

"Um, okay," says the waitress, a girl who I recognize as a senior from when I was a freshman.

Once she leaves, Mitch turns to me. "I used to hate coming to Chinese restaurants when I was a kid because they never bring bread out or put crackers on the table, so my mom always asked for those crispy things —"

"Wonton strips." I have to stop myself smiling. "That's what they're called."

"Yeah. Well, they're delicious."

We look over the menu in silence. As the waitress approaches with our drinks, Mitch leans in and whispers in my ear, "You can order whatever you want."

I'm tempted to point out to him that everything on the menu is about the exact same price, but instead I thank him.

Once the waitress takes our orders, Mitch holds a wonton out for me. "You want one?"

I shake my head. "I saw that you guys won last night."

He nods. "Just barely, but, yeah. A win is a win."

We sit in silence for a moment as the local radio station plays over the speakers and our feet brush up against each other.

Mitch coughs into his fist. "So I guess Ellen Dryver's your best friend, right?"

I reach for my glass of water and do that thing where your mouth can't quite find the straw. "Yeah. She is." I tell him some about Lucy and Mrs. Dryver and how Dolly Parton brought us all together.

"You're, like, a die-hard Dolly Parton fan? I mean, isn't she really old?"

I don't know if there's a how-to-go-on-a-first-date-without-making-a-total-fool-of-yourself handbook out there, but if there is I'm pretty sure 'fessing up to your weird Dolly Parton obsession is not on the do list. But I feel this intense sense of loyalty to her that I can't shake. "Okay, so here's the deal: yes. I am a huge Dolly Parton fan. But there's something you have to understand about Dolly Parton fans: we're nuts. And since there's such a high level of crazy amongst all of us, I am, in comparison, not as batshit as most others. Like, there are people out there who have devoted their lives to creating ceramic Dolly Parton dolls. Some people even leave their jobs and families behind just to be near her."

"Okay," he says. His brow crinkles together, and I can see that he's really making an effort to understand. "Okay, but on, like, a scale of one to ten?"

"On a scale of one to ten, ten being total nut job, I guess Ellen and I would be fours. Maybe fives? Mrs. Dryver is a total eight, but not quite a nine because she hasn't had plastic surgery. Yet. And I guess Lucy was about a seven."

"Was?" he asks.

The memory of her sinks through me and settles deep in my bones. "Was. She died in December of last year."

He sits back. "Oh, wow. Hey, I'm really sorry."

"Thanks. It's fine." I reach for a wonton. "What about you? Who's your best friend?"

Please don't say Patrick Thomas. Please don't say Patrick Thomas.

He pops all the fingers on his right hand and then his left. "I'm close with all the guys on the team. It's hard not to be. But I guess I'd have to say Patrick Thomas."

I bite down on my lip and give myself five seconds to come up with something to say. One . . . two . . . three . . .

"You cringed," he says.

"What? No, I didn't."

He laughs. "Yeah. You did. It's fine, really."

My shoulders slump. "Okay." I shift around in the seat to get a better look at him. "It's just that he's such a —"

"Dick."

"Yes. Exactly. And you're not."

"I've known him forever. Sometimes I still think of him as that same kid from when we were really little, and then I remember that he always was a dick."

I get what he's saying. When you've known someone for so long, you don't see the same things in them that everyone else does. But then when you're friends because of who you were and not who you are, it's hard not to find the common thread that stitches you together. Still, I guess it's not my job to police his social life. "Okay, I can buy that."

He shrugs and then drums his fingers on the table. "Uh . . . so, what's your favorite holiday?"

"Fourth of July, I guess?"

He wipes the sweat from his forehead

using a napkin. "I'm a Halloween kind of guy."

The waitress swoops in and places a bowl of egg drop soup down in front of each of us.

"I hate Halloween." I always have.

El loves Halloween and drags me to a different party every year. But, as a kid, I never fit into the costumes and was always left with whatever we could scour from my mom's and Lucy's closets. I guess the magic of being someone else is lost when you can never quite shed your own skin. I drew the line in fifth grade when my mom sent me to school as the modern-day queen of England in her old yellow suit with my hair curled up high and sprayed white. All the other girls in my class went as princesses or pop stars or witches. I mean, fat kids have enough problems finding clothes. The added pressure of Halloween is unnecessary.

"You're missing out on Halloween. Big-time."

I want to tell Mitch why I hate Halloween because I feel like maybe, being pretty big himself, he'll understand, but I'm not sure how to form the words or even if I'm ready to peel back that layer of myself to let him see. Just 'cause he's a big guy doesn't mean I can tell him all of my Fat Girl Secrets.

We slurp our soup in silence until the busboy brings our dinners. After we've finished eating, Mitch pays for our meal using all five-dollar bills.

At my house, Mitch gets out of the car to open the passenger door for me.

"Thanks for dinner," I say.

"My pleasure to feed you." He holds out his hand for me and I stare at it for a moment before he solidly shakes my hand.

"Um, good night."

And that is my very first date. Dolly Parton, my dead aunt, our favorite holidays, best friends, and a handshake. Now I have to sit next to him in class for the rest of the year.

I can't even bring myself to call Ellen for the blow-by-blow. Making out with Bo next to a Dumpster felt more romantic than that date. I like to think I'm not high maintenance or anything, but is it so bad to want some chemistry? A little bit of spark that makes me feel like we're the only people in the world for ten minutes.

Inside, Mom is sitting at the kitchen table on the phone, taking notes in a bedazzled notebook. "It's that we can't really choreograph the dance routine before registration." She pauses. "Yes, I trust your abilities, but this year is all new blood, Judith. And I — Hold on a moment." She cups her hand over the receiver and turns to me. "Who was that who dropped you off?"

"A friend." On the other line, Judith is still yammering on about the pageant choreography, which has really never looked like anything more than measured walking. "I'm going to bed."

Upstairs, I sift through the stacks of Lucy's records before placing one on the player. I watch as the needle follows the grooves of Dolly's voice.

Twenty-One

Last night was my first night at the Chili Bowl. No one, I mean *no one,* comes into the Chili Bowl. If my first shift was any indication, it is mathematically impossible for the electricity to still be on.

At the end of the night, when Alejandro locked the door behind us, he sighed through his nose and said, "Just not chili season yet."

I can't imagine the time of year makes all that much difference when South Texas is only known to have two seasons: Hot as Balls and Not Quite as Hot as Balls.

Because I had nothing to do last night except relive the most awkward date ever, I compiled a list of pros and cons regarding my most recent life choice.

PROS AND CONS OF WORKING AT THE CHILI BOWL

Pros

- I can wear jeans. No more polyester dresses that zip up the front.
- I don't like chili, so I won't be stuffing my face any time soon.
- No Bo.
- No drunk teenagers who want chili five minutes before we close.
- Minimal cleaning because of the whole no-one-comes-here thing.
- It's quiet.

Cons

- I smell like chili.
- Fewer hours = less money
- No Bo.
- It's too quiet.

Bo is everywhere. His lips red as ever. In fifth period, I feel his eyes on me like a shadow. Sometimes I find myself roaming the halls, not quite realizing what I'm doing until I catch a glimpse of him.

But not only that. My whole mind has turned against me. Every time I blink, all I see are my flaws. My body in a fun-house mirror. Hips too wide. Thighs too big. And a head too small for the rest of me. Before this summer, I'd always been happy in this skin. Proud even.

But then came Bo. Since that first time we made out in the cab of his truck, I've felt myself cracking. Something about the way his skin felt against mine drew all these doubts to the surface that I didn't even know I had.

I thought that when he went away, so would these feelings. But they're there, and the best I can do is try to ignore them.

I ask Miss Rubio for a bathroom pass. I don't have to go to the bathroom, but I need out. Fifth period has become this horrible little slice of hell where the volume in my head is turned up.

I let the combined aromatic scent of metal and sweat shock my senses as I walk through the hallways and to the nearest bathroom.

I'm splashing my face with water when the door swings wide open and a voice calls, "Hello?"

"Um, yeah?" I pull a paper towel from

the dispenser.

"Willowdean?" Bo holds the door open and glances back to the hallway. "Is anyone else in here?"

"Are you kidding me? This is the girls' bathroom!"

"I need to talk to you." He walks in.

"There could be girls in here."

He shakes his head, his brown hair swishing. "They would've said something by now."

"You can't be in here."

"Give me five minutes."

I emit a heavy sigh and lean up against the door, prepared to stop anyone who might try to come in. "What?"

"You quit." He crosses his arms and holds a wide stance. "What did I do?"

I pull my ponytail loose to let my curls breathe.

"Are you trying to get me to kiss you?" he asks.

"What? No. Why would you say that?"

"Then put your hair back up."

Jaw slack, I stare at him, waiting for him

to say something else.

He doesn't look away. "I'm serious."

I flip my hair over and gather it into a ponytail so that he can't see the blush spreading across my cheeks and down into my chest. With my teeth, I pull the hair tie off my wrist and whip my head back up, hoping that the redness is gone. Or that maybe he'll think it's from hanging my head upside down. "Listen, you're in one of my classes. Things didn't work out between us. But I can't work with you *and* go to school with you."

"Things didn't work out? You ended it. I didn't even get a choice."

"Yes, you did. You made choices all summer." *But so did I.* "Listen, I can't do this. Okay? I can't."

He shakes his head, but that doesn't stop him from leaving.

I wash my hands over and over again, trying to force the noise out of my head.

The door to the handicap stall swings open and my heart jumps. Hannah Perez with her mouth of too-big teeth. Her combat boots smack against the tile until she's there standing next to me. As she

185

watches me in the mirror, she reaches over and turns the faucet off.

I should be scared that Hannah might tell someone about me and Bo. But the sad truth is that no one will listen to a girl like Hannah Perez. That doesn't stop me from feeling completely exposed, though.

I leave without drying my hands, rubbing them against my jeans instead. Once I'm in the hallway, I gulp down air like I've been suffocating.

TWENTY-TWO

"No. No. No." I lay my head against the steering wheel and try the ignition once more. "Come onnnnn!" Sitting up, I smack my hand against the wheel, but all my sweet car gives me is a honking yelp.

She won't start. My sweet baby Jolene is dead in the water. It's Tuesday morning and the universe hates me.

I watch as my mom walks down the driveway and past her car with her lunch box and purse in hand. She taps on my window with the hard acrylic nail of her index finger. Once. Twice.

When I don't budge, she opens my door wide. "Let's go. I'll give you a ride to school."

I slam my head against the headrest and let out a totally warranted sigh.

"Well, aren't you just having a come-apart?" Mom calls over her shoulder as she walks back up the driveway to her car. "I'll call Bruce to see about getting her looked at, but in the meantime your pained sighs aren't doing you a lick of good."

The whole way to school my mom flips between the oldies and the Christian radio station. We're not very religious, but going to church is part of Mom's personality. It's not even an act or anything, just her social outlet, I guess.

At school, she lets me out at the carport where all the freshmen and every other car-less soul hangs out. "Can you get a ride home with Ellen? I've got a pageant meeting."

"Yeah, I'll figure something out."

I'm halfway up the walkway when I hear: "Dumplin'! Dumplin'! You forgot your phone!"

My whole body goes straight like a steel rod. A few pimply-faced boys laugh. My mother's nickname for me is . . . whatever. I can't remember a time when she didn't call me Dumplin'. It doesn't bother me, I don't think. But it's not something she really calls me outside of the house — for obvious reasons. I mean, who really wants to be called a ball of dough in public?

I walk quickly back to the car, and Mom hands me my phone. "Please don't call me that outside the house, okay?"

She smiles. "Just my little pet name is all. Hey, dinner on your own tonight?"

I nod.

"Pageant season," she adds again by way of explanation.

I take the phone and speed walk back up the sidewalk. Near the entrance, leaning up against a pole, is Patrick Thomas. He smiles, but it's more of a sneer. I wish I were invisible. But he sees me. And whatever decision he's just made about me can't be undone.

After second period, Mitch follows me out into the hallway. "Hey, I texted you a few times yesterday. I thought maybe we could hang out on Sunday. We could see a movie or something. I'd say Saturday, but coach wants us to come in and watch film for next week's game."

I keep walking. He grabs my hand,

stopping me.

"Who's your girlfriend, Mitch?" calls a freshman with his hands cupped around his mouth.

"We're not dating!" I yell back.

Mitch's cheeks flush red.

I yank my hand away and head in the opposite direction. I feel like a terrible person. But today is not my day, and I don't have it in me to play along with him like we might be anything more than friends.

Still, I owe him an apology.

"Will!" he calls after me.

I don't turn around. As I take the corner, I hear: "Oh, hey! Dumplin'!" Patrick Thomas drags each letter out. He grins as he points over my head. "And Mitch! My man. Finally met a lady your own size."

I've been teased enough in my life to know that there are several ways to react to a bully. It only took me crying once in the second grade to realize that tears only lead to more bullying.

Lucy always said to ignore bullies. That

they thrived on attention, and if you paid them no mind, you took away their fuel. I think that, for the most part, this is true. But Patrick Thomas is one of those jerks who needs no reason to keep talking. He likes the sound of his own voice that much.

Slight shock registers on Patrick's face as I take deliberate steps toward him. I think of him making oinking noises outside of Millie Michalchuk's car. I remember how he decided that Amanda Lumbard's corrective shoes made her look like Frankenstein. No one stands up for themselves to Patrick Thomas. Not even Hannah Perez, who is as rough around the edges as they come. The guy gives you a nickname and it sticks. But I won't be called Dumplin' by him. Nope.

Patrick is totally unprepared when I knee him square in the nuts. His expression transforms, all the blood draining as it heads south. He howls, but it's more like a small screeching dog. I clap my hands over my mouth.

I'm as shocked as he is. I had pictured it in my head. I saw myself walking up to him, shaking my finger in his face as I told him what I really thought of him. But then my body took over and this primal defense mechanism, said, *No, we will not stand for this.*

Mitch pulls me back by my shoulders. Teachers swarm the scene, and I'm carted in the opposite direction.

This is probably bad.

TWENTY-THREE

My mother is livid. And mortified. And many other things. But I have stopped keeping count.

Her fingers squeeze the steering wheel so tightly that I'm surprised her nails don't pop off. After leaving Mr. Wilson's office, she walked to the visitor parking lot like it was a race. I ran to keep up.

We drive home in silence. Mom barely slows the car as she turns into the driveway and comes within inches of the fence.

The car isn't even in park and I've got the door open and am off for the backyard. I slide the glass door shut behind me even though she's only a few feet behind.

I plop down on the couch and it's mere seconds before Riot is curling into a circle in my lap.

"You're grounded."

My mother has never grounded me. Ever. No spankings. Nothing. I'm no angel, but I've never really done anything worthy of punishment.

I pick Riot up and place him on the cushion next to me before standing. I don't want him to get in the crosshairs of whatever is about to go down.

"For what?" My voice is too big for our house. "For biting back after some guy called me that hideous nickname you've been calling me my whole life?"

She wraps her arms around her waist and shakes her head. I notice a rash of white hair at her temples that I've never seen before. "You're being so sensitive about this."

"Maybe, Mom, you haven't noticed, but this is about so much more than that dumb nickname. You'll never come out and say it, but I know you can't stand that your daughter looks like this." My arms flail wildly.

"What are you talking about?"

"Don't play dumb. I see it every time

194

you turn on a weight-loss show or tell me about your friend who lost a ton of weight on the latest fad diet or when you inventory our pantry every time you come home to make sure I haven't eaten the whole goddamn thing."

Her chin quivers and the possibility of her crying at this exact moment fills me with rage. "I want you to be happy."

"I *am* happy," I say, every syllable perfectly even. I don't know how much truth there is to that, but I can't imagine that fifteen or even fifty pounds would change how much I miss Lucy, how confused I am by Bo, or the growing distance between me and El.

"But that's what you think 'cause you don't know better. You're missing out on so much." She takes a step toward me. "Boys and dating. That kind of stuff."

I scrub my hands down my face. "You have got to be kidding me. News flash, Mom: a man will not cure my troubles."

"I just —" She stops herself.

"Mom, I do want to date. I want to have boyfriends. I deserve that. Even if you think that I don't." I want for it to feel as true as it sounds.

She throws up her hands. "You're doing what Luce used to do when we were girls. You're taking my words and turning them into something else."

My head shakes back and forth without hesitation. "No, Mom. All Lucy ever did was show you how ridiculous you sounded."

"This has nothing to do with Luce, all right? She's gone and it's no thanks to the way she lived her life. I wish you wouldn't idolize her so much." Her eyes fill with tears that don't quite spill. "She'd still be here, you know. If she'd just lost the weight."

My body is the villain. That's how she sees it. It's a prison, keeping the better, thinner version of me locked away. But she's wrong. Lucy's body never stood in the way of her happiness. As much as I will always love Lucy, it was her own decision to stay locked up in this house.

"I was a big girl, too. You know that. Me and Luce both were."

"I've heard it, okay? I've heard all the stories about how you trimmed down before high school. Good for you. You entered a small town beauty pageant and won. Quite literally your crowning achievement. Forget college or getting a job that doesn't require you wiping old people's asses. Never mind that. Because you slimmed down enough to score a fake-ass crown! You must be so proud."

A tear trickles down her cheek and she says, "Well, I think that's more than you can say for yourself." She wipes away the tear.

"Lucy was more a mother to me than you'll ever be."

Her lips squeeze together. "No work. No going out. Not until your school suspension is over. I'll be home at six."

I take off upstairs and Riot follows at my heels. On my bed, I curl up on my side and listen to the sound of my phone vibrating against my desk as I get text after text. All from El I assume. I take the Magic 8 Ball from where it sits on my nightstand and hold it with all of its answers to all of my unasked questions tight to my chest.

TWENTY-FOUR

I stay in my room all day. Our old pipes notify me as Mom begins to do the dishes after work, and the floorboards announce her as she climbs the stairs. Before locking herself in her own room, her shadow hovers at mine, darkening the gap between the closed door and the floor.

Riot stretches his legs, pushing his paws against my chest, before jumping off the edge of my bed and rubbing himself against my bedroom door. When I don't move, he meows, letting me know that his sympathy has run short.

I crack my door and let him out as I flip on the light.

In the mirror, I find a drooping and smudged version of myself. I grab a pen from my dresser and jot down a note on my forearm to call Alejandro and tell him I won't be in for the next couple days. Judging by my first few shifts, I don't think my absence will be such a burden.

Careful not to make any noise, I navigate my way downstairs in the dark and swallow down a tall glass of water in three gulps. It feels silly, but my mother has conditioned me to need water any time I cry. That was always her remedy. *Calm down and have a glass of water, Dumplin'.* Like, I might need to refill my well of tears before I run out.

Upstairs, the Magic 8 Ball lies on my bed, right where I left it. My phone vibrates, so I pick it up.

ELLEN: Oh my God. Are you okay?

ELLEN: I've called you like eight times and you know I hate talking on the phone. CALL. TEXT. SMOKE SIGNAL. MORSE CODE.

ELLEN: Is it true about Patrick Thomas? I told Tim to kill him.

ELLEN: He said he might after dinner.

ELLEN: Okay. Really freaking out now.

Fine, I type. *Just —*

I stop and hit the damn call button because all I want right now is my best friend. The phone doesn't even make it through a full ring before she picks up.

"Holy shit. Oh my God. Holy shit."

"Hey," I offer, my voice scratching against the receiver.

"Are you okay? What even happened?"

I sigh into the phone and it feels so good to not be chastised for it. Then I tell her. I tell her about Mom calling me Dumplin' in front of the carport, with all the freshmen and Patrick Thomas standing around, waiting for the first bell to ring. I tell her about the incident in the hallway, and how I'd never been made to feel so small for being so large. She curses and coos and does all the things that make calling her the right decision.

She goes off on a tirade about "piece of shit ninth-graders and their tiny peens" and how Patrick has failed his driving test so many times he can't try again until he's eighteen.

I tell her about the argument with my mom. "And I'm suspended for the rest of the week. Hopefully that will give everyone at school enough time to forget and let this whole thing blow over." The noise from my mom's television stops abruptly. "Also, I'm grounded."

"Wow. Okay, so this is the worst day ever, right? But the good news is that since this is the worst day ever, tomorrow can only be better. Even if it's by a little bit."

I laugh. It feels good. "I guess we'll see." A yawn pushes up from my chest. "I don't get how crying can make you so tired."

"Adrenaline or something."

"Smart."

"Hey, you probably don't want to talk about this right now, but you have given me zero details on your date."

"Yeah, well there's not much to say. It was incredibly . . . unremarkable."

"Aw, man. I had high hopes for Mitch."

"I'll talk to you in the morning."

"Hey," she says. "I love you. Listen to some Dolly. She'll make you feel better."

TWENTY-FIVE

I waste the days of my suspension on the couch. After school, Ellen comes over with my homework before my mom gets home. We watch television in silence and although I want to ask her about school and if she's heard anyone talking about me, I don't. Tim drops her off and picks her up, but he never comes in. I like Tim, but I like him even better for not inviting himself in and for letting me have El for these few hours.

At first, my mom and I operate on our own schedules and in the evenings it's like someone's come in and divided the house with red tape. When I leave my room, she stays clear and when she leaves her room, I stay in mine. But slowly, our paths wind closer and closer until Saturday morning when she says, "I've got an all-day pageant planning meeting today. We're gearing up for open registration. There's tuna salad in the fridge."

It's not a truce, but it breaks the silence.

Mitch texts me a few times, telling me he's sorry for the scene he caused and that Patrick has a big mouth. I tell him I'd rather not talk about it, but I know it's me who should be doing the apologizing.

El works all day Saturday and is going to a party afterward, so I am left alone. I have been stuck in this house for so long that I think the wallpaper is moving.

I hate that there's never anything good on TV on Saturday afternoons. It's like even the networks are trying to get you off your ass and have a life. I guess whoever does the channel scheduling has never been grounded on a Saturday.

Maybe it's the boredom, but Lucy's room calls me like a siren.

Her bed is perfectly made with Gram's homemade moss-and-cream-colored quilt folded up at the foot of the bed with my mom's steamer in the corner.

In Lucy's nightstand, I find more newspaper clippings, but these are mostly of Mom. Mom's in the *Clover City Tribune* all the time. I think she even dated the editor for a while, but he ended up marrying the girl who did his dry cleaning.

The stack of clippings is thick with grainy photos of Mom in her crown and dress. The same dress every year, posing with a different Miss Teen Blue Bonnet. I dig deeper in the drawer, coming up with a weathered gallon-sized bag of documents. Contracts, pamphlets, bills. Until I stumble upon a totally blank pageant registration form. Dated 1994, three years before Mom won in '97. Mom would have been too young to enter. But this can't be right. Lucy thought the pageant was a joke. Or I thought she did.

My aunt wasn't a timid woman, but even at her slimmest, I can't see her ever entering this pageant. The blank form feels like empty promises of what could have been. I look over the application and imagine her handwriting there. The form asks for the usual: name, DOB, and address. But it asks for things that make me cringe like height, weight, hair color, eye color, career ambition, and talent.

I try to mentally piece together this puzzle, but it's useless. There is no answer.

The only thing left in this particular drawer is a red velvet box with a Christmas ornament inside. A white iridescent globe with puckered red lips wrapping around its circumference alongside Dolly's signature in gold. A souvenir from Dollywood — a place Lucy had always wanted to visit. El's mom had won a set of airline tickets at work, and she immediately offered the second ticket to Lucy. They would go to Dollywood, like they'd always dreamed.

They made plans. They looked at hotels and rental cars. They drove the three hours to the closest airport only to find that Lucy would have to purchase an extra seat on the plane because she wouldn't fit in one. The airline was kind, she'd said, but firm. In the end she was too mortified, and decided to go home rather than take up two seats on the plane. Mrs. Dryver brought home the ornament for Lucy. You knew it was expensive because instead of a metal hook, it hung by a red velvet ribbon.

I shuffle back to my room with the old pageant registration form and the ornament. I spend the rest of the afternoon studying the form and am surprised to find that the only real requirements are that the contestant be between the ages of fifteen and eighteen and that their parents give consent. For all the requirements I've made up in my head, I can't wrap my mind around how simple it is to compete in the pageant and how many girls are actually eligible.

An obscene thought crosses my mind, and before it becomes anything more, I stuff the registration form away in the bottom drawer of my dresser.

My mom's voice fills the house as she comes in through the back door. "I don't think she's in the right state of mind to be an active member of this committee. I'm sorry, but this town is not ready for an opening number set to Beyoncé." I can't help it. I laugh when my mom says "Bay-yonsay." "Even if it is one of her tamer songs — or so she says — I am not taking the flak for that."

I plop down on my bed. Riot trots in

from downstairs and spreads himself out in front of me until I scratch his chin.

"Well, ready or not, registration opens this week," Mom says.

I grab my Magic 8 Ball from my night-stand and give it one good shake.

Signs point to yes.

TWENTY-SIX

On Sunday morning, I've got this major emotional hangover. Last night I made a decision — a really stupid decision. I tell myself that I don't have to hold myself to anything because no one else even knows about it except me. If I chicken out, I will be my own sole witness.

It's kind of like when you see someone drop their lunch tray at school, but no one else notices. Nobody will know if you don't help them. But you'll know.

I flip-flop back and forth all day, not even really paying attention to the fact that my mom and I have been sort of civil today.

After dinner, I lock myself in my room to catch up on some required reading. But instead I find myself looking over the registration form again. I can't imagine it's changed much since 1994. The idea of me in a poufy gown, gliding across a stage like I own it is ludicrous.

There are so many things that Lucy never did. Not because she couldn't, but because she told herself she couldn't and no one made her believe otherwise. I won't lie to myself and say that Lucy was the picture of health in the last few years, but that's such a horrible reason for her to have deprived herself of the things she wanted most. It's not even that I think she wanted to compete in the pageant so badly. But it's that, even if she wanted to, she wouldn't have.

I pick up my phone and hit the call button.

"Hey! Your sentence is almost up," says El.

"I need to tell you something."

"Okay."

I could chicken out now and tell her never mind. Or I could tell her about Bo and how some parts of me can't let him go. Even now when my head is full of so many other things. But instead, I say, "I'm entering Clover City's Miss Teen

Blue Bonnet Pageant."

The line is silent for a second, a second almost long enough for me to say, "Just kidding!"

"Oh. Hell. Yes."

"You don't think I'm crazy?"

"Well, you're totally nuts, but this is going to be awesome."

"I don't know about that."

"Have you told your mom?"

I rub my forehead. "Christ. No. I haven't really figured out the logistics. I just know that I want to enter the pageant. Not like I can hide it from her."

"She's going to freak."

"Yeah, well, she's always been embarrassed by me. Why not give her a good reason?"

Ellen doesn't say I'm wrong even if she thinks so. "We need to game plan. What are you doing tomorrow?"

"Working, but I don't think Alejandro will care if you come and hang out."

"Okay. Me. You. Tomorrow night."

I hang up and put the old form away. Now that I've told El, she won't let me back down.

I try to sleep, but not even Dolly does my nerves any good.

TWENTY-SEVEN

Ellen and Tim pick me up in the morning so that I won't have to face the carport because I am officially Patrick Thomas's public enemy number one.

But except for a few whispers, school is relatively calm. Everyone seems to have suppressed the memory of or sort of gotten over last week's incident.

At least that's what I think until lunch. People crowd in groups all passing around phones. Most laugh. Some shake their head in disgust. In the lunch line, I peer over a girl's shoulder. She turns to me, her voice bubbling with laughter, and says, "Have you seen this?" Her arm's outstretched, holding the screen within inches of my face.

Hannah Perez. Her school photo on the screen sits alongside a photo of a horse, with his gummy mouth of giant teeth on full display. Just like Hannah. Except hers are even more crooked. The caption for the picture says: *HaaaaaaAAAAAaaannah.* I hear it in my head in Patrick Shit-for-Brains Thomas's voice.

"That's not funny," I spit.

The girl whips her phone around, holding it to her chest, with her face twisted in confusion. "Um. Okay."

I know very little about Hannah except that she is quiet and stubborn. In third grade, during art, we all sat coloring hand turkeys for Thanksgiving. I hadn't heard Hannah speak all year, but then I took the marker that sat in front of her — one she didn't even appear to be using — and she slapped it out of my hand, yelling that I should've asked for permission first. The only other memory I have of her is from fifth grade when she snapped at a teacher who kept calling her Afri*can* Ameri*can*. Which actually made sense because she's Dominican.

As I'm walking to my next class, I hear things like, "So horrible," or "I'm sorry, but she's hideous," or "Why doesn't she get braces?"

That last one is the sentiment that stays with me all day because Hannah shouldn't have to get braces. Maybe she can't afford them or maybe she's scared to get them. Either way, she shouldn't have to fill her mouth with metal so that some shitheads will leave her alone.

In fifth period, Bo sits with his arms crossed tight over his chest. His cheek is bruised and a scabbing cut clusters at the corner of his lip. I want to know what happened. Who he got in a fight with.

But it's not your business, I remind myself.

When he sees me, his brow furrows, and his lips fall into a deep-set frown, breaking his scab. He pulls the sleeve of his sweatshirt over his hand and pats it to his mouth.

After school, I meet Ellen in the parking lot. "Did you see all that stuff about Hannah?"

I nod. "She must have lost it when she found out. Does anyone know who did it?"

"Tim says some guys on the golf team,

but that they can't get in trouble because no one can prove anything and it didn't happen at school."

"That's such bullshit."

Tim and El drive me home and wait for me to change into my Chili Bowl uniform shirt. They drop me off at work and Ellen promises to come back for me later with her mom's car.

I brace myself for Alejandro. He's got to be pissed that I missed so much work, but when I walk in, he asks, "You're not still grounded, are you?"

I shake my head.

"Good. 'Cause I don't cross moms. Anyone's mom. So if you're lying, you can go home."

"Not lying," I say. "Totally free."

Around seven, Ellen walks in. "Sorry, my mom would only let me take the car if I ate dinner with them."

"It's cool."

She hoists herself up on the other end of the counter and whispers, "This place smells like onions and BO. I still don't get why you quit Harpy's for this shitter."

"Better pay," I lie as I lean forward, practically laying my upper body on the counter. "How much do you think I can get a formal for? This pageant isn't going to be cheap."

She shrugs. "Maybe a couple hundred bucks. You could try Goodwill, too."

The cowbell above the door rings. I stand up, totally caught off guard by the prospect of a customer. Ellen doesn't budge.

Millie Michalchuk waves at the two of us as she walks in. She smiles at me and an immediate guilt for any less-than-nice thing I've ever thought about her weighs me down like an anchor.

"Hey, Millie." Ellen gives a short wave.

"So what can I get you today?" I ask.

She drops her keys down on the counter, and there are at least twenty-six key chains on her key ring with all of two keys. "A pint of house chili." She pauses. "And some crackers."

"You got it."

After she pays, Millie picks up some plasticware from the condiment bar while I spoon her chili out from the pot.

"So," Ellen says, "the registration fee can't be more than two hundred bucks, right?"

"I guess. I have five hundred and sixty-eight dollars in savings, so if the whole thing costs more than that, I'm going to have to get a second job." I press the lid down on Millie's to-go cup. "Here ya go!"

Her eyes skip back and forth between El and me before taking her chili and walking out the door.

El watches as Millie pulls out of the parking lot. "That was weird-ish."

"Yeah," I say. "Well, she's kind of weird all on her own."

We hang out all night and when Alejandro comes out from his office, Ellen slides off the counter and pretends to be a customer. He runs the nightly report on my register and as he's walking back to his office, he calls over his shoulder, "Tell your friend we're hiring!"

TWENTY-EIGHT

I run into school, shielding myself from the rain with my backpack held up above my head. I stop to wipe my feet on the doormat.

"Will?" Millie stands off to the side against the lockers, wearing floral leggings with a matching tunic.

I step toward her to get out of the way of incoming students. "Hey. What's going on, Millie?"

She pulls on her backpack straps so that they dig into her shoulders. "I heard you talking last night to Ellen. About the pageant."

I'm taken aback. "Yeah, we —"

She leans in and whispers, "You're entering, aren't you?"

"I . . . well, yeah. I am."

A wide grin spreads across her face, pushing her cheeks up and out. She claps her hands together like I've done some sort of trick. "That's amazing."

I turn toward her so that my back is to the stream of students. "Listen," I say. "It's not a secret, but I don't wanna make a big deal of this, okay?"

"Yes. Right, of course."

Something about her smile makes me uneasy. "Okay."

When I catch up with El later that day, I tell her about my odd exchange with Millie.

She grabs my shoulders and leans into me. "Will, you're, like, her inspiration."

I shake my head vehemently. "Am not."

"Oh my God, you have a little fan club."

"Eat shit." A small speck of me swells with pride.

The rain brings in a few customers in search of chili. It's the most business I've seen at once here. I serve up a few bowls, and without looking up to see who my next customer is, I say, "Would you like to try our new white bean chili?"

"Uh, yeah. A cup or a bowl or whatever." That voice.

I don't look up. "What do you want, Bo?"

"I came for some chili. This is a chili restaurant, isn't it?"

Words bubble in my chest, but none of them are right. None of them say exactly what I want. Because I don't know what I want. "Can I get you anything else?"

He bites down on his bottom lip. It disappears beneath his teeth. I love his teeth. They're all so perfect, except the front two. They overlap. Just slightly. It's like the universe decided he was too perfect and had to give him one tiny flaw. "No," he says.

I watch as he walks back across the street with his to-go cup of chili. He pulls his visor from his back pocket and tugs it down on top of his head as he jogs into Harpy's.

■ ■ ■ ■

Over the next two days, I open my mouth at least twelve times to tell my mom that I'm entering the pageant. But I can't. I can't have this conversation with her. It's like I'm holding out this last bit of hope that I'll show up for registration and she'll squeal with delight. She'll tell me that she's always dreamed of me entering the pageant and following in her footsteps. She'll say that she didn't want to push me. She wanted me to find my own way.

It's a dream I don't want to wake up from.

TWENTY-NINE

I've always known that the pageant was this huge part of my mom's life, but it's never been more than background noise for me. When I was little and she had meetings or rehearsals to attend, I usually stayed home with Lucy or went over to El's. The pageant and everything it encompassed was hers alone.

Registration takes place downtown at the Clover City Community Center. Downtown Clover City is a picturesque square with a gazebo at the center. The block always smells like fried chicken thanks to Frenchy's Fried 'n' Such, which is the diner to end all diners.

El and I sit outside on a bench while I count out the two-hundred-dollar registration fee.

"You didn't by any chance get your

mom to sign your form, did you?" she asks.

"Nope." Entering the pageant requires parental consent. And in this moment, my greatest fear is that my mom will say no. In front of all those people.

On the other side of the square, a short, wide person frantically waves their arms over their head.

"El." I squint. "El, who is that?"

She looks up. Her jaw drops.

"Hey! You haven't gone in yet!" yells Millie. "Perfect timing!"

"She loves you," says El. "She is in love with you." She stands up and uses her hand as a visor from the sun. "Is that . . . is that Amanda Lumbard with her?"

I nod.

"We're signing up, too," says Millie.

"Is this gonna take very long?" asks Amanda. "My mom's going to kill me if I'm late to pick up my brother."

I look to Ellen. She shrugs.

Millie fixes her hands on her hips. "I get that you don't want to make a big deal of entering this pageant, Will. And, if I'm being honest, I don't even really know what your personal reasons for doing this are. But you're doing it. And that's important. I want to be a part of that. We both do."

"She made me come," mumbles Amanda.

Millie rolls her eyes. "I tried to get Hannah Perez on board, but she said no."

"Actually," adds Amanda, "she told you to shove a pageant sash up your piggy ass."

I told Millie that I wanted to let this fly under the radar, but with these two, I might as well take a front-page ad out in the *Clover City Tribune.* I'm not doing this to be some kind of Joan of Fat Girls or whatever. I'm doing this for Lucy. And for me. I'm ready to go back to being the version of myself I was before Bo. I'm entering this pageant because there's no reason I shouldn't. I'm doing this because I want to cross the line between me and the rest of the world. Not be someone's savior.

I shake my head. "This isn't a good idea."

"All my favorite things start as bad

ideas," says Millie.

"Millie, people are cruel," I tell her. "I know that. And so does Amanda, I'm sure."

Amanda nods. "Haters gonna hate."

"But doing this pageant is the ultimate KICK ME sign on your back. You don't need my permission, but I don't want to be responsible for that."

Millie's shoulders slump.

Ellen kicks her toe in the dirt. "They should do it. If Millie and Amanda want to enter the pageant with you, they should. Viva la revolution and all that."

"No," I say. "Y'all should go home."

Amanda shrugs and starts to walk off, but Millie stays put, silently asking for an appeal.

Ellen grabs my hand and squeezes it tight.

I sigh. "Registration for the revolution is two hundred bucks."

Inside, the community center sounds like the gymnasium during girls' phys ed. High-pitched conversations bounce off the ceiling, echoing and multiplying until the voices of twenty sound like the screeches of a hundred.

Cliques of girls sit at round tables with white tablecloths, the same ones my mother ironed in our living room last night. The legacy girls with mothers and sisters who have been crowned. Athletes trying to beef up their college résumés. The cheer table, which consists of anyone who does anything at a football game that doesn't include a ball. And the theater and the choir girls, of course. All of them wear dresses. Like, Easter dresses. Precious little garden dresses with matching cardigans. While we are wearing nothing more than jeans and T-shirts.

I turn back to Amanda and Millie and try to give them an encouraging smile that doesn't say I-have-no-clue-what-I'm-doing-I-feel-like-I'm-naked.

El squeezes my hand. "Let's do this."

We weave in and out of tables and as we draw to the front, a silence sprinkles over the room, until the voices are nothing more than a low buzz of questions.

At the registration table sit two former pageant queens, Judith Clawson and

Mallory Buckley. Only former winners are invited to participate as members of the planning committee. Judith is at least twenty years Mallory's senior, but both their smiles are as glittering white as the crown brooches on their cardigans.

"Hi. I'm here for registration."

Both women smile with their lips closed. Judith whispers into Mallory's ear, who then stands and says, "Pardon me."

Judith examines my application. "You'll need to get your talent approved by the first week of November."

"Right. Of course."

Her eyes travel between the form and me as she reads over my weight and height. "I'll need your mother's signature, dear."

"Willowdean." As if on cue, my mother grips my elbow as Mallory rushes past her to reclaim her spot.

Mom pulls me off to the side and through a set of French doors. I watch through the glass as Amanda and Millie hand in their applications. I have this urge to go back in there and stand with them, like I've somehow abandoned them.

Ellen stands behind them and flashes me the thumbs-up.

"What do you think you're doing?" Mom's voice is a harsh whisper.

I stand up straighter with my fists dug into my hips. "I'm registering as a contestant."

"This isn't some joke."

"Do you see me laughing?"

"And who are those other young ladies with you?"

"They're my friends. And they want to enter the pageant, too."

"Is this some kind of ploy for attention? Are you trying to get back at me for something?" Her voice rises with every word and while I'm not willing to break eye contact, I can feel the eyes of every person in the registration room on us.

"Oh, are those the questions you ask all the contestants? I didn't see them on the form."

She points a perfectly polished pearl-pink finger in my face. "Don't you do this. Don't you drag these poor girls into our issues. This pageant isn't some joke for you to make an example of me."

"Why does it have to be that? Why do you have to make that assumption, Mom? How come I can't enter the pageant without it being a joke or revenge?"

She crosses her arms with her lips pursed together in a tight knot. "You can't enter unless I sign the release."

I knew it would come to this. "And why wouldn't you?"

Her voice softens. "Besides the fact that I'm unsure your intentions are pure?" She licks her thumbs and wipes a spot on my shirt above my chest. "I don't want you to embarrass yourself."

I open my mouth, ready to snap back.

"And more so, it's not fair for you to subject those girls to this. They'll be ridiculed, Dumplin'." The nickname burrows beneath my skin in a way it never has before.

There are so many things I could say, but instead I cut right to the bone. "Mom." My mouth is dry. "If you don't sign that form, you're saying I'm not good enough. You're saying that most every girl in that room right now is prettier and more deserving than me. That's what you're telling me."

A long silence sinks between us.

My mother has never encouraged me to enter the pageant. I remember sitting in the kitchen with El the summer before freshman year, decorating our new matching day planners when I ran upstairs for more markers. When I came back down, I lingered in the shadows of the hallway as I heard my mom say, "Ya know, dear, you might think about entering the pageant when you turn fifteen." El brushed her off, and I waited a few beats before sitting down at the kitchen table. That day was, like, realizing for the first time that the religion your parents subscribe to doesn't work for you.

I watch my mom, waiting for her to crack.

"Fine," she says after a long moment. "But don't you dare expect any special treatment or allowances."

El's eyes are wide as she watches us file through the door. I see the question on her lips.

I nod once.

Mom walks past me to the table and signs her name to my form.

THIRTY

I sit at a table with Ellen, Millie, and Amanda as my mom stands in front of the registration table and claps her hands together, silencing the room. "Welcome, ladies." She clears her throat. "You are about to embark on a path that has been weathered by many before you and will be by many after you. Clover City's Miss Teen Blue Bon—"

The heavy door at the back of the room creaks loudly and every head, including my own, turns.

"Am I too late for registration?" asks Hannah Perez, her tone flat.

My jaw drops. Along with everyone else's.

With her clipboard in hand, the younger woman from the registration table rushes to Hannah. She looks over her form and instructs her to take a seat.

Hannah sits by herself at an empty table.

My mother clears her throat again. "One, two, three. Eyes on me." She pauses for a moment. "As I was saying, the Miss Teen Blue Bonnet Pageant is a treasured tradition with a rich history. Former titleholders have gone on to become business owners, physicians, and beloved mothers and wives. We even have a mayor amongst us." She goes on to explain the origins of the pageant and how it went on hiatus during World War II and again when Kennedy was assassinated.

I have never seen my mother in command of a room like she is right now. She stands with her back straight and speaks with her voice projected. She owns this. But, I guess, what surprises me most is how captivated everyone is. Including my table. Here, in her element, she's not my mother. Here, she is Rosie Dickson, Clover City's Miss Teen Blue Bonnet 1997. Here, she is royalty. *Y'all hail the queen.*

"Now if you haven't already declared

your talent, you have until the first week of November to notify us. Don't forget: the board must deem your talent appropriate. So save the sexy, understand? You will also need to have your formal, swimwear, and talent costume approved by the Wednesday before the pageant."

She waits for some nods from her audience. "Wonderful. I'd like to introduce you to my cohorts this year. This is Mrs. Judith Clawson, Miss Teen Blue Bonnet 1979." The older woman stands and curtsies. "And this is Mrs. Mallory Buckley, Miss Teen Blue Bonnet 2008." She pauses for quiet applause.

"A yes from these women is a yes from me. A no from them is a no from me."

The two women walk the room and hand out hot-pink folders with the Eighty-First Annual Clover City Miss Teen Blue Bonnet logo printed across the front in gold script.

"Look around for a moment." She pauses as we stiffly stare at one another. "Somewhere in this room is the next Blue Bonnet. The bad news is that only one young woman will wear this year's crown. But the good news is: she's sitting among us. You'll notice that this is the eighty-first anniversary of our pageant. We have wonderful things in store for you all, including a beautifully choreographed opening number —"

"No one said there would be dancing," mumbles Amanda.

". . . and the promise of front-page billing in the *Clover City Tribune.*"

Mallory (she's so young I can't bring myself to call her Mrs. Buckley) makes the rounds at our table, and hands us all folders. Including El.

"Oh," I whisper. "She's not doing the pageant. Just here for moral support."

Mallory, whose auburn hair is curled in bouncing ringlets, smiles at me like I'm speaking a foreign language, and hands El a folder anyway.

"Ellen," I whisper.

She turns in her chair and opens the folder as she thumbs through the pages. "Yeah?"

My mom still droning on, I lean over and say, "That was weird, right?"

"What?"

"With Mallory just now."

"How was that weird?" she whispers back as she skims through the papers in the folder.

I feel my eyes widen. "You entered the pageant."

"Isn't that what we came here to do?"

"Thank you, ladies," says Mom, her voice ringing like a bell. "Feel free to mingle with one another. Don't forget: only you can put the *friend* in friendly competition. There's a refreshments table on that back wall, starring my famous sweet tea, of course."

Applause echoes in my ears. "You can't do the pageant. That wasn't part of the plan."

Everyone around us migrates toward the back of the room. "What are you talking about?" She's not whispering anymore. "This is all we've been talking about for days."

"You can't be serious."

"Why? Why is this such a problem?"

"You're — you could actually win. We're not here to win. That's not the point." I can hear how ridiculous I sound.

"Are you fucking kidding me right now?"

I don't know what to say. There is nothing to say.

"Have you thought about the fact that I feel as out of place here as you do?"

"You have to back out. El, for me, you've got to. Let me have this one thing."

"What? Let you have what? You can't pick and choose who joins the revolution." She makes air quotes as she says "revolution."

I hear the logic in her voice. I recognize the truth there. But if El entered, she could really win. And that's why she could ruin this.

I remember that night, two years ago, as we sat at the kitchen table and I pretended that I hadn't heard my mom tell her to enter the pageant. It shouldn't have mattered to me, but it did. It was a moment I'd kept locked away deep inside of me, and now it was all I could see. On a loop. She was my mother. She lived at the end of the hall, and in all that time, she'd never extended an invitation to me.

I deserve to be selfish, I think. I deserve to make something about me.

"You already have everything," I say. The perfect parents. The perfect job. The perfect boyfriend. "Let me have this."

El shakes her head. "That's not fair. You can't put that on me. Maybe Callie was right, Will. Maybe we're outgrowing each other. Holding each other back. I miss out on lots of things because of you. I can't believe you would even think of asking me not to enter."

All the sorrow and bitterness I've felt over the last few months is clumping together into one giant fit of rage. Holding each other back? "Callie? Really? I can't believe you talk to her about us. Sorry I can't be some mindless friend for you who sits around and tells you how fucking flawless you are, okay? Just go ahead and say what you mean. We don't hold each other back. *I* hold *you* back, isn't that right?"

She doesn't answer.

"I'm not your goddamn sidekick or your chubby best friend." I take a step closer to her. "This whole pageant thing *is* about me, El. I am making this about me."

Her face turns an angry shade of red. "You're a shitty-ass friend, Will, and I'm done wasting my time. I'm not backing out of this." And then she leaves.

THIRTY-ONE

On Monday, Ellen ignored me. And I deserved that. I expected it. We're both quick to anger, but Ellen is always ready to forgive. It's something I've come to count on. But then came the weekend without even a text. On Tuesday, not even Tim acknowledged me. And that's when the knot in my stomach turned into panic.

Today, I have to talk to her. I don't know who's wrong and who's right, but I'm not prepared to go through this without her. I catch her in the hallway, after second period. It'll be fine, I tell myself. We're like an old married couple who can't even remember what they were arguing about to begin with.

"Hey, Ellen! Hey."

She stops and turns to me. Her whole

241

body is taut and closed off.

"What the hell am I even going to do for my talent?" I ask, trying to pretend like nothing happened.

She opens her mouth, and my heart raps against my chest as I wait for her to say something. But then she shakes her head and walks off.

Callie pushes past me and gives me a dirty look before running after my best friend. "El-bell!"

The tears well up behind my eyes all day long, waiting to burst. I leave school as fast as I can. My mom has decided to let me take her car to and from school as long as I drop her off at work every morning. The second I am outside of the parking lot, I let the tears run. Dripping down my cheeks. Big, thick, and heavy. Like angry drops of rain against a windshield.

She should understand. Of all people she should know. I roll to a stoplight and close my eyes for a moment, but when I do, the only thing I see is that day when we were fourteen. It's selfish and it's wrong, I know. But I'm not perfect and neither is she. When you love someone enough, you accept their flaws. You make sacrifices to keep them sane. I need her to keep me sane. I need her to sacrifice this for me.

Behind me a horn blares, reminding me that I am behind the wheel of a three-thousand-pound hunk of metal.

At home, I pull into the driveway. I've got two hours to kill before I have to pick my mom up.

I yank my rearview mirror toward me and dab at my eyes. *Dab,* my mother would say. *Wiping only makes your eye-spuffier.*

I get out of the car, but pause with my hand on the door handle. "What are you doing here?"

Mitch stands on the crack where the driveway meets the street. His jeans are half tucked into his boots and his baseball cap is fraying and trimmed in sweat stains. "I saw you crying."

I slam the door shut. "So you followed me?"

His cheeks flush red. "To make sure you were okay. Not to be, like, creepy."

"Right." I hike my backpack up on my

shoulder. "Well, I'm okay." I realize that outside of awkward small talk, we haven't really spoken since the ordeal in the hallway. I owe him an apology. "Aren't you supposed to be at practice?"

He shrugs.

"Come on," I say.

He follows me through the backyard, and I tell him to sit down on one of our rusted lawn chairs.

"You want some peach tea?"

He pulls his cap off to reveal a matted head of hair and uses his forearm to wipe the sweat from his forehead. "Sure."

In the kitchen, I drop my bag on the table and pour us each a glass. We're in that weird time of year where we experience every season all in one day. I guess most people might call it autumn, but in the South it's this unruly combination of winter-spring-summer-fall. Regardless, iced tea is a year-round delicacy.

I sit down across from him and hand him a cup. "My mom's tea," I say. "My gram's recipe."

"Thanks."

We sip for a few moments.

"I'm sorry about that day in the hallway," I say. "When someone said something about us dating."

"It's fine." He rubs his fingers up and down the back of his neck. I think every girl has a spot — a spot on a guy that makes her melt. For El, it's hands. For me it's that place where their hairline meets their neck. I love that feeling of brushing the tips of my fingers against a guy's buzzed hair. And when I say a guy, I mean Bo with his slim silver chain peeking out from the edge of his collar. Because he is the only guy.

Except maybe he doesn't have to be.

"I don't know why people have to go on dates," Mitch says. "If we called it hanging out or something, there'd be so much less pressure. But a date, God, that's like some huge thing to live up to."

"Yeah, it is." Bad first date aside, there's something so comforting about Mitch. He feels like the kind of person you don't have to ask to stay because he probably won't ever leave. I reach down, tug a flower from my mom's flower bed, and twist it around in my fingers until it's limp in my hands. "I entered the Miss

245

Teen Blue Bonnet Pageant."

"You know," he says, "if you try smiling, you might win that thing."

I smack his shoulder. "You don't think it's weird?"

"That you entered?" His mouth slips into an easy smile. "Why would I think that?"

"I don't know. I guess I'm not much of a beauty queen."

"Well, the whole thing doesn't really strike me as your type of scene, but if you ask me, you're overqualified for the job."

Heat stains my cheeks. "Thanks."

"I want us to be friends," he says.

I need a friend. I need one so bad. "I want that, too." I stand up.

He gulps down the rest of his tea and stands, too, tucking his hands in his pockets. "I oughta get to practice."

"Saturday," I say. "I'm off work. Let's hang out."

"I'm sorry for whatever made you cry," he says.

I wait for him to ask what happened, but he doesn't, and I like that about him.

Thirty-Two

Me, Amanda, and Hannah sit in a tiny booth at the back of Frenchy's with Millie at the end of the table in a chair. As we were seated, Millie took one glance at the booth and said, "Well, that looks like a squeeze."

The waitress's lips turned into a deep frown, but Millie shrugged it off and asked for a chair. It's the type of thing that would have stopped Lucy from eating here, but Millie doesn't seem all that bothered.

After we place our orders, I say, "So, have y'all thought in terms of the talent show?"

"I kind of want to do something having to do with soccer," says Amanda. "Like, some kind of trick." She bounces her legs so hard that the whole table shakes. She's one of those people that just can't sit still.

"You play soccer?" I ask as Millie leans forward with both elbows on the table. I just never really thought someone with uneven legs would be as into sports as Amanda is.

"Well, I mean, I'm not on the team. But I kick the ball around with my brothers."

Millie gives her an encouraging smile. "I don't see why you wouldn't be able to do that. I remember a few years ago Lacey Sanders's older sister did a first-aid demonstration."

Hannah leans back with her arms crossed. Her bangs are overgrown and hang above her eyelashes so that she's all hair and mouth. Like a talking wig. "Maybe I should dress up like a horse and trot around the stage for five minutes."

Millie turns to me, discomfort in everything but her smile. "What about you, Will?"

"I don't know." I never stuck with dance classes or did violin or any kind of organized sport. My talents consist of watching television, being Ellen's best friend, sighing, and knowing the lyrics to nearly every Dolly Parton song. "But we need to figure out things like dresses and pre-interview stuff, too."

"I'm not spending any more money on this shit," says Hannah. "I'll wear jeans up there if I have to."

"Maybe we could make you a dress?" asks Millie, her voice creeping so high it almost cracks.

Hannah doesn't answer. It's hard for me to look at her without wondering how much she really gathered from that day with Bo in the girls' bathroom. We've said no more than a handful of words to each other and she knows a secret so big that I've not even told my best friend.

"So what do we need to know?" Amanda asks as she chews on a piece of hair. "Like, last time everyone was dressed up and we looked like friggin' idiots. It was like amateur hour."

"Well," I say. "There's the dress, the talent, and the interview. I mean, there's not that much more to it. The whole point is to walk up there and not fall on your face and to try to make it look like your fake eyelashes aren't stabbing your eyeballs. Oh, and swimsuits. We have to figure those out, too."

Millie chews at the skin around her thumbnail.

Hannah crosses her arms and stretches her whole body out, eating up more and more of Amanda's booth space. "We are so fucked. Your mom runs the thing and that's all you've got?"

"It's not like I'm some pageant groupie, okay? I never gave a whoop about the whole thing until last week. I'm sorry if this is something you feel like you can't do, but too late now, sweetheart."

Millie makes a long slurping noise as she finishes off her soda. "Well, um, Will, if you don't mind, I have a few things to add." She places her soda down and sits up straighter. "There's more to pageants than dresses and talents. It's about show-manship. Or showwomanship. And pride. So many pageant winners go on to do big things. Look at Miss Hazel" — our local talk show radio hostess — "and Dr. Santos. It's about the full package."

That's when it hits me. Millie buys into this stuff. This isn't a joke for her. This is the real deal.

"None of us are the perfect contestants," she says. "I think we can all agree to that. The key is playing to our strengths. Not to toot my own horn, but I think I've got the interview in the bag. Amanda, when you wear your corrective cleats, your soccer tricks are awe-inspiring."

I almost hold my breath, waiting for her to get to me so that she can somehow enlighten me.

"Hannah, don't take this the wrong way, but I've seen you in a swimsuit, and well, you go, girl." The edge of Hannah's lip quivers, and I swear to Christ, if Millie can make her smile, it will be nothing short of an act of God. "So, like they said at orientation, it's the eighty-first anniversary of Miss Teen —"

"Wait. What's *my* strength?" I ask.

She smiles. "Your confidence, of course."

I zone out completely. How can she see something I can't feel? And what's the point in acting confident if I'm not? I never thought I cared about what I saw in the mirror. But Bo ruined that. It's supposed to be easier to like yourself when someone else likes you.

But that can't be true. No matter how much I tell myself that the fat and the stretch marks don't matter, they do. Even if Bo, for whatever reason, doesn't care, I do.

Then there are days when I really give zero flying fucks, and I am totally satisfied with this body of mine. How can I be both of those people at once?

"Do you have anything else to add, Will?" asks Millie.

I blink once. Twice. "No. No, I guess not."

Hannah slides out of the booth. "I'm out of here."

Amanda slurps her soda until the straw screeches loudly.

I turn and call after Hannah, "What changed your mind? When Millie first asked you, you said no, right?"

She turns back. "I get called a freak every day. I might as well make a show of it."

"Straight from the horse's mouth,"

mumbles Amanda after Hannah's a safe distance away.

Millie kicks her underneath the table. "That wasn't very nice."

"Well, neither is she," says Amanda.

THIRTY-THREE

This time I tell Mitch that we can meet at his house. He invites me over to watch movies and I guess I just assume that his parents will be out for the night.

When the front door opens, I find the female version of Mitch wearing a light yellow T-shirt with kittens rolling in yarn. This woman who can only be Mitch's mom throws a dish towel over her shoulder and brings me in for a hug. "Oh my word!" she says. "Mitch said you were pretty, but he didn't say gorgeous." She lets go of me for a second before grasping my cheeks and pulling me in through her front door.

The entryway of Mitch's house is a bottleneck. Small and congested. But his mother doesn't move. "Let's get a look at this face." She slides her thumbs across my cheeks like she's wiping away tears.

"Mom!"

She steps back and I see Mitch there in the narrow hallway, his cheeks a deep magenta.

"Hey."

"Hey, Will." Mitch clears his throat. "Uh, Mom, we're heading upstairs."

His mom nods. "Leave the door open."

"Mom, we're fine!" Mitch waves for me to follow him up the stairs.

"For the Holy Ghost!" she calls after us.

Hanging on the posts at the head of Mitch's bed are his mum garters from freshman and sophomore year homecoming. Mums are one of those things that are so specifically southern that I both love and hate them. The best mums are homemade with giant artificial chrysanthemums on cardboard backing with huge streams of ribbon hanging from them. Since they're for homecoming, they're made in school colors and the ribbons usually have glitter letters that spell out different things, like you and your boyfriend's names or your school mascot. It used to be that girls would pin them to their shirts, but, like most things in Texas, they've only gotten bigger. Now, mums are so heavy that they have to be worn around your neck. And guys — especially football players like Mitch — wear miniature versions of garters around their arms. It's all pretty ridiculous, but in a Dolly kind of way.

On the walls of his room are a few random video game posters, but one in particular sticks out to me. A girl's torso takes up most of the poster. She holds a machine gun with a horde of zombies behind her. Taped over whatever she might be wearing is a knee-length dress made out of a paper grocery bag. I point to the poster. "What happened there?"

"Ugh, my mom. It's my favorite game — or at least it was before the sequel came out — and she always hated the poster." He lifts the paper bag dress to reveal a low cut crop top and olive green shorts so tiny they could be underwear. "She wasn't too crazy over me having a half-naked girl in my room. Even if she was 2D. This was her compromise. Every time I take it down, she cuts a new dress."

"Why don't you just take the poster down?"

He sits on the edge of his bed. "I don't know. I like the game. I don't really care about the naked girl."

"Okay?"

He waves his hands, like he's trying to erase what he said. "Not that I don't like naked girls. I mean, I don't go looking for naked girls. I" — he takes a deep breath — "I meant that I play the game because she's a badass. Not because you can see her ass cheeks." He whispers those last two words.

"It's okay," I whisper back. I pull out his desk chair and sit down because it's too weird to sit on a boy's bed.

"So you want to hang out here and watch a movie or something? We could go out, too. I figured keep it low-key?"

"A movie sounds good."

"Okay. Cool. We can watch in here on my laptop. Or in the living room."

"In here is fine. Or the living room."

"We can sit on my bed or I could sit on the floor and you could sit on —"

I sit down next to him on his bed. "Calm down." I'm so used to being the spastic one, the one who needs to take a deep breath. It's sort of a relief to not feel like I could fall off a cliff at any moment. "This is fine. It's not like sitting on your bed is going to get me pregnant."

"You should tell my mom that."

I laugh. "Well, at least we left the door open for the Holy Ghost."

He dims his lights and pulls out his laptop, which he sets up on a pile of pillows in front of us. "So if you want, they made a movie out of that video game or we could rent something online."

"I kinda want to see what this zombie movie is all about."

We settle back as the glow of the laptop washes over us. The movie is just as the video game poster advertised except the main character doesn't wear a brown-bag dress. I can tell that Mitch has seen this thing hundreds of times. His lips move with the actors as they say his favorite lines of dialogue. He laughs a few beats before every joke and grimaces before every scary part and, seeing as I've never much liked scary movies, I can appreciate the warning.

I almost miss most of the ending, because instead of the movie, my eyes focus in on Mitch's hand as it inches toward mine.

I should pull my hand away.

His pinkie brushes mine.

Then the laptop explodes.

Well, actually the hospital full of zombies in the movie explodes, but since I'm not paying attention, it scares me so much that I scream.

"What in baby Jesus's name are you subjecting that girl to?" hollers Mitch's mom.

"*Final Death 3!*" yells Mitch.

"I'm fine, ma'am!" I call back.

The credits roll, sending his room into a near pitch-dark. "You hungry?" he asks.

I am starving. "I could eat."

"There's that taco stand down on Dawson. We could walk and hang out for a little while before you go home."

I follow Mitch to the kitchen where his mom is tallying up receipts on one of those old calculators with the receipt paper. "You two hungry?"

"Actually, I think we're going to walk down the street to Taki's Tacos."

She takes her reading glasses off and they hang around her neck, bouncing against the kittens and their balls of yarn on her shirt. "Well, why would you do that when I went grocery shopping this morning? I'll make salami sandwiches. Or there's some leftover chicken spaghetti casserole, too." She turns to me. "Not to brag, but my chicken spaghetti casserole is something to behold."

"We want to get out of the house, Mom. Why is that such a big deal?"

"It's wasteful is all." She puts her glasses back on. "But it is a Saturday night. Be home before midnight."

The taco stand is on an old car lot. Weeds creep up through the cracks in the pavement as a reminder that the focus here is tacos and not landscaping. Next to the stand is a rusted playground set that looks like it was plucked from a city park and dropped in this parking lot. We sit on a bench at the edge of the circle of light put off by the taco stand to get as far away from the mosquitoes as possible.

After we eat, we wander into the playground. I sit on a swing and so does Mitch. The chains groan against his weight.

"Good tacos," I say.

He nods. "Did you like the movie?"

"It was . . . bloody. But I liked it."

"So you really entered the Miss Teen Blue Bonnet Pageant?"

"Yeah. Yeah, I did. I'm pretty screwed. I need a talent and I've got nothing."

I walk back in the swing and let the momentum push me forward as I pump my legs. "Not to mention these other girls ended up entering because I did. It's like I'm supposed to be guiding them or something. But I don't even know what I'm doing. And I feel responsible for them, ya know?"

Mitch stands up behind me and gently pushes me every time I swing back. "Maybe if you worry about figuring your own stuff out, you can help them with their stuff."

He pushes me back and forth a few

times while I let that thought simmer.

"Hey, Mitch?"

"Yeah?"

"You're really good at football, right?"

"That's what people tell me."

"I bet you'll get a scholarship out of here."

For the first time, Mitch doesn't respond.

"What?" I ask. "You don't think you will?"

"I don't know. I guess I will." He stops pushing me and sits down again in the swing beside me facing the opposite direction. "I never really like doing the things I'm supposed to like. I'm good at playing football. But the whole season feels like something I have to get through."

It's a hard thing for me to grasp. The idea that you can be so good at something and still not enjoy it.

"Being a guy in a town like this people expect things from you. You're supposed to play football and hunt and fish. Growing up, I didn't have a lot of friends, but

I had Patrick. We'd go hunting on the weekends with our dads."

"You hunt?" I ask. I shouldn't be surprised. Tons of people hunt here. It's disgusting, but it's not like I've sworn off meat, so I'm not one to talk.

"Well, sort of," he says. "I've been hunting since I was a kid. I'd go out with my dad and he'd let me have half a beer while we waited for whatever animal was in season to show itself. But whenever it came time to shoot, I always missed. For a while, I blamed it on me being a bad shot. My dad would get so mad at me. I'd miss the mark. Just barely. Then he started to realize that it was on purpose."

I feel this prickle of warmth in my chest for him. I think maybe it's the things we don't want to talk about that are the things people most want to hear.

"We were in seventh grade, and my dad was harping on me real bad. Patrick and his dad were there. It was deer season. I hit one." His voice trails off. "It was an accident. He was a big proud buck. My dad slapped me on the back. I remember feeling like I was choking."

"I'm sorry." The words sound so lame.

Like they did when people said they were sorry about Lucy.

He stands and pulls my swing back by its chains. I feel him let out a long breath against my neck. "I know guys aren't supposed to cry, but I cried a bunch that night. And I guess that's when I decided being good at something didn't mean you had to do it. Just 'cause something's easy doesn't make it right." He lets the chain go and I kick my feet out into the stars.

That night, I dream that I am inside Mitch's video game, wearing the tiny shorts and a shredded shirt. My body isn't some Photoshopped dream version of itself. My thighs are thick with cellulite and my love handles hang over the waistband of my shorts. My golden waves are done up big and high in an old-school Dolly perm. Like the girl in Mitch's game, there are guns, ammo, and knives strapped to my back and thighs with a bazooka resting on my shoulder. I am a total badass. A fat badass.

I run into an abandoned civic center. The revolving door pushes against months of debris as I enter the building.

They come slowly at first, but then they multiply. Zombie beauty queens. Everywhere.

I wait until they're almost too close before I fire the bazooka. Gone. Particles fly. I duck. They're dead. Like, really dead this time.

But there's still one left. One graying zombie, dressed for the best day of her life in a torn red gown. Her crown is bent and broken and her sash is too faded to read. She walks toward me, one foot dragging as it scrapes against the marble floor.

I reload my bazooka.

THIRTY-FOUR

There are a few things — like the swim-suit segment — I didn't consider before signing up for the pageant. But what I really didn't prepare myself for was the group dance number.

Me, Millie, Amanda, and Hannah sit in a row against the back wall of Dance Locomotive, the only dance studio in Clover City. I know this doesn't look easy, but it can't be much harder than walking in choreographed circles.

My mom stands at the front of the room in a dance skirt, a leotard that's working a little too hard, super shimmery nude tights, and black character dance shoes. Flanking her are Mrs. Clawson, in her turquoise wind suit that swishes every time she breathes, and Mallory Buckley, in her white yoga pants and petal-pink

267

sports bra. I catch my mom eyeing Mallory several times with the slightest bit of contempt, and it gives me a sick satisfaction.

Everyone is toned, tanned, bleached, and in matching workout gear. Whereas I wore the same pajama pants I slept in last night. Amanda in her soccer shorts and Millie in her matching sweat suit are slightly more prepared, but Hannah rounds us out in black jeans and a black T-shirt.

"Let's stretch it out, ladies." My mom sits down in front of us with her back to the mirror. Everyone falls into their preferred positions. Including Mrs. Clawson, who is doing standing windmills. Her face puffs red as she counts her breaths with each rotation. By some miracle, her perm doesn't move an inch.

My mom sits with the bottoms of her feet touching and her legs bent into a butterfly position. "This year's theme is 'Texas: Ain't She Grand?'"

"Yes," mumbles Hannah, "because grammar is make-believe."

Amanda laughs, and Millie kicks her in

the shin with her tiny little Keds-wearing foot.

I reach forward to touch my toes, but my stomach and boobs stand between me and my thighs.

"At the end of rehearsal, you will each be assigned a Texas landmark to plan your opening number outfit around. Everyone is asked to wear a denim skirt, plaid shirt, and cowboy boots. Beyond that, you are welcome to create whatever you like in homage to your landmark. For example, if you were given our state flower, the blue bonnet, you could wear a headpiece made to look like blue bonnets. This is an opportunity for the judges to get a taste of your personality and see how well you do with an assigned task. Take advantage, ladies."

Ellen sits in the front row with Callie, who is of course competing in the pageant. They wear matching workout gear with Sweet 16 stamped on their hips. We haven't spoken in two entire weeks. The last time I went two weeks without talking to Ellen was when her parents rented an RV and took her up along the West Coast. I wrote her a letter every day she was gone and left them in her mailbox. I went mad without her, and when she got back, both of our moms let her spend the night for two nights in a row.

This is so much worse. Because she's right there. She's at the other end of the room, and if I call out to her, she won't answer. I've almost apologized so many times, but I've waited too long now. And a part of me still thinks — no, knows — I'm right.

We all stand up to learn the routine. Millie leans over, standing on her tiptoes, and says, "You should talk to her."

"What are you talking about?"

She pushes up the sleeves of her sweatshirt. "Ellen."

"Grapevines!" says my mom over the twangy music. "Five counts left. Five counts right. Bekah!" she calls. "Come up here, so the girls can see your technique."

Bekah blushes, but obeys my mother. Just looking at her annoys me, and really I've got no good reason. She's good at everything. She's pretty, too. And she's humble.

I spend the next hour tripping over my feet, trying to keep up with the endless grapevines and turns as we all weave in and out of one another. I catch my mom watching me in the mirror as I trip over Amanda's platform shoe and have my ass handed to me by a hardwood floor. In the end, my mom was right to call Bekah forward, because she knows what the hell she's doing.

At the end of rehearsal, I am sweating in places that I didn't know could sweat.

Millie's got this crazed look on her face and a huge sweat ring around her neck. "That was so cool," she says. "What landmark did you get?"

I hold up the slip I drew from the bowl. "Cadillac Ranch." A place I've only ever seen in pictures. Something you gotta understand about Texas is that it's freaking huge. I know tons of people who have never even left the state. I remember hearing that, depending on where you start, you could drive for a day and still be in Texas. "What about you?"

She grins. "The Stockyards. Up in Fort Worth." Only Millie could turn a live-stock market into a pageant-worthy headpiece. If her optimism were contagious, I'd be betting on myself to win this whole thing.

THIRTY-FIVE

I've heard that at bigger schools, dances aren't really a thing anymore. There are too many students, I guess. But, unfortunately for me, dances are very much alive and well at Clover City High. And, outside of prom, the hottest shit in town is the Sadie Hawkins Dance. Because a sister can't just ask a guy out like it's some normal thing, girls have gone to great lengths to make sure that their Sadie Hawkins proposition is the most elaborate.

Then three years ago Macy Palmer reinvented the wheel when she asked her boyfriend Simon to the dance by employing the Twelve Days of Christmas. I am not kidding. Every morning this kid came to school and was greeted by anything from three hens to twelve drummers drumming. And the guy was already her boyfriend! It's not like he suspected she'd ask someone else. (Let the record show that they both graduated. She was four months pregnant while he had one foot out the door thanks to a golf scholarship.)

After that, it was no longer acceptable to ask a guy to Sadie Hawkins by baking him a plate of cookies or by wearing a T-shirt with his football number on the back. Now, not only do you have to muster the courage to ask a guy out in the first place, but you've got to do it with style.

Freshman year wasn't so bad because Ellen hadn't started dating Tim. Last year I faked sick. But this year, with everything that's happened, I don't notice the banners and the signs announcing ticket sales.

After a full five hours of walking through a minefield of Sadie Hawkins proposals — including a cheerleading pyramid during lunch — I have one hour to go. I slide into my desk next to Amanda.

She looks up from her phone. "So did

you ask anyone?"

"No. You?"

She shakes her head. "Nah. I figure let the chips fall where they may and see who's left tomorrow. I wouldn't bother, but we're gonna have to ask a guy to escort us at the pageant. Might as well cross two things off my list."

I drop my head into my hands and moan. I forgot about the escorts. My desk jolts like someone's kicked it. I whip around to see Bo walking to his seat at the back of the class.

I secretly love seeing him like this, in the clothes he chooses each morning from his closet. I wonder if he's deliberate. Or if he's one of those people who gets dressed in the dark because mornings are such a total violation. Or maybe he gets up super early and goes for a run or eats eggs or some other thing that morning people do.

Or maybe it's none of your business anymore, I tell myself.

"Millie asked Malik. From the newspaper," says Amanda. "He's kind of hot if you can get past the unibrow. Or if you think unibrows are hot."

I turn back to her, grateful for the distraction, but suddenly very conscious of exactly how I'm sitting. Maybe if I sit up straighter, my back fat will disappear.

"How'd she do it?"

She laughs. "She sang to him. With a ukulele."

I cringe with embarrassment for her. Everyone probably laughed. "What happened?" I whisper.

"Well, he said yes." She says it like, *Duh, why would he not?*

"Wait. Seriously?"

"He's doing the pageant thing, too. It was sweet. And he kissed her on the cheek. More action than I've seen."

Class drones on and I wonder how much of a jerk it makes me to expect that Millie would've been humiliated. If she had asked my opinion beforehand, I would've told her what a sweet idea it was, but I would've done everything in my power to stop her from going through with it. And it's not that I don't think she deserves to go to the dance and have an escort. I just don't want her to be the butt of anyone's joke. I would never wish that on anyone. And, yet, Millie's been there. She's been the punch line.

But there she is, doing her thing, not giving a hoot what anyone else thinks.

It almost hurts to know that she's putting herself out there so fearlessly. It's like seeing an old friend you've drifted from and remembering all the shared experiences you used to have.

Class lets out and I'm pushed out the door in a current of students. I can hear Bo talking back and forth with José Herrera about calculus and then about a party.

In the hallway, a wall of girls stops us. They stand with their hands joined, like a game of Red Rover.

"Sorry for the delay," one of them says.

"This will only take a minute," adds another.

Bekah Cotter stands behind the row of girls in a pair of tiny denim shorts, gold flats, and an oversized white T-shirt that's been tied into a knot at the small of her back. In iron-on letters the shirt reads *Go to Sadie Hawkins with me . . .* She spins a baton between her fingers, waiting for the crowd to settle.

Amanda stands behind me, bouncing on her toes. "Just looking at those shorts gives me a wedgie."

Bekah takes one deep breath and, without announcing herself, she spins the baton in the air, throwing it over her shoulder and catching it as she does gymnastics so sharp and quick you can barely keep up with her. It's amazing, and still, it's nothing nearly as involved as I've seen her do at football games. Her pageant talent is going to kill.

She throws the baton in the air and does some sort of crazy spinning flip, then she lands with her back to us and catches the baton as it's about to hit the floor. With her ass in the air, it's clear who she's asking to the dance. On each pocket of her denim shorts, in glitter paint, are the letters *B* and *O.*

The guys from World History push him up to the front of the crowd. He smirks and I can barely watch him as Bekah takes his hand. Bo glances to his side, and I know he sees me. But there's no second for decision or thought. He nods.

And now they're Bekah and Bo. Bo and Bekah.

I push Amanda out of the way and move against the flow of students heading for the parking lot. Keeping my eyes on the ground, I watch the sea of feet until I've found a bathroom. I sink down to my knees and dig through my backpack, looking for something. My phone? A grenade?

At the bottom of my bag is a permanent marker. I uncap it, turn to the mirror, and, like the totally sane person I am, begin to write on my face.

I didn't actually consider the logistics of getting from point A to point B when I was scribbling across my face. After looking myself over in the mirror, I realize that there is no turning back. Even if I want to. I guess it's called permanent marker for a reason.

Walking to the parking lot as quickly as I can, I flip my hair over my head like Cousin Itt and rely on whatever sight I have through the strands, praying to Baby Jesus that I don't get hit by a car.

And there he is. Walking to his car.

279

"Mitch!" I yell. "Mitch!"

This is a bad idea. I think it's actually safe to say that all my ideas are bad ideas.

He turns. "Will?" Deep concern lines his face. "Did something happen? Are you okay?"

When I'm within a few steps, I flip my hair back, letting him see my face.

His concern fades into confusion. "snikwaH eidaS ot oG?"

"Shit," I say. "I wrote it in the mirror."

He glances down, trying to hide his smile from me as he twists his toe in the gravel.

"So you wanna?" I ask. "Go to Sadie Hawkins?"

"I don't know." His cheeks swell. He's a boy struck with relief because I haven't forgotten his birthday. I am a hideous person. "Are you gonna wear a dress?"

"Are you?"

He slips his hands into his pockets. "Yeah, I'll go with you." He reaches forward and rubs my forehead with his thumb. "That's permanent, isn't it?"

"Forever," I say.

His eyes flood with light.

I should've added, "As friends." *Go to Sadie Hawkins as friends?* But it's too late now. I won't ruin this for him, though I worry I might have only done it for me.

THIRTY-SIX

It's Friday night and I'm spread out on the couch watching a daytime talk show I'd recorded about second cousins claiming to be telepathic.

Mom's in the kitchen dyeing a tablecloth for the judges' table.

The announcer on the television show gives the cousins some kind of test, asking them questions they should be able to answer with their "abilities." The first twin goes fifty-fifty and blames it on the time zone change and her jet lag from flying in from Louisiana to New York.

When the show goes to commercial, my mom sits down on the love seat and unhooks her apron from around her neck. "Woo," she says. "Gotta let that sit for a bit." She picks the remote up and mutes it.

"Wait," I say. "Pause it. I don't want to accidentally see what happens."

She fumbles with the remote for a minute before passing it to me to pause. "Let's talk for a minute."

This is going to be about the pageant, and how I'm not taking it seriously enough. Or how she thinks I'm going to embarrass myself somehow.

"Since Lucy passed, we haven't had her disability coming in."

So not what I was expecting.

"And her life insurance wasn't much, but it was floating us these last few months."

I sit up. It takes me a moment for my vision to adjust. "Are we selling the house?"

"No, no. Nothing like that. This place is paid off in a few years. I think I can make things work until then. I don't want you worrying about that."

"Okay . . ."

"But I can't afford to get your car fixed."

There it is. My heart sinks. I know it's

stupid to worry about something like a car when there are obviously other things like food and utilities to think about. Especially when we don't technically need that car. But that little red thing is my freedom in physical form. Clover City feels even smaller and more removed without my Jolene.

"I'm sorry, baby."

"How much is it going to cost?"

"About three thousand dollars."

I nod. That's at least a year of working at the Chili Bowl.

"Maybe we can start a little jar? Like, throw the day's pocket change in."

I lie back down, and hit play on the TV. If I were a better daughter, I would tell her it's fine and that I understand. I may not be the daughter she expected, but she never lets me go without.

The cousins are back on. Audience members laugh quietly as they so obviously get question after question wrong.

My mom stands and pulls the apron back over her neck.

Before heading to bed, I sit down at my desk in my room with Riot curled into a pile in my lap. My emails are mostly junk mail, but buried beneath that is one from Lucy's address.

My stomach twists like a corkscrew. I open the email.

But it's spam. Some piece of junk about interest rates.

I sit back in my chair and let my body exhale. If I'm getting junk mail from my dead aunt, then maybe other people are, too.

I log out of my account. It takes a few tries, but I finally guess her password. *DUMBBLONDE9.* One of her favorite Dolly songs and her favorite number. I'm about to shut down her account, but I find myself distracted by the months of messages just sitting here. This in-box full of unopened messages is the truest reminder that we are temporary fixtures in a permanent world.

I click through a few. There's nothing that really catches my eye until the fifth

page. The subject line reads: DOLLY
PARTON NIGHT.

THIRTY-SEVEN

Cardboard stars and crepe streamers hang from the rafters, but they're not enough to make me ignore the lingering body odor and forget that we're in the gymnasium. The music reflects off the walls, reminding everyone that this place was not built for the acoustics.

"This is cool," yells Mitch into my ear.

"Yeah." Except it's not. There are maybe fifteen people dancing, while everyone else spreads out on the bleachers. There's this weird hormonal energy in the air that I've never noticed before. Maybe because students are getting away with an insane amount of PDA that would never be tolerated during normal school hours.

Ellen sits perched on the bleachers with Callie and her boyfriend. Tim's got one arm draped over El's shoulder and his head is leaning so far back I think he might be asleep. Callie's boyfriend is overattentive and rubs his hand up and down her thigh in a weird way that makes me shiver while she and El whisper back and forth, sharing secrets, I'm sure.

I catch Callie pointing at me, and turn away. "Hey, I'm going to run to the bathroom."

Mitch's lips form a question, but he just nods.

In the bathroom, I turn the faucet on high and let the hot water rush over my hands until they're red. I hate that I can't just go in there and tell El about what a fool I made of myself when I asked Mitch to this thing. This distance between us started months ago. I know that. But maybe she didn't. Maybe you only ever notice the distance when it's you who's being left behind. I should've shut my big mouth and not said anything about the pageant, but Ellen signing up somehow felt like scoring points for the other team. I don't know.

"Can I give you some advice?"

I stand up straight, my brain coming

back from its tangent. "Hi, Callie."

She watches me in the reflection of the mirror. "I know El has been, like, super good to you since you guys were kids. But you telling her she couldn't enter the pageant? That was a shit thing for you to do."

I feel naked. Like, somehow, in the midst of all of her anger, El might have revealed every little one of my secrets and insecurities. "Callie, listen, I don't know you, but I don't have to know much to know that I don't like you. So back off and mind your own business."

"Whatever." She throws her hands up. "Ya know, she's better off without you. At least now you're not around to drag her down." She turns, but then whips back around to add, "And you wanna know what else? If you would put a little effort in and take care of yourself, you'd be surprised how much of a difference it would make. And I don't even mean that in a rude way. I'm just being honest." Reaching down the front of her dress, she re-tucks her boobs into her bra. "By the way, despite what you and your friends might think, this pageant isn't some feel-good after-school project where you get an A for effort." She walks off. Which is good because I'm about two steps away from breaking her nose.

The door swings shut behind her, and I listen as her heels clack against the linoleum floor.

Maybe she's right. Maybe my life would fall into place if I could shed a hundred pounds. I'm holding back the tears brimming in my eyes. Maybe it all comes down to me and this body.

Mitch is dutifully waiting for me behind the DJ, who isn't actually a DJ, but instead the varsity basketball manager armed with an iPod and speaker access.

I knock his elbow with mine. "Let's dance."

Mitch follows me out to the dance floor where I find Millie and her date, Malik. Amanda's with them, too.

I'm kind of starting to love Amanda. She's brusque and odd and the opposite of everyone else I know. She's the type of person who overcommits to tapping her foot to the music and takes every joke too far. Right now, with her head bopping and her limbs flailing, she almost looks like one of those one-man bands, but without instruments.

I introduce them to Mitch even though we've all gone to school together forever.

Amanda elbows me in the side and whispers, "Not bad. But he's no peach-butt."

"What about you?" I ask. "Did you ask anyone?"

She leans in, but doesn't stop moving her head. "Options were limited, so I decided to fly solo."

"You're not solo!" yells Millie. "You're with us. Right, Malik?"

Malik takes Millie's hand. "Yeah, of course."

My damn heart explodes. Because, to me, Malik and Millie are homecoming/winter formal/spring fling/prom king and queen combined into one.

The next song starts up and it's the type of song that makes people rub their crotches together. Because they're horrible human beings, Millie, Amanda, and Malik abandon us for the refreshments table.

The space around us is filling in with horny teenagers. Mitch must see the panic in my face. He takes my arms and wraps them around his neck. His meaty hands barely touch my waist, but I suck in as deep as I can. I can't help it. And, in the midst of the grinding and sloppy making out, we begin to slow dance.

"I like takin' it easy," Mitch says. He is the epitome of southern gentleman in his creased khakis, plaid pearl-snap shirt, and brown boots.

Slowly, I let my body ease into his.

We dance slow to fast songs and fast to slow songs, creating our own rhythm.

Patrick works his way over to us, basically dry humping as many girls as he can on his way. "Hey, man," he says to Mitch. "I'd be careful with this one. She's violent." And then to me he says, "The baby maker still works. In case you were wondering."

I shake my head. "God save us all," I say.

Patrick rocks back and forth on his heels. "I hear you got some of your friends to join the pageant with you. You better make sure they know it's a beauty contest and not a livestock show."

He's gone before either of us can respond.

Mitch takes a step forward, but I squeeze his arm, pulling him back.

"You know he's disgusting, right?" I say.

"I'm not saying you're wrong."

I only see Bo and Bekah during one slow song, like the kind of couple who have their pictures taken in white shirts and jeans or the kind who go on family vacations together during the summer.

And I hate it.

I rest my cheek against Mitch's shoulder. Bo glances up, but this time I don't look away. There on the floor of the gymnasium, our eyes meet. And I can imagine that it's us dancing out here, all on our own. Not because the room is empty, but because no one else matters.

"I went to a dance in middle school," Mitch says. "My mom made me. I had to wear my Easter Sunday suit. I was the only kid that dressed up."

My eyes stay with Bo and I am acutely

aware of the fire licking against my rib cage. "Did you have a date?" My voice is far away.

"No one really had dates. I mean, you know, there were people who called each other boyfriend and girlfriend, but that was it."

Bekah says something and, after a moment that feels like good-bye, Bo looks away. The two of them slip off behind a wall of people.

I watch the empty space left by Bo. "Did you dance with anyone?"

Mitch drags his finger up and down my spine, and I know that this little bit of contact is a leap for him. "Nope. Just sat in a folding chair next to the chaperones all night. Hung out with some guys doing layups on the other side of the gym. But no dancing."

"Well." I lift my head. "You're dancing now."

He grins. "Worth the wait."

Later, as we're walking to the parking lot with sounds of the dance winding down behind us, my kitten heels dangle from my fingers, and Mitch holds his arm out for me. Inside the dance, the rules didn't apply. I was allowed to lean my head on his chest and let him wrap his arms around me because it was a dance and that's what you do at dances. But out here, outside of that bubble, it's different. I don't want to be the one to lead him on and turn this into something it's not.

He smiles. I hook my arm through his because I've ruined so much lately and I'm not ready to add this night to the list.

"You're still not talking to Ellen?"

"Nope." I hadn't told him the exact circumstances, but I told him we'd gotten into a fight — a real one. I didn't really want to share more and he hasn't asked.

"You guys have been inseparable forever. I remember when we were doing *Where the Red Fern Grows* in sixth grade and we were reading book reports in front of the class."

I nod. "She always cried when we got to the part with the dog." She hated that book. El's not the type of person who can read something that's made her cry and think it was good because it touched her. No, books or movies that make Ellen cry infuriate her. Like, it's some kind of betrayal.

"So you finished reading the report for her."

"She practiced it in front of the mirror dozens of times. She was so pissed when she started crying." I pick my head up after realizing I'd been leaning against his arm this whole time.

He opens the car door for me. "How long are you going to let this go on?"

For a split second, I think he's talking about me and him. "She's got new friends anyway," I say after he slides in behind the wheel. "I guess I'm no match for Callie."

"Listen," he says. "I obviously don't know the whole story here, but good friendships are durable. They're meant to survive the gaps and the growing pains."

THIRTY-EIGHT

Amanda Lumbard is a horrible driver, but since Millie couldn't use her mom's van tonight, she's the only one of us who has access to a car that both works and can fit all four of us comfortably.

"That was sweet of your mom to let us borrow her van," says Millie.

Amanda shrugs it off, her foot weighing down on the gas. "She was actually kinda excited to hear I was going out with friends. Even if it is a Tuesday night."

I nod along. I didn't really give all the details when I invited them via group text.

ME: Hey, so I think we can all agree that we've got some things to work on before this pageant. There's this pageant-ish event going on in Odessa tomorrow night and I think we could pick up some pointers.

HANNAH: My dance card is full.

ME: We're going to need transportation, too. My car's out of commission.

MILLIE: Sitting here with Amanda. We're in. She can drive. Can't wait!

HANNAH: Fine. I'll go.

The half truth is that I feel responsible for the three of them and I thought maybe we could use some pointers for the pageant. I'm not trying to be a ringleader or anything, but if I hadn't started this whole thing, we wouldn't be in this boat.

The whole truth is that I needed a ride. That's kind of horrible of me, I know. But I paid for Amanda's gas, and her mom's van isn't cheap to fill up. So I'm absolved, kind of.

As we speed farther and farther away from town, I listen as Millie and Amanda bicker back and forth over some series of books they're reading while I sit in the back with Hannah and a crumpled paper in my hand.

DOLLY PARTON NIGHT!

Come see your favorite Dolly Parton impersonators duke it out for the crowning glory of best little whore in Texas! Winner gets bragging rights and a one-year supply of Avon lipsticks courtesy of our very own Kiwi Lavender! The Hideaway on Palmer and Fourth, Odessa, Texas
Doors open at 8! Show starts at 9!

As we pull into the parking lot, Millie turns to me. "You're sure this is the right place?"

I check the cross street and point to the hot-pink sign that blinks THE HIDE-AWAY. I recognize this place from the picture of Lucy that Mrs. Dryver gave me to keep. "This is it."

"What kind of pageant would be in a bar? This is a bar, right?" she asks.

I clear my throat. "I think it's probably best if we keep an open mind. And I didn't say it was a pageant necessarily."

Hannah laughs. "This should be good."

We all pile out of the car.

Amanda stands in the flickering pool of

light below the sign. "My mom's van is safe here, right?"

None of us answer.

There's a short line at the door with a group of gay guys in front of us. Or what I assume to be gay guys. This is going to sound totally Podunk of me, but I've never actually met a gay person. Well, I mean, someone who was open about it. There are gay people in Clover City, I'm sure, but the ones I've heard of have been treated as urban legends or cautionary tales. Lucy had lots of gay friends online because, as she put it, Dolly Parton is the patron saint of gay men.

There are moments in my life when I feel like I know everything and that I've left no rock unturned. But things like this remind me of how small my world is.

"Y'all, I think those were gay guys," whispers Amanda after they go through the door.

Hannah rolls her eyes. "You're a fucking Einstein."

Amanda is undeterred. "How do they get their eyebrows so perfect?"

The man standing at the door is a big,

burly guy with a belly, but all he's wearing is a pair of jeans and a leather vest.

It's hard to imagine Lucy at this place, but then I think of the bright blue eye shadow I saw her wearing in that picture, and it doesn't seem so impossible.

"IDs," he growls.

"Uh, for what?" asks Millie.

"Eighteen and up," he says.

My stomach sinks to my butt. "That's not what the email said," I tell him.

"Well, that's what I say," he says.

Hannah pushes past Millie and Amanda. "Listen, we drove here from Clover City. Do you even know where that is?"

He grunts.

"That's right," she says. "Of course you don't, because it's a sad little town that no one's ever heard of. We drove two hours to get away from that shitter and you can't be telling us it was all for nothing."

He licks his lips. I almost think she might have cracked him. I mean, look at us. Millie's wearing a polyester pantsuit and Amanda's in a pair of soccer shorts — I think they might even be the same ones she wore yesterday. We don't look like the kind of girls who are capable of drinking the place dry. Well, Hannah might.

"Nope," he says. "Sorry, kiddies. No can do."

"But look at this email," I tell him, like that will somehow make a difference.

He takes the paper from my hand and his gaze hovers at the top of the page before he says, "This isn't your email address."

I swallow. "It's my aunt's. Lucy."

Carefully, he folds the paper and hands it back to me. He pulls four fluorescent orange wristbands from his vest pocket and fastens them around our wrists.

My mouth drops wide open.

"If any of you even look at the bar, you're out." He holds my elbow while the others file in. "Lucy was good people."

I nod and silently thank her for this little bit of magic tonight.

Inside we find a small table off to the

side of the stage and far, far away from the bar. The waiter walks by, glances at our wristbands, and brings back four waters.

Millie scoots her chair in close and smooths down her hair. "There's a whole mess of men here, don't y'all think?"

Hannah looks around for a moment, and the expression on her face shifts. "Give me that email."

I lean away from her. "What? Why? No."

She reaches for my pocket and despite me pushing at her hands, rips it out. Millie and Amanda are in their own worlds, absorbing their surroundings. Hannah takes a second to glance over the email. "Holy shit," she says.

The lights begin to dim. "What?"

She shakes her head. "Oh my God. You don't even know, do you?" She smacks her hand on the table, laughter spurting from her mouth. "Millie," she says. "Your mama's gonna make you wash your eyes out with soap when you get home tonight."

Millie's mouth forms an *O,* but that's

all I see before the club goes completely dark except for a few runner lights by the bar.

Over the speakers comes a low, sultry voice. "Tramps, vagabonds, ladies, and lords, welcome to Dolly Parton Night at the Hideaway!"

The crowd cheers.

"First to grace our stage tonight is the lovely Miss Candee Disch! Let's make her feel welcome, y'all."

A spotlight hits center stage on a tall woman with a huge blond wig. She wears a floor-length velvet gown in lime green. Her makeup is exaggerated and her lips are bubbly and drawn on. The music starts and I know the song within only a few notes. "Higher and Higher."

"Your love has lifted me," she sings. "Higher, higher, and higher." Then the tempo speeds up and even though she's straight and lean, her hips appear like magic and she's shaking, working the stage with everything she's got. I am totally taken. So much so that I don't even think to watch for reactions from my friends. I sing along with the song, and not until she's about to walk off the stage do I realize that Hannah is in absolute hysterics.

My eyes have adjusted to the darkness. Millie turns to me, her expression still in that same *O* shape it was in when the lights went down. "Willowdean," she says. "Correct me if I'm wrong, but that was a man. A very lovely man."

I glance around. Men holding hands. Girls with their arms around each other.

"This is better than reality TV," says Amanda.

The crowd applauds as Candee Disch curtsies. "Let's hear it for the iconic Britney Swears!"

Another woman enters from offstage, and I see it now. The rough edge of her square jaw. Her broad shoulders. The stubble beneath her makeup despite her close shave.

This is a drag show.

I sit up straighter in my chair.

My stomach flurries with excitement. For the first time since that night when I sat in the back of Bo's truck, watching the meteor shower, I feel like my life is happening.

"I'm almost impressed," says Hannah.

We watch as drag queens every shape and size and color give it their all and leave everything they've got on that stage in this dingy little bar out in the middle of West Texas. They wear sparkling, elaborate costumes with incredible high heels and insane wigs. Each of them is their own brand of beauty. There's even a duo with a woman cross-dressing as Kenny Rogers for a rendition of "Islands in the Stream."

My favorite, though, is a short Asian queen named Lee Wei. She wears a baby-blue minidress with sequins so long that every time she moves, she's a blur of motion. When the spotlight zeros in on her and the song begins, it only takes one note before the whole bar loses it. "Jolene."

It's cliché, I know, but if I had to listen to one song for the rest of my life, it would be "Jolene." Everyone loves it, but I like to think it takes a special kind of heartbreak to really call the song your own. I mean, Dolly Parton — THE Dolly Parton — is singing to some mysterious Jolene who she thinks is more beautiful and more worthy than her, begging her not to take her man. It's catchy and everyone knows the words, but to me, it's this reminder that no matter who you are, there will always be someone prettier or smarter or thinner. Perfection is nothing more than a phantom shadow we're all chasing. If I could sing worth a lick, this would be the song I'd sing for the pageant.

By the end of the song, I'm wiping away tears I didn't even realize I was shedding.

The four of us leave at the end of the night with this look of wonder plastered to our faces, like we've spent the last few hours sitting too close to the TV.

As we're walking to the van, someone calls to us from the back door. "Hey! Kiddies!"

I turn. It's the bouncer from earlier. "Y'all go on," I tell Millie, Hannah, and Amanda. "I'll be there in a sec."

The burly man sits on a stool, holding the back door open with his back. "Name's Dale," he says. "You enjoy yourself tonight?"

I nod. "I think it's safe to say that this

has been a formative experience in my life."

"Seems like a fair thing to say about most drag shows."

I nod back to the van. "My friends had fun, too."

"Lee!" he calls behind him as he stubs out his cigarette beneath his boot. "Honey!"

Lee Wei, the queen who sang "Jolene," saunters out the back door. She's even shorter and somehow rounder without her high heels. She looks from me to the bouncer, and smiles, even though she obviously has no idea who I am.

"You 'member Lucy?" Dale asks. "Used to come around here with Suze Dryver."

El's mom. Oh Jesus. I wish El had been here tonight. It's the only thing that could have made the whole experience even more perfect.

Lee holds her hand to her chest. "Oh, sweet Lucy! Of course I do." Her voice is deeper than I expect.

"This is her niece," says Dale.

I nod. "Willowdean."

Without a moment of hesitation, Lee reaches for my hand. "I am so sorry," she tells me. "Lucy was a real gem. She had a kind, open heart. We were so sad to see her go."

"Th-thanks," I say, and I don't really know why, but I add, "I've been real lost without her. Like, she was this compass I didn't even know I had."

She nods, and Dale presses his lips together in a thin line. "You email the club's address if you ever need anything," he says.

Lee steps forward and plants a kiss on my forehead. "There's nothing good about losing someone," she says. "But maybe Lucy wasn't supposed to be your compass forever. Maybe she was there for you just long enough so you could learn how to be your own compass and find your own way." She winks at me. "The universe is a strange thing."

I leave Dale and Lee there at the stage door and hop into the backseat of the van.

"What did they want?" Amanda asks.

"Just told me not to come back until

we're eighteen."

"You've got lipstick on your forehead," says Hannah.

"I know." I want to leave it there forever as a blessing. The last permission I need to be my own role model.

THIRTY-NINE

One week turns into two, and I realize that Mitch and I have begun to spend lunches and almost every moment not dedicated to work or the pageant together. I almost even tell him about the drag show at the Hideaway, but it's like trying to explain your favorite part of a movie to someone who's never seen it — you'll never do it justice.

We both settle into an easy type of routine where I come over and watch him play video games, even taking the controls myself a few times. I stay for dinner one night, but it feels too much like trespassing.

From what I gather, Mitch and his mom eat dinner together every night while his dad takes his meal on a TV tray in front of his recliner. I watch him walk in from work, grab a beer, and wait in the living room for his food to be brought to him.

The three of us eat at the dinner table in total silence as our silverware scratches against plates. I want to ask Mitch about it, but it feels like a secret I'm not meant to know.

A few days later, we sit at lunch, talking about what we want to do after graduation when he brings it up all on his own.

"I don't know if I can leave my mom," he says. "I mean, he doesn't, like, hit her or anything. But they don't talk. Not at all. And I kind of hope that maybe it's me who's the problem, so that if I do leave, it'll get better."

"Why don't they get divorced?" A single-parent home is all I've ever known, and Lucy more than made up for some deadbeat dad. My real dad was some guy passing through town. He stuck around for a while, but not long enough to be more than some guy. He's in Ohio or Idaho. Wherever the potatoes come from.

He smiles in a broken kind of way. "My mom doesn't believe in divorce. She gets really upset every time I mention it."

Just as I'm about to respond, Tim walks right past us. "Hang on a sec," I say as I'm already leaving to follow him. "Tim!" I look around for any sign of Ellen as I follow him up to the lunch line.

I cut past three freshmen to squeeze in behind Tim. "Tim, come on. Talk to me."

He reaches for a tray and so do I.

"We're friends, too, ya know," I remind him.

He takes one of the bowls of mac and cheese from beneath the heat lamps. "I know that, Will."

I check over my shoulder once more for El even though I didn't see her in second period.

"She's sick today," he says.

The lunch lady tries to offer me a plate of chicken-fried steak, but I wave her off.

"You've got to get her to talk to me."

He shakes his head. "When has anyone ever had any luck making Ellen do anything?"

He has a point. "Come on, Tim. Something. I can meet you guys one day in the parking lot or maybe you can tell her you want to meet her in the gym and I'll show up instead."

"I'm not tricking her into talking to you. I don't wanna get in the middle of this."

Tim pays for his food as the lunch lady eyes my empty tray. I take a bowl of green Jell-O and hand her a few dollars without waiting for my change. "You can't tell me she's not miserable without me."

"Listen, I'll try, but I just don't see how I can make something happen."

I nod my head like a madwoman and pretend he didn't say that second half. "Thank you. Thank you so much."

"I really hate that Callie girl," he says.

Relief floods my chest. No stronger bond than a common enemy.

I hurry back over to the table where I left Mitch. "I am so sorry," I tell him.

He's unfazed. "Can't beat a Jell-O craving."

I shove a spoonful in my mouth. I could have at least gone for the red bowl.

"Hey," Mitch says. "Not to put you on the spot, but my mom's been talking about making you a homecoming mum, and I wanted to make sure that wouldn't be awkward or anything."

I smile. "No, that wouldn't be awkward or anything."

The door chime at the Chili Bowl so rarely rings, which means I always find myself startled when it does.

Ron, my former boss, walks in. Because of the log cabin interior and maroon accents, he looks like a candy cane in the middle of a lumberyard with his red-and-white-striped shirt and white pants.

"Ron," I whisper, circling around the counter. "What are you doing here?"

"Maybe I want chili," he says, a little too loudly.

I cross my arms over my chest and give him the best cut-the-shit stare I can muster.

"All right." His voice drops a few degrees. "Listen, we're desperate and super shorthanded. I've got Lydia working sixty-hour weeks covering your old shift because everyone we hire leaves when they find something better. She's threatening to quit on me and I can't afford to see her go."

My head's shaking before he can even finish.

"Hear me out." He puts one hand up. "You left in an awful hurry. I may be old, but I'm not dumb. I don't know what happened, but whatever it was, I promise the boys will be on their best behavior. I grilled each of them — Marcus and Bo — after you left, and I got nothing." He shakes his head, and I see the lines of exhaustion crowded around his mouth and eyes. "Give us a second chance. I'm begging you, Will."

I open my mouth to say no, but nothing comes out. Ron's always been so kind to me, and I think I owe it to him to at least pretend that I'll think about it. "I'll let you know by the end of the week. I'm going to have to think on it."

He holds his hands up. "Fair enough. Fair enough." He pulls his wallet from his back pocket. "I'll take a cup of chili."

■ ■ ■ ■

I only see a few more customers for the rest of the night, which gives me far too much time to think. At first, I'm logical. *You don't make nearly as much money as you used to at Harpy's and your car's stuck in the shop. At least Harpy's is busy enough to make the time go by faster.*

Then I remember how lonely these last few weeks have felt. Millie, Hannah, Amanda, and Mitch, too, are okay — great even. But they're no Ellen. The thought of going back to Harpy's feels like comfort food. And not just because of Bo. I miss Marcus and Ron, too.

Bo was the reason I quit. The reason why I couldn't bear to work there anymore. But now that anger I've trained myself to feel seems false. Like a pretense of what I thought it should be. And it's pretty obvious he's over me, too. I don't know for sure, but I've heard whispers about him and Bekah. And if I don't think about what it felt like to kiss him, then I can tell myself that they're cute together. That they match. And maybe the burning that could only be jealousy

317

will go away.

Before leaving work, I scrub everything down and refill the already stuffed condiment bar. *I'm still thinking,* I tell myself. *I haven't made up my mind.* I say good night to Alejandro and get in my mom's car.

Rather than turning left out of the Chili Bowl, my foot presses against the gas pedal, almost flying across the street and into the parking lot of Harpy's. I have crossed the line in the sand.

The dining room doors are locked, but I bang on them anyway.

Marcus turns the lock and lets me in. "Whoa. Hey! What's going on, Will? You smell like onions."

Bo watches me from behind the counter with wide eyes and a twitching jaw.

I can't look away. "Ron in his office?" I ask Marcus.

If Marcus would look up from the lock instead of fiddling with his huge ring of keys, he'd see everything that happened between Bo and me because in this moment it is so obvious. So open. So public. It's all right there, splayed out like an open-heart surgery.

"Yeah, I think so." He locks the door behind me, finally. "But you still haven't said what you're doing here."

I don't answer him. The butterflies in my stomach carry me through the break room and to Ron's office. I knock on the open door.

Lydia is sitting in front of his desk on a crate. She turns at the sound of me. "Oh, thank Christ. The prodigal cashier has returned." She stands and takes her pack of cigarettes from his desk. "I'll leave you to it." And once her back is turned to him, she gives me the tiniest smile as she closes the door.

Without bothering to sit, I turn to Ron. "I want a raise. And I'm going to need a couple days off for . . . for this thing I have."

Without hesitating, Ron says, "I can do a seventy-five cent raise. And I'll work with you on your schedule. We'll figure it out."

"Okay." I didn't expect that to be so simple. "Well, then it's a deal."

"You're back?"

I nod. "I'm back."

"That chili was really bad. I tried to eat it, but Lydia kept gagging every time she walked by my office. I think she was kidding, but still."

"It's pretty horrible."

He chuckles. "I'm glad to have you back." He stands and walks me through the kitchen to the front. We pass Bo and his eyes follow us all the way to the door. "Are you okay to start on Monday?"

"I'll be there."

He holds his hand out for me to shake, and I do.

I walk to my car as Bo's gaze follows me; the feeling of it starts as a ball of heat in my chest and spreads like a sunrise.

FORTY

I gave Alejandro my notice, and he kind of looked at me like, *What took you so long?* He promised me that I'd always have a job at the Chili Bowl and asked me to give Ellen his number. I slipped the folded scrap of paper in my pocket and swore to forget about it. I was all nerves when I told Mitch I was going back to Harpy's, but he shrugged it off and kept playing his video game. It occurred to me then that he had no reason to be upset. For the first time, not telling him about my history with Bo felt like a lie.

My first night back at Harpy's is quiet. Marcus berates me with endless questions about the Chili Bowl, like, "Who makes the chili?" or "Is it true you guys don't wash the pots?"

Bo keeps to himself in the kitchen, but we play a game of Catch Me If You Can with our eyes over the heat lamp counters. When Bo's on his break, Marcus leans over and says, "He almost got fired a couple weeks after you left."

"What?" The way Ron made it seem, he couldn't afford to fire anyone, so I can't imagine what Bo could've done that was bad enough to get fired.

"Ron had Bo up on the front counter while he worked the kitchen, which was a bad idea to begin with, and these guys from his old school came in, and Bo refused to serve them. Just flat-out told them they weren't welcome. The dudes made a big deal about it. Even their parents made a big deal about it, and basically the only way Bo could keep his job was if Ron only kept him in the kitchen."

"Whoa."

"He's one crazy dude. I feel like he's either going to murder everyone or be, like, a movie star. There's no in between for that guy."

I like that about Bo. You were either for him or against him.

Marcus goes off on a tangent about different schools that his girlfriend, Tiffanie, is looking at and how he's going to a community college near whatever school she chooses. He doesn't really pause to ask me a question or get my take on any of it, but he seems to take comfort in talking without someone lecturing him on why he shouldn't be planning his life around a girl. I don't know. Maybe Tiffanie and Marcus will go off to school and graduate and get married and live happily ever after. But I don't want to be the asshole he worked with at a fast-food restaurant who planted a seed of doubt in his head.

After cleanup, I take my bag out of my locker and find a red sucker there. I try not to smile as I slide it into my purse.

Bo says nothing. He doesn't even make eye contact with me. But as we're all walking out the door, I unwrap the sucker and pop it in my mouth.

It's a cherry-flavored olive branch.

■ ■ ■ ■

When I get home from work, I find my mom on her knees with Lacey Sanders standing on a step stool in a formal gown and Bekah Cotter on my couch, tapping away on her cell phone.

"Hi, Dumplin'," says Mom through the straight pins between her teeth. "Lacey, how's this hemline, dear? You can't go any higher on those heels, you hear?"

Lacey smacks her gum and blows a bubble. "Roger that."

Lots of things happen around pageant season, but Mom altering dresses in the middle of our living room is not one of them. There's also the fact that with Bekah sitting here in my house, my brain is going into high-alert mode like one of Mitch's video games. Red letters flash above Bekah's head. TARGET. TARGET.

I feel weird going upstairs with all of them down here, so I sit on the couch and lightly click my tongue until Riot comes out of hiding.

Bekah glances up from her phone and

turns to me. "Oh, hey. You work at Harpy's. You must know Bo." She doesn't even know to be threatened by me because why would she?

Lacey spins around and I see the terror on my mother's face. "Lacey, honey, you have got to stay still."

"Sorry, Miss D." She blows another bubble.

I glance down at my uniform. "Well, I did over the summer, and I just started back there again today. Why?" My tone is sharp, but Bekah doesn't seem to notice.

"He's a strange one," says Lacey.

"He's my escort," says Bekah. "For the pageant. Well, I haven't asked him. But he's going to be. I think."

"Hey," says Lacey. "He might be quiet" — *as shit,* she mouths — "but at least he'll look good in a tux. Maybe he'll let you twirl his baton?"

I could barf. On her shoes.

"Girls!" my mother shrieks.

Bekah grins. "We went to Sadie Hawkins together," she says by way of explanation.

Against his protests, I tuck Riot beneath my arm and stand to go upstairs. "Nice dress, Lacey."

I sit on my bed, still dressed in my uniform and compose texts to Ellen that I'll never send. I check for messages from Tim I might have accidentally missed. Anytime I see him at school, I look for some kind of meaningful eye contact, but the best he's given me is a curt head-shake.

After a while, my mom knocks on the door and enters without waiting for my permission.

"I'm doing some alterations this year for extra cash." She pulls the elastic out of her hair and combs her fingers through.

"You could have told me." Bekah Cotter. On my couch. I'm not even safe in my own house. But then I notice the deep circles beneath my mom's eyes. "I'm sorry," I say.

She nods. "You missed Ellen. She was here with her mom."

"She was here?" My eyes are immediately thick with tears waiting to spill.

"Only gettin' her hem fixed. You know that girl. Can buy a darn formal straight off the rack and it fits like a dream."

"Yeah." I don't even know what she's wearing for the pageant. Or what her talent will be. Or if she's started on her prop for the opening number.

"What's going on with the two of you anyway?"

"Me and El?" I shrug. "Just having a difference of opinion, I guess."

"Y'all will figure things out. Me and Luce always did." She comes in a little further and sits at the foot of my bed. I try to picture the last time I saw her perched there, but nothing comes to mind and it's like one of those memories you tell yourself is real, but it's not. You just wanted it to be. "Have you thought any about your wardrobe for the pageant?"

"Uh, no. Not really." I bite down on the skin around my thumbnail. "Mom, do you miss her?"

"Miss who?"

It kills me that she doesn't instinctively know. "Lucy."

"Luce," she says and it comes out like breath. "Yeah. Of course. All the time."

We're both quiet for a moment.

"The year I won Miss Teen, she stayed up all night sewing sequins on my dress. I bought the thing at a consignment shop. I told her no one would notice a few missing sequins, but she wouldn't have any of it. 'The difference between winning and losing is all in the details,' she said."

So much of my memory is filled with their arguments that I sometimes forget that more than anything else, they loved each other.

She stands up. "The dresses from Cindy's are pretty pricey and she'd have to order something for you, but maybe we can put something together ourselves."

I want to appreciate this, that she can take off her former Miss Teen Blue Bonnet hat and be my mom. But it doesn't feel like enough.

"Sometimes," I say, "I think I can't miss Lucy any more than I already do, but then something like dress shopping comes up, and I remember all the things she won't be here to see."

For the first time in a very long time, my mom says nothing. I never realized how much was lacking from my relationship with her until Lucy wasn't here to fill in the gaps. It's the two of us now, fumbling around in the dark.

FORTY-ONE

It's homecoming, which means school is a total joke. The day's schedule is full of pep rallies, contests, and alumni tours. When I sit down for second period next to Mitch, there's a huge blue, yellow, and white mum spread out across my desk. Long, glittery ribbons hang from a cluster of fake chrysanthemums, and hot glued to that are two miniature stuffed teddy bears. One in a football uniform and the other in a pink dress and a tiara. Mums are like good food. The best kind is homemade.

"Oh." I suck in a breath.

"You don't like it?" asks Mitch. He wears a small version of my mum around his arm. His hair is combed and his jersey is tucked into his jeans. "My mom can go overboard, and well, I can't really —"

I sink down into my chair. "No, it's not that," I tell him. "I love it. No one's ever given me a mum before. Thank you. Really."

"But?"

I sigh. "I have to work tonight."

He smiles, but the rest of his face is heavy with disappointment. "I guess you can't get out of that, huh?"

"I wish I could." I really do. "But I just started back, and I'm going to have to take off time for the pageant, too."

He squeezes my hand. "It's cool. At least tomorrow's Halloween."

For a moment, I'm distracted as Ellen and Callie file into the classroom, laughing back and forth about the costumes they have planned for tomorrow night. I hated dressing up with her. She'd always try to put together some couples costume that suited both of us, but no matter how hard she tried, it never quite worked. She doesn't even look in my direction.

There are lots of things I can't remember. Like, the periodic table. My mother's birthday. Or my locker combination at work.

But if there's one thing I can't forget, it's those words we spat at each other.

Maybe we're outgrowing each other. Holding each other back. I miss out on lots of things because of you.

I hate it. I hate that she thinks she's better off without me. Like I'm this sad, fat girl stepping on her heels.

I know I should apologize.

But maybe she should, too.

I wear the mum all day long. It's so big I have to wear it around my neck. Hannah and Amanda make fun of me. Millie thinks it's adorable. But by the end of the day, my neck is sore and my shoulders are hunched from the weight of it.

For Halloween, Ron asks us to wear costumes because the elementary school PTA is hosting a trunk-or-treat party in our parking lot. Like I told Mitch on our Most Awkward Date Ever, Halloween isn't my thing. Outside of school parties, my mom never really took me anywhere for Halloween. Well, except to church "harvest parties," which were just covers for Halloween parties. Besides, we were only able to dress up as biblical characters. If you're a guy, that's not a big deal, but if you're a girl all you've got is Eve (leaf bikini, anyone?), Esther, the Virgin Mary, or a prostitute. Plus, all that's in my costume arsenal is the Betty half of Betty and Wilma from the Flintstones costumes that El and I wore a few years ago.

Ron's dressed in all black like Zorro with a plastic sword tied to his hip. "Well, I figured none of y'all would come dressed." He drops a cardboard box down on the counter. "I borrowed some hats and whatnot from the church drama department."

Marcus picks a devil headband from the top and holds it up for inspection. "What is this, some leftover from last year's Hell House?"

Ron takes the devil horns from him and drops them back in the box. "Let's maybe stick to the less controversial stuff. And the candy is for the kids only. No teenagers." He walks outside to the popcorn machine on the sidewalk where he'll be handing out complimentary bags of popcorn.

Bo takes the blue-and-white-striped conductor hat and then reaches over my shoulder to grab a lollipop from the bowl of candy. Despite Ron's request, Marcus goes for the devil horns, and I reach for the sequined flapper headband with a big white feather.

Besides the rare kids' meal, it's pretty quiet. I get bored enough to clean out the employee fridge. When I'm done, I find Callie and her boyfriend, Bryce, standing in front of the counter. Bryce is wearing jeans and a T-shirt cut to look like a Peter Pan tunic, while Callie is supposed to be some kind of warped version of Wendy Darling in a sexy blue nighty.

"What are you doing here?" Each word comes out like acid.

"Whoa," says Callie. "Someone's attitude is turned up to ten."

The bell above the door chimes and the situation goes from bad to worse. Ellen is dressed like Tinker Bell, and really, besides being one of the tallest girls I know, she makes the perfect Tink. Tim is dressed as Hook. Unlike Bryce, he's actually committed to his costume.

I hate it. I hate their dumb coordinated

costumes. And I hate the way El looks like I'm violating her by breathing the same air.

Tim's eyes go wide for a second while El studies the floor. I try not to gasp. He did this. He made this happen. I would've preferred he not bring Callie and Bryce, but this is my chance. I've got to take it.

Ellen looks up. "I didn't think you worked here anymore." That's all she has to say. After all these weeks of silence, that's all she's got.

"I came back." Despite our audience, this moment feels starkly personal. "Hi, Tim."

He nods in my direction, and does nothing more to acknowledge me. I want to call him a traitor, but it's obvious whose side he's on.

"Let's go," says El.

"That's it? I haven't talked to you in weeks and that's it?" I can sense Marcus and Bo watching now, too.

Callie turns to Ellen. "You don't owe her anything."

El's eyes don't move. "I'm doing pretty

good on my own, so, yeah, I guess that's it."

The four of them leave and, as they do, Tim shrugs in my direction.

Marcus and Bo know better than to ask me what's going on.

Marcus spends his break in the parking lot as he travels from trunk to trunk with a paper Harpy's bag.

"Like the feather," says Bo from the kitchen as he points to my hair.

I forgot I was wearing this thing. All I've been able to think about is Ellen. I can't believe that happened. This part of me kept holding on to the hope that we would break the silence somehow — and it would be fine. But it's not. I touch my hand to the feather, letting the edges tickle my fingertips. "Yeah. Thanks."

"I'm glad you're back."

I nod. I'm glad I am, too. This little grease hut feels like a slice of normal. And so does he. I wish that wasn't true, but it is.

He pulls the conductor hat off and repositions it on his head. "And I'm sorry you felt the need to leave."

"It's okay." I stack and restack the same pile of to-go bags before asking, "Are you missing Holy Cross?"

He smirks. "I actually miss my uniform."

"What? Why?"

"I don't know. It's kind of nice to not have to think about clothes in the morning." He brushes his thumb along his lower lip. "I guess you could say I'm not a morning person." Hearing him talk this much after two months of silence is like a downpour after a drought.

"And then my brother hates it." He chews the skin around his thumb for a second before adding, "But it's my fault we had to leave HC."

I'm about to ask him why, when Marcus walks back in. "Y'all, those moms are not foolin' with that candy."

Heat spreads to my cheeks, like we've been caught making out.

At the end of the night, we all walk out together, the two of them laughing about Ron's Zorro costume. Bo still wears the conductor hat, and I can't even look at him without smiling like a total idiot.

Outside, Mitch is leaning up against my car.

It's horrible of me, but I resent him being here. I'm like one of those people who doesn't like for their food to touch. I need for Mitch to stay on his side of the plate.

"Hey," I say to Marcus and Bo. "I'll see y'all later." I turn to Mitch. It might be physically impossible, but I feel Bo's eyes on my back like a weight. "Um, hi? Nice costume."

Mitch is dressed like Indiana Jones in khaki pants and a bomber jacket with a wide brim hat. "It's Saturday night," he says. "It's Halloween."

I laugh. "Which basically means I want to go home."

He shakes his head. "Nope. Not happening. I'm going to show you why Halloween is awesome. Let's go. Get in."

"I don't have a costume."

He shrugs. "You're a fast-food employee. Or a candy striper."

My feelings for him swing from hot to

cold and back. I don't want him here. I want him here. He's crowding me. He's not close enough. I feel a smile flicker on my lips. "Okay. Prove me wrong."

FORTY-TWO

In the car, I text my mom to let her know
I'll be home a little late, but there's
another message waiting for me.

BO: glad you're back.

I bite in on my lips, making them disappear, and drop my phone into the cup
holder.

Mitch drives us to Stonebridge, the
richest neighborhood in Clover City. I
guess maybe it's not rich by normal
standards, but it was built in the last ten
years and it's gated. The gates are always
open, but whatever.

After parking on a random street, he
tosses me a pillowcase.

"Wait. We can't go trick-or-treating this
late."

"It's not that late."

"It's past midnight."

"Well, we are." Mitch doubles back. "Forgot something." He runs back to his car and comes back with a brown whip twisted around his fist.

"Are you shitting me with that thing?"

"What? It makes the costume more authentic."

We walk down the center of the street for a while, looking for a house with the lights still on. The pavement is smooth and pale, nothing like the patch-riddled street I grew up on. Every house is huge and hulking, but crammed together with only slivers of plush, green grass between them.

When this place was first being built, my mom and Lucy used to drive through here every few weeks with me in the backseat. We watched as all the houses were built and each street added. I remember being in awe of the new street signs, like some virgin territory had been discovered and we were some of the first to visit it. I had no understanding of how small Clover City was, but, to me, this was where all the glamorous people lived. Movie stars, musicians, models. And back then, my mom was still glamorous to me. I thought the three of us would get our fancy house someday.

The first house we stop at is redbrick, with a huge bay window and a glowing chandelier visible from the street. Mitch rings the doorbell, and I stand half behind him. It's late and whoever answers isn't going to be thrilled to have two teenage kids at their doorstep.

No answer. Mitch rings again.

I start walking back down the sidewalk. "No one's answering. Let's go."

"Wait!" says Mitch.

The door creaks open to reveal a woman in a bathrobe, with water dripping down her neck and her hair wrapped in a towel. She's too old to be my mom, but not old enough to be my grandma. "Can I help you?"

Mitch holds his pillowcase out without hesitation. "Trick or treat!"

The woman looks like she's woken up in a different time zone. "Oh." She holds her wrist up to check the time, I guess, but there's no watch there. "Right."

She closes the door almost all the way, and returns moments later with a bowl of candy. Without hesitation, she dumps half the bowl into Mitch's bag.

He nudges me forward, and, despite how foolish I feel, I open my pillowcase.

She pours out the remainder. I guess this lady figures if two high school kids have the balls to go trick-or-treating this late at night in the nicest neighborhood in town, we deserve some candy.

Bathrobe Lady pats her stomach. "I shouldn't keep all this in the house anyway."

Mitch tips his hat. *"Gracias, señorita."*

As we're walking down the pathway, he bumps into my shoulder. "See," he says. "That was fun."

Most of the houses we visit have reactions like Bathrobe Lady, don't answer, or turn their lights off when they see us outside.

At one house, an old man in boxer shorts answers. His face is perpetually frowning with wrinkles so thick he could be melting. "Get outta here, ya damn hooligans!" he yells.

"Trick or treat!" says Mitch over the sound of a small dog yelping behind the man.

"Oh, I'll trick ya." The man opens the door fully to reveal a shotgun at his side. "I'mma whip y'all's asses!"

Mitch grabs my hand. "Run, run, run!"

We haul it down the driveway and around the corner as the old man's heckling laugh echoes behind us.

When we're a safe distance away, I stop with my hands braced on my knees. We're both heaving. "That. Crazy. Bastard." I take a fresh gulp of air. "Could have killed us," I say.

"Nah," he says. "He wanted to scare us."

I stand up straight, letting the muscles in my back stretch. "Mission accomplished."

I hold up my bag of candy, much heavier than I ever expected it to be. "I think it's time to call it quits."

Mitch holds a finger up and winces a little. "One more house," he says.

"Please?"

Beneath the moonlight, he looks different. Almost mysterious. And maybe cute. A small laugh escapes me. "One house," I say. "Choose wisely."

He settles on a huge white house with a long driveway down at the end of the cul-de-sac.

Mitch rings the doorbell, and after a few minutes, an exhausted woman in a witch hat and a sweat suit answers the door. "Oh, darn," she says before Mitch even has a chance to say trick or treat. "We ran out a little while ago."

"Indiana Jones!" cries a boy in a pirate costume a few feet behind her. It's a homemade costume. The kind pieced together with great attention to detail. "So cool!"

Mitch beams.

"It's okay," I say to the lady. "We're just out foolin' around. We should head home."

She wishes us a good night.

We're halfway down the driveway before we hear the kid yell, "Hey! Hey! Wait up!" Pirate Boy is sprinting toward us with a plastic pumpkin dangling from his fingers. He skids to a stop in front of us and holds out a piece of candy for each of us. "I like your costume," he says to Mitch.

"Thanks, little man. Your pirate costume is pretty cool." Mitch doesn't talk to him like he's some little kid. Because to Mitch, he's not. To Mitch, everyone's somebody.

The kid runs back inside to where his mom is waiting at the doorway.

We sit on the curb with our candy at our feet. It's the first night this year that feels like fall might actually be on its way, and each breeze sinks into my southern bones.

"I told you Halloween was awesome," he says.

I lie back on a patch of rich people grass (real Texas grass is crunchy and brown) between the road and the sidewalk. "It was okay."

"When that kid saw me, he saw Indiana Jones. Not some guy who botched play after play in last night's game. Or some dude who plays video games all day. To him, I was someone else." He lies down next to me.

"But doesn't it kind of feel like you're hiding from yourself?" I turn to him; the grass tickles my cheek. "I get not wanting to be yourself. But isn't it almost sadder to pretend otherwise?"

"I don't know. I think you gotta be who you want to be until you feel like you are whoever it is you're trying to become. Sometimes half of doing something is pretending that you can." He turns on his side and props himself up with his elbow. "Like, that first time I talked to you, you terrified me. You kind of still do. But the more I act like you don't, the less you actually do." He pauses. "Terrify me, I mean."

I get what he means, because I think I've played pretend my whole life. I don't know when, but a really long time ago, I decided who I wanted to be. And I've been acting like her — whoever she is — since. But I think the act is fading, and I don't know if I like the person I am beneath it all. I wish there were some kind of magic words that could bridge the gap between the person I am and the one I wish I could be. Because the whole fake it till you make it thing? It's not working for me.

"What?" he asks.

I shake my head and clap my hands over my mouth, smiling against my fingertips. "I terrify you?" The thought of it makes me feel bad, but it's kind of nice, too. To not feel like the one who's about to jump out of their skin all the time.

Mitch pulls my hands down, away from my face. His palms are sweaty, and I'm realizing how close he is. I can see the pores in his nose. "I think the good stuff is always supposed to be a little bit scary," he says.

His lips brush mine. I stay very still as he curls his arm around my waist. We don't kiss with our tongues, just with our mouths open. I can feel the terror and exhilaration in his trembling touch.

But I am not terrified. Not at all. And it's then that I know this moment is a lie. I know what I should be feeling and it's not there.

FORTY-THREE

The next day is like someone has dropped an atomic bomb in our house. It starts when my mom gets home from church and decides to try her pageant dress on.

"Dumplin'?" she calls from her bedroom. "Baby, my zipper's stuck."

I trudge up the stairs. My mother has fit in her old pageant dress every year since she was crowned. Including the year she gave birth to me. From the way Lucy told it, the house was a Jazzercise fun house, and it was a close call, but she did it.

I've seen this dress — a sea-foam-green sequined bodice with a chiffon skirt — so many times that it's not even pretty anymore.

Since the house is so old, there's no

actual master bedroom upstairs. Just a shared bathroom at the end of the hallway. It's weird to think that my mom's and Lucy's rooms are the same rooms they grew up in their whole lives. I imagine them as teenagers slamming doors in each other's faces or sneaking back and forth from room to room. I've heard so much about their lives together before me, but sometimes I wonder about what they chose not to tell me and it's those blanks that I like to fill in.

I walk down the hallway and reach for the glass knob and open the bedroom door.

Oh shit.

From the doorway, I can tell that the zipper isn't the problem. There's a good one-inch gap between the fabric across my mom's back.

Sweat dampens her forehead as she waves me closer.

I make a show of pulling on the zipper for a minute or two before saying, "Uh, Mom? I don't think the zipper is the issue."

She whirls around and looks over her

shoulder so that she can catch her own reflection. "Godammit," she spits.

Okay, so my mom has maybe said the Lord's name in vain two times in her entire life. And only once that I can really remember.

"Unzip me."

The zipper slides down like a sigh of relief.

She sits on the edge of the bed, holding the front of the dress to her chest. "Okay, so I'm gonna have to go on a cleanse and add in some cycling and Pilates classes." She says Pilates like "Pee-lates," the twang in her voice becoming more and more pronounced with the added anxiety. "I think Marylou's got a class I can get into tomorrow night."

"But I have to go to work," I say. "I need the car."

She looks up at me with her eyebrows raised, like, this is a crisis and I do not understand the gravity of the situation. "Well, sweetheart, we're going to have to make it work. You keep taking the car to school and I'll have it in the evenings. Most girls your age don't even have cars.

We get what we get. We don't fret."

I don't bother fighting her on it.

I sit in the break room picking on the apple my mom gave me when she dropped me off. I swear, when she pulled into the parking lot, she held her breath, like she might catch some extra calories if she inhaled too deeply near so much trans fat.

I expected to hear from Mitch yesterday. A follow-up call of some sort to make sure we were cool after Halloween. Or maybe, like, a customer service call to rate my satisfaction. But nothing.

I woke up yesterday morning and had to convince myself that he'd actually kissed me. It wasn't a bad kiss. There just wasn't that heart-stammering feeling I had had with Bo.

Today, though, he was his usual self. With no mention of The Kiss. I started to think that maybe he really was someone else that night, and it was the magic of Halloween. But the guilt and regret I feel are all too real.

Then, at the end of the day, when we

walked to the parking lot, he took my hand firmly in his. It was hard not to feel like we hadn't skipped a step somewhere. I wasn't about to embark on another relationship that was all action and no definition. Before I left he handed me a small hardback book called *Magic for the Young and the Young at Heart.* "I remember you saying you needed a talent. For the pageant."

I shoved the book in my backpack and thanked him.

"There's a note inside," he said. "But read it later."

There's a knock on the break room door, even though it's open.

"Hey," says Bo.

I smile involuntarily. "Hi."

"I wanted to make sure you got home okay the other night." He fiddles with his fingers, and then shoves his hands in his back pockets. "I felt weird leaving you with that guy, but I recognized him from the dance." He clears his throat. "You guys must be pretty close, huh?"

My cheeks burn. "Oh, right. Yeah, that

was Mitch."

He coughs into his elbow. "Cool."

A slight laugh slips from me. "Cool."

He turns on his heel and heads back to the kitchen.

I release a slow breath through my pursed lips. I think that must have been the tamest interaction of all time. And I feel like I'm on fire.

After we close up, the first thing I notice outside is the lack of my mom's car. I'm dialing her before the back doors even close.

"Hello?" Her voice is thick with sleep.

Dammit. "Mom?"

"Oh, Dumplin'!" I can hear her grabbing her keys and slamming the sliding glass door. "On my way, baby!"

The line goes dead.

Marcus and Bo watch me.

"You guys go on," I say.

Marcus nods his head toward where Tiffanie's waiting for him in her car. "You wanna bum a ride?"

"Thanks, but she's on her way."

Marcus and Bo share a look. "I'll wait with you," says Bo.

Marcus nods a "thanks" to Bo and leaves.

"I can wait inside," I tell him. "Ron'll be here for a while still."

"It's cool." He digs his keys out of his pocket. "Let's wait in my truck." He must see the pause in my expression. "Just sittin'," he says. "I'll even put the armrest down."

Once we've settled, Bo is indeed true to his word and lowers the armrest between us.

We sit in silence for a while, listening to the hum of the road at our backs. The scent of him hits me, all artificial cherry and aftershave. I guess I stopped noticing it over the summer, but it's been a while now since I've been in his truck. I don't quite understand how something can feel so comfortable and foreign at the same time. Like, déjà vu.

I reach forward and flip through some stations. Bo says nothing about me commandeering his radio.

"I can't hear Dolly Parton anymore

without thinking of you."

My stomach flips as I laugh nervously. "Well, lucky for you she's not on the radio too much anymore." My voice comes out more abrasively than I mean for it to. But really, I love that I've staked my claim on his memory. Except that I can't think of Dolly without seeing El or Lucy. And that doesn't seem very fair.

"Why Dolly?" he asks. "I don't really get it. She's so . . . fake."

"Her boobs are, yeah. Obviously." I trace patterns on the armrest, looking for the right words. "She's the kind of person who looks like she's never had a bad day. I guess she's sort of my guru. Like, her music is good, I guess. But it's *her* that makes it good. With her big hair and fake boobs. I've never seen anyone who's living the life they set out to live like she does."

He studies me, but doesn't say anything. "It's like every day is Halloween for her." Mitch in his costume flickers in my memory. "But for Dolly, it's not dress up or make-believe. It's her life. And it's exactly how she chose for it to be." I stop myself before I get too cheesy.

"Huh." He crosses his arms and sinks down further into his seat. "I've always thought of her as some kind of cartoon character. But maybe not."

The Harpy's light above us cuts out and we let the radio do the talking.

"No car?" he asks after a while. "What's the story there?"

I lean my head against the headrest. "It wouldn't start. About two months ago maybe." Is that all? It feels like it's been forever since everything happened and I entered the pageant. And since I lost Ellen. "It's been in the shop ever since. Can't afford to get it fixed."

"I feel ya," he says. "Money's supposed to make things easier, but it's always doing the opposite. I sort of wish we worked on a barter system."

His words grate on me. Bo's gone to private school for the last few years, and that's anything but free.

"What?" he asks.

I shake my head.

"No. Come on. Out with it."

After a long moment, I say, "Well, I

mean, you went to Holy Cross. I get that you're trying to be nice, but I don't think it's fair to say you actually know what it feels like to be broke."

"Wow," he says. "That's a pretty broad assumption."

Headlights flood the cab of the truck from behind us. "Whatever," I say. "You asked. Good night. Tell Bekah I said hi."

I slide out of his truck and slam the door behind me.

He rolls down the window. "Just so you know," he calls to me. "Not everyone who goes to private school is rich. Especially not the poor kids who can play basketball."

The window rolls back up, dividing him from me, before I have a chance to add anything else.

My cheeks burn with embarrassment. But more than anything, I'm confused. Why wouldn't he tell me about being on scholarship?

My mom gets out of her car and runs up to Bo's window. I watch from the other side of the truck as she uses one knuckle to knock on the glass. She talks in the high-pitched voice she only uses when communicating with "menfolk." Bo says something and her whole face lights up. She touches his forearm and holds her other hand to her chest. "Bless your heart, Bo!" I hear her say.

She walks to the car and I follow. "Uh? Mom?"

We get in the car and she says, "I'm so sorry, Will. That Pee-lates kicked my behind and I was out like a light the second I got home."

"It's fine," I grumble as she's turning out onto the street. "But what was that about?"

"Your sweet coworker. Bo, he said his name was?" She laughs, and out of the corner of her mouth says, "That boy's jawline could cut glass."

"Mom."

"I said we were shuffling around, sharing a car, and I appreciated him waitin' on me." She turns, but not hard enough for her blinker to stop ticking. "But then he said y'all work the same schedule and he could drive you home every night."

"Mom! You said no, right?" Panic rips

through me. Click. Click. Click. The blinkers are still going.

"Well, why would I do that? He was so kind to offer. Don't let me stand in the way of a good deed."

I sigh. A huge dramatic sigh.

"Willowdean," she says. "Enough with that sighin'. Count your blessings." She pulls into our driveway. "Especially the good-looking ones."

"I hate you," I say as I climb out of the car.

"Well, aren't you a wretched thing," she calls after me. "And maybe do your hair before your next shift! A well-styled head of hair is a head above the rest."

FORTY-FOUR

The bell for World History rings and I barely make it through the door before Miss Rubio shuts it behind me.

I stop. Right there, in Amanda's usual seat next to mine, is Bo. I think my brain is dribbling out my ears. From the back of the room, she shrugs and mouths, *Peachbutt wouldn't move.* I wave my hand at the air to tell her it's fine. But really it's not, because what the hell is even happening?

Seating for World History isn't assigned, but no one has budged since the first day, so it goes without being said. Knowing Amanda, there was a confrontation when she saw him in her seat, but someone had to lose. And it wasn't Bo.

He sort of half smiles when I sit down, and says, "Willowdean." And that's it.

That is the only word he says for the whole damn period.

When the bell rings, I scramble out the door as fast as I can.

I meet Mitch in the parking lot and his face brightens because he thinks this stupid grin on my face is for him. *No,* I want to tell him. *Don't give me that sweet smile. I don't deserve it.*

The next day, Bo's there again in Amanda's seat. I watch from the corner of my vision as he brushes his knuckles across his chin. I want to touch him. It seems inevitable. He's a negative and I'm a positive and all that stands between us is a matter of time.

Like yesterday, he says my name at the beginning of class, but this time adds, "I'll see you tonight."

There is a chorus of bees in my stomach as I listen to Bo whistling in the kitchen. Bo always whistles when he thinks no one is listening. But normally it's no song in particular, just a hodgepodge of tunes. But tonight his lips press together and whistle "Jolene" by Dolly Parton. Which turns my knees to mush.

Ron comes out from his office and hums along as he restocks the receipt paper. With a few minutes to go before closing time, Marcus barks, "Don't you know any other songs?"

The whistling stops for a moment as Bo flips a burger. The burger lands, sizzling against the griddle, and he begins to whistle again.

Marcus watches us curiously when, at the end of the night, we both walk toward Bo's truck.

I get into his truck just as his phone rings. He picks it up, and I watch as he listens for a moment. The vein in his neck bulges, his head shaking. Through his clenched teeth, he says something and hangs up before sliding in behind the wheel.

"Who was that?"

He chews on the inside of his bottom lip for a moment. "My brother."

"Oh."

"He just needs me to pick him up after I drop you off." He stares straight out into the field behind Harpy's. "We don't really get along."

I don't have any siblings, but I know what it feels like to butt heads with someone you see every morning and every night.

"I envy him sometimes," he says. "It wasn't the same for him when our mom died. I don't know how true it is, but sometimes I think I absorbed more of the blow than he did."

I nod. I knew Lucy in a way my mom never did, and it's hard not to feel like I carry the heavier burden because of that. "I'm sorry," I say as we're buckling our seat belts. It's like a hot potato that I've been holding on to for days. "For what I said about you going to private school."

He grips the steering wheel and cranes his neck back while he reverses out. "It's fine."

We sit at the stoplight in silence until it turns green. "What happened then? You were on a scholarship, I guess?"

"Yeah." I love the way he drives with one hand anchored to the bottom of the wheel as he uses his palm to spin it when he turns, like he's driving an eighteen-wheeler or something.

"Left on Rowlett," I say.

"I was in eighth grade when one of the Holy Cross dads saw me playing. I don't want to say I was really good, but I guess I was. I just didn't know it because no one gives two shits about basketball in this town."

"Except at Holy Cross," I say. Holy Cross is too small for a football team, but their basketball team always wins district and sometimes state.

"Yeah, so I guess a bunch of the dads got together and talked to my dad about me going there. But we couldn't afford it. Not with everything that had happened with my mom. You can't give high school kids sports scholarships. At least not according to the athletic association they compete in. They put together this academic scholarship for me. And for my brother, too. My dad said I couldn't go unless he went."

"But you said it was your fault that y'all had to leave, right?" I point to my driveway a few houses down. "This is me up here on the left."

"I blew my knee out at the end of the season last year. We didn't have insurance then, so I'm not really sure how everything got paid for. More of those rich dads, probably. But I wasn't going to be playing anytime soon."

The car idles in front of my house. I wish the drive home were three times as long. "But you were on an academic scholarship? They wouldn't take that away from you."

He crosses his arms. "After my injury I got in a fight with a guy on my team. Collin, that kid who swung by Harpy's over the summer."

"Over what?"

He shakes his head. "What every guy gets in a fight over. A girl."

The air in his truck is dense, and I can feel it all the way down to my bones. "The girl who was with him?"

"Amber. We dated for two years. But I was a shitty boyfriend to her anyway."

I want to ask him how, but I don't know if I want to know the answer yet.

"I broke Collin's collarbone. He broke my nose. When we went to enroll for the next year, they said funds had dried up. The donor had to pull their donation. And now my little brother hates me."

"He misses it?"

He smirks. "Yeah, that kid was a king there. He'd been dating the same girl since seventh grade. Who does that?" He shakes his head, still smiling. I can see what he doesn't say: that he loves his little brother more than is healthy and would probably play on a busted-up knee to make him happy. "He's a freshman now. He took the whole thing worse than I did. And then because he's fifteen and everything's shit when you're fifteen, his girlfriend broke up with him. Said she couldn't do long distance."

"Long distance?"

"Yeah, the place is about a ten-minute walk from our house."

"Wow." My hand hovers over the door handle.

"Let me walk you to the front door," he says.

"No, it's fine."

He persists. "Really."

"We actually use the back door."

"Why?"

"The front door's jammed. It's been

like that for a long time."

"So why don't you fix it?" he asks.

"I don't know. Just one of those things we never got around to. And now we're so used to it that it doesn't matter."

His lips twitch like he's got something to say, but he stays quiet.

I let myself out of the truck and hold the door open a second as a thought forms in my mind. "Why have you been sitting next to me these last two days? In class. You can talk to me at work."

He does that thing again where he brushes his knuckles across his chin. "I guess I would rather talk to you everywhere."

Behind the fence, in my backyard, I smile.

I dump the contents of my backpack on my bed, hoping to at least do some homework before I fall asleep. Splayed out between my textbooks, with a bent cover, is the how-to magic book that Mitch gave me. I pull it to my chest and slump down to the floor. I'd completely forgotten about my talent — or even the pageant — for a few days. Bo coming back into my world, if only in the tiniest of ways, turns my brain into a vacuum, where nothing else can exist, because I'm so consumed.

But I don't want that. I can't want that.

Thumbing through the pages, I find several different tricks, but none of them grab me. A note slips from the pages, and I unfold it.

Will, when I was a kid, I went through a magician phase where I wore capes and top hats everywhere. I thought maybe you could use some magic of your own. — Mitch

I slide the note back between the pages and sigh. It's ridiculous. Me, performing silly magic tricks. But what else is there for me to do? I don't have a self-defining talent like Bekah or even something I stuck with long enough to fall back on.

I lean back against my bed with the book in my lap, and begin to practice the motions of hidden coin illusion. This feels like settling. A missed opportunity. But I don't think that makes it wrong.

I try to channel that spark of energy
that made me enter the pageant in the
first place. But that little bit of magic is
nowhere to be found.

FORTY-FIVE

When I pick my mom up from work the next day, she's got a dress bag draped over her arm. She holds her hand up as she gets into the car. "Before you say anything, hear me out."

"Okay?" But I can't hide the apprehension in my voice.

"Debbie and I hit up a few thrift stores on our lunch break, and I knew you hadn't gotten a dress yet. And well, you have to get the dress approved in a few weeks, so you don't have much time. You may not realize it, but you can't just buy a dress off the rack. That's not how it works."

I know I need a dress, and I know I'm dragging here. But there is no recipe for disaster so guaranteed as my mother clothes shopping for me. We've been there. We've done that. We still have the bruises.

"It's a little on the simple side, but that means we can add our own touches. Like it was custom made."

I promise myself that I'll at least try it on. I will give her the benefit of the doubt.

Mom lets me get dressed in her room so I can use the big mirror. The door clicks shut behind her, and I realize how odd it is that she doesn't stay. She roams the house all the time in various states of undress, searching for a stray sock or ironing her scrubs. It's not as if she ever instilled modesty in me. But there came a point, maybe around the time I was eleven or twelve, when my mom stopped sitting in fitting rooms with me or brushing her teeth while I was in the shower. I guess it could be that she was trying to be intuitive to whatever privacy needs she figured I might have. But the thought tickling in the back of my mind says that she's not interested in being reminded of this body I wear.

Whether or not it's true, it still hurts.

I have to give it to her: the dress isn't

horrible. It's red — the perfect shade of red that's reserved for sexy nail polish and fast cars — with a sweeping neckline and straps that hang off my shoulders on purpose. My shoulders don't create the sharp lines I've seen on actresses and models. Instead they slope at the edges, but still I like the dress.

Until I zip it.

It zips.

But that doesn't mean it fits.

Christ. The fact that I'm able to get the zipper over my hips is a lesson in inertia or just willpower. The fabric pulls against the seams, threatening to tear if I even look at a chair the wrong way. And the top is pretty huge. I can actually tuck my arms in. (In case I get cold or something.)

"All right," I call to my mom. "Come on in!"

My mom stands behind me, and I can see both our reflections there in the mirror. I watch as her gaze travels over me, and her lips dip down at the corners when she sees the way the fabric stresses against my hips.

Our eyes meet, and she catches herself.

Her mouth presses into a smile. "Surely we can let it out a few inches," she says. "And tuck it in up top." Her voice is too high and her smile too big, but I don't care. I can ignore those things. Because she's making an effort to meet me where I am. "What do you think?" She pulls the top of the dress back, bunching the spare fabric in her fists.

I can almost imagine what it might look and . . . I like what I see. "It's good. I'm only going to wear it for twenty minutes, right? We can make it work."

I sit in the third row of the school auditorium. Millie sits beside me, reading a paperback romance, and beside her sits Amanda, her feet bouncing as she drums her fingers on her thigh.

Today is the day we all have to have our talents approved for the pageant. All I've got is the one magic trick I learned from the book Mitch gave me. The rules state that a contestant should prepare a sample, so I'm hoping this is enough.

Hannah squeezes down our aisle past Amanda and Millie. "I'm out of here as soon as they give me the okay."

"Don't you think it would be polite to stay for everyone else's talents?" asks Millie.

Hannah plops down in the seat beside me, but doesn't bother to answer.

Millie's patience for Hannah is slowly slipping, and I get this sick joy from that. I would love to see cheerful little Millie lose it on Hannah's grumpy ass.

Once the crowd settles, my mom gives her spiel and says that costumes for the talent portion will need to be approved at the same time as the rest of our wardrobe. "The surprises," my mother says, "are for the audience."

First up is Bekah Cotter who — ta-da! — twirls a baton like a freaking superhuman. This time, however, Bo's name is not stamped to her butt cheeks. It's really not fair how much I can't stand her. She's maybe said twenty words to me, but the thought of Bo, in a tux, escorting her at the pageant turns me into this version of myself that makes my eyes burn.

Then there are five girls in a row who sing songs from either *Les Miz* or *Chicago*. Karen Alvarez's *Chicago* performance is deemed too sexy and she is given one week to come up with another song. She slinks off the stage, holding her songbook to her chest. I can tell she's mortified, but it smells of pageant scandal and I kind of love it.

"Amanda Lumbard?" calls Mallory Buckley.

Millie pats Amanda on the back as she reaches down under her seat for a duffel bag. Once she's onstage, I notice that she's not wearing her Frankenstein orthopedic shoes. I mean, these still have a thicker heel on one side, but they're more athletic-looking.

"I guess this isn't very traditional, but it's what I'm good at." Her voice shakes a little. She squats down and opens her gym bag to retrieve a soccer ball. Without any further introduction, she begins dribbling the ball back and forth between her knees. It's kind of amazing. She head butts the ball a few times and even kicks it over her head, but the ball never hits the ground.

Here she is doing something I could never even dream of doing with my two legs of equal length. After a few more tricks she tucks the ball beneath her arm, grabs her bag, and walks offstage.

Millie and I clap like madwomen, while the rest of the auditorium is quiet as the committee makes its decision.

It takes doubly as long as it has for everyone else, but finally my mom says, in a not-so-impressed tone, "Well, that wasn't our usual fare, but it'll do."

"So I'm approved then?" asks Amanda.

My mom nods.

Amanda smiles, all goofy and relieved as she sits back down.

Next is a monologue from *Much Ado About Nothing,* which is actually pretty good, but will be totally lost on the judges.

"Willowdean Dickson?"

I reach into my backpack for my prop and walk down the aisle to the stage.

As a kid, I remember standing onstage during school productions. The intense lights always made it impossible to see the audience, and that always made the whole thing bearable for me. But today the theater is lit and the stage lights are dormant.

"I can start now?" I ask.

I try not to count all the girls sitting in the audience because if I start I might not stop.

Mrs. Clawson, who sits next to my mom, nods.

I hold up an empty water bottle and pull a quarter from my pocket. "I'll be doing a magic trick." My mom's face is unmoving. "I plan on doing other tricks, too, but this is just a sampling." I wait for someone to tell me that that's okay or that I shouldn't worry, but I am only greeted by silence.

So here's the quick and dirty of how this trick should work: I take an empty water bottle, which I've sliced a sliver of an opening in. I am to hold the water bottle so that the audience cannot see the cut in the side. After banging on the bottle and proving how normal it is, I hold up a quarter and slap it through the small cut in the water bottle. Bada bing. Bada boom.

"Here in my hands I hold a perfectly normal water bottle. One that I drank out of this morning to take my vitamins." If I can make my voice sound all magician-y, maybe no one will notice what a hack I am. I tap the water bottle all over. "Totally average water bottle."

I hold up my quarter. From the front row, my mom squints. I uncap the bottle to show that I cannot fit it through the top. The room is so quiet. Is this why magicians always tell jokes? Or play really intense music that sounds like lasers? I display the quarter once more before gripping it between my fingers like the book said and slapping it into the side of the bottle and through the crack I had created.

"Voilà!" I say, which might be cute, except I've spoken too soon. I shake the water bottle, but besides the few stray drops from this morning, it's empty. I hadn't checked to make sure that I was hitting the right side of the water bottle.

"On the floor," calls Callie from the third row where she sits beside Ellen.

Ellen. She chews on her bottom lip.

Her in the audience. My shitty talent. This fully lit auditorium. I'm wasting my time with this pageant. I don't think this is what Lucy imagined when she stashed that old registration form away in her room. And it's no one's fault but my own. Tears threaten at the corners of my eyes, but I force myself to hold them back.

I look down, and there at my feet is my quarter. Quickly, I bend over to pick it up before shoving it through the other side of the bottle.

Worst magic trick of all time.

The only applause comes from Millie. Of course.

"I'm still learning," I say.

I stand at the edge of the stage as the committee members — my mom included — converse back and forth. Finally my mother says, "Approved." But her face says it all. Disappointed. Underwhelmed.

I squeeze past Hannah and Millie to get to my seat. "Weak sauce," whispers Hannah.

"Oh, like you have anything better planned," I snap.

"Hannah Perez," calls my mother.

Hannah stomps across the stage in her army-navy surplus boots.

Then — thanks to the kid in the sound booth — her music begins to play. It's a song I remember hearing on Lucy's record player: "Send in the Clowns." It's the type of song that settles in your bones and makes you sad for a reason you can't quite pin down.

Hannah's voice isn't even all that amazing, but she really sings it. Like, she wrote it herself. The music crescendos and so does her voice. I stop seeing Hannah with her usual sour face and her huge teeth and her fading black clothes. And all I see is this girl who sings this heartbreaking song because she gets it even when the rest of us don't.

The music cuts out in the middle of it fading, and there's a brief silence before every single person in the auditorium claps.

When the applause fades, my mom says, "Hannah, that was lovely." And she says it in a way that says, *Now, that is how you do it, Dumplin'.*

Hannah nods and takes the steps two at a time. She doesn't say thank you. Just grabs her backpack from where it sits at her feet and leaves.

I watch every single talent. Callie does sign language to the *Titanic* song, which I've got to admit is kind of a surprise. Millie plays "Somewhere Over the Rainbow" on the xylophone, which isn't incredibly impressive, but suits her still. And Ellen clogs to some German folk music. She was on a clogging team all the way up until seventh grade, and she's as bad at it now as she was back then.

It makes me smile, and she sees me, but doesn't acknowledge me. When she's done, I clap too loud and even my mom turns around.

As my mom and I are driving home, she lowers the volume on the radio at the stop sign before our house and says, "That talent approval was the only favor you'll be getting from me." She pulls a deep breath in through her teeth. "I get that you don't take this pageant seriously, but maybe you could at least pretend to."

She's right. It's not fair to her or Amanda or Millie or Hannah. When I get home, the first thing I do is sit in front of my computer with Riot curled around my feet as I compose an email. The subject line reads: SOS.

FORTY-SIX

In the light of day, the Hideaway is nothing more than peeling paint and sticky floors.

Beside me Hannah teeters back and forth in three-inch heels. "I'm not wearing these in this pageant."

Lee Wei has us all lined up on the stage in high heels while Dale, the bouncer/owner, sits at the bar sipping on a tall boy. The email I sent to him was as transparent as I'd been in a long time. I told him about finding the old registration form in Lucy's dresser and about Millie, Amanda, and Hannah. *I've gotten myself in too deep,* I told him. *And not only am I going to make a fool of myself, but I'm taking these girls down with me. We need help. The kind you can't find in Clover City.*

Because, the truth is, we have no idea what we're doing. We don't know how to walk or pose or present ourselves. I don't want to go up there and be the fat girl who fell on her ass and fumbled her way through some magic tricks. I'm not naïve. I know I won't win. I don't even want to. But I want to go up there and prove that there's no reason I can't do this or shouldn't be able to.

On my other side, Millie is surprisingly silent with her knees locked in place.

"Are you okay?" I whisper.

She concentrates on the dark spotlight above her. "I'm trying to concentrate on not falling."

"Bend your knees!" calls Lee.

Hannah yanks a thumb in Amanda's direction. "I don't get why she doesn't have to wear these spiked torture devices."

Amanda grins innocently.

"Hannah," says Millie. "You know —"

Lee interrupts with a no-nonsense tone. "Because life is not a river and we're not all headin' in the same direction."

Hannah rolls her eyes.

"And, sweetheart," Lee adds. "Your attitude needs a makeunder."

I asked Lee and Dale to sacrifice their Friday afternoon, and here we are, moaning. "Come on, y'all."

"Let's get this over with," says Hannah.

Lee clears her throat. "The first thing you've gotta nail down is your walk. Your walk makes you a queen. Because, ladies, it ain't anything that comes out of your mouth that counts as your first impression. It's all" — she swings her hips to the right and then the left — "about the motion in the ocean."

From the corner of my eye, I spot Millie chewing relentlessly on her nails.

Lee instructs us to sit down while she shows us exactly what she means, and all of us sigh as soon as our asses hit the chairs. She struts up and down the stage, her heels making a distinct thwacking noise with each step. "You see how I'm walking with one foot in front of the other. Pretend you're taking a sobriety test —"

"They're in high school," grunts Dale.

"Then they should know exactly what I'm talking about, right, girls?" The only one of us who nods her head is Hannah. "So you act like you're walking down a yellow line. And none of those baby steps. Your stride should be as long as your forearm, at least." She takes another lap. The way she moves in her silk robe and endlessly tall heels transforms her from some short chubby guy dressed as a woman into a glamazon. Maybe I'm seeing what I want to see, but it's hard to think she's anything less.

"You can't hold all your weight on your heel. It's not fair to make those poor little spikes hold you up all on their own. Distribute the work to the rest of your foot. Now, one of y'all try."

I raise my hand. I can do this. I can so do this.

Dale whistles.

Carefully, I take the steps.

Lee sweeps her arm out, lending me the stage. "Give the girl some music, Dale!"

I pull in a deep breath. I don't recognize the song, but it's enough for me to ignore the way my toes pinch together and how the balls of my feet feel like they're on fire. My first few steps are long like Lee said, but slow and tentative. She's right about walking toe to heel with one foot in front of the other. It makes your hips swing, which sets your whole body in motion, like a downhill bicycle. Once you're going, you can't stop. As I turn around at the other end of the stage, Dale whistles again. I walk with purpose and with the knowledge that if this room was packed, every eye would be on me.

Lee claps for me and wraps her arms around my waist. Her head presses against my boobs, and for a brief moment, I remember that she is a he. I wish every day of my life could be this absurd. I want Lucy to see this. To see that I've connected the dots of her fragmented life, and here I am.

I watch as Hannah trips across the stage, falling not once but twice. Halfway through her walk back across the stage, she tears her heels off and throws them into the empty audience. And the whole time she's laughing, which isn't something I can say I've seen her do much of.

Millie's walk is measured and careful. Lee reminds her over and over again to keep her eyes on the horizon and not on her feet. A few times she holds her hands up for balance, but she makes it. And Amanda, she's so comfortable in her own shoes that she barely requires any coaching.

Before we drive home, the four of us sit at the bar while Dale makes virgin cocktails for us and not-so-virgin cocktails for Lee.

Lee tells us about stage makeup and what kinds of clothes make statements until she's had so many cocktails that her head is slumped against the bar. "I wish I'd known girls like you when I was in high school."

"Why?" asks Hannah. "You like being made fun of?"

Lee shakes her head. "No. No, I wish I would've had friends that were going after things they weren't supposed to have. I was so scared of myself at that age. I was so scared that all the big things I wanted would never be anything more than wants."

Dale comes around the other side of

the bar. "I better get you home before I have to open tonight."

Lee sits up. "It got better," she says. "Look at me. I'm living my dream. I'm in love. I'm happy. But I waited for that to happen to me. And y'all are making it happen now. Y'all are going for it."

We sip our drinks for a moment. I don't say anything, but her words bring something inside of me to life. Like, I'm using a muscle I forgot I had.

"Thank you for helping us today," says Amanda. "Even if I can't wear heels."

With the help of Dale, Lee pops off her bar stool. "Child, you don't need heels. You're fierce all on your own."

She walks down the row of us and kisses each of our cheeks. Millie reaches to hug her, and Lee doesn't pull away. As Dale is getting her in the car, we gather our stuff and load up into Amanda's mom's van.

The drive home is quiet. Not even Hannah has anything snarky to say. Millie makes us stop at a grocery store for a thank-you card. We each sign it, and Millie promises to drop it in the mail.

There's something different about us. I can feel it. It's not a walk. Or a makeup tip. It's not anything you can label or take a picture of, but I feel it like you do a birthday — nothing you can see, but something you intuitively sense.

FORTY-SEVEN

"Dumplin'! You have a guest!"

I storm down the stairs. Bo volunteered to pick me up, but I specifically told him to text me when he was outside. I guess he's not one for following directions.

Last night as I was getting into bed, my phone chimed. I should've known better but, for a second, I thought it might be Ellen.

BO: hey you wanna study for that World History test this weekend?

I replied yes without even stopping to think if I should.

Now Bo stands in the kitchen next to my mom, who's still sipping on her coffee. She makes a show of turning her back to him and wiggling her eyebrows at me.

"I'm going to Bo's to study, Mom."

Her cheeks are so red she could be drunk. "You two behave."

Bo slides the door open and waits for me to walk out first.

"Don't you forget to get that quote from your dad, sweetie!" she yells to Bo in a singsong voice.

We round the corner into the driveway. "What was that about?" I ask.

"Uh, yeah." He motions to my house. "We were talking about that front door. My dad, he's a locksmith. But he fixes doors a lot, too."

We drive in silence for a while before I say, "My mom's a total nut. I'm sorry."

"You guys look alike."

I try to swallow, but my mouth is dry as can be. No one's ever said that about me and my mom. It was always Lucy. *You look just like your aunt.* I'm not ashamed of that, but I like the idea of looking like my mother's daughter.

"In a good way," he says.

■ ■ ■ ■

Based on what Bo told me about him being on scholarship, I figured he didn't live in a new neighborhood, but I wasn't quite expecting this. His house — with its well-maintained lawn — sits on a street of sagging roofs, chipping paint, and overgrown yards.

Bo pulls into the crumbling driveway. "This is my place."

I follow him up the walkway to the front door, which has a hand-painted sign hanging from it that says: *Unless you're selling cookies, no soliciting, please.*

Bo's house is warm, but not uncomfortably so. It's one story, and considerably smaller than mine. The furniture is at least two decades old, but it all matches. I wonder what it must be like for his step-mom to live in the house his mom made.

The place smells distinctly of incense, which doesn't at all match everything else. I wonder if maybe my house smelled anything like me to Bo.

I don't know where I expected Bo to live, but it was not here.

"Let me introduce you to my step-mom."

I follow him the short distance from the front door to where the incense is burning in the kitchen. Bo's stepmom is cursing at the ice machine in the freezer. A small puddle of water with stray cubes of melting ice floats at her feet. She's not as polished as she was when I saw her at the mall, but she's still pretty in a way that my mom isn't. In an unprepared way. Without the manicures and the makeup and the hair spray.

"Loraine," says Bo, "this is Willowdean."

She whips around with a big steak knife in her hand. "Oh!" She laughs and drops her arm to her side. "The girl with two names. I remember you."

Bo nods.

She smiles and hugs me with one arm. Not the knife-carrying arm.

He coughs. "Everything okay with the ice maker?"

She holds the knife up again, like she's about to stab something. "Oh, just all frozen inside. Trying to break some of it up so your dad doesn't have to deal with it. He got called out on a job during breakfast."

"We're going to study in my room," says Bo.

Loraine's eyes bounce back and forth between us. I'm waiting for her to say something like, *Maybe you should study out here* or *Leave the door open.* Instead she says, "Let me know if you need anything."

His room isn't dirty, but lived in. There are traces of him at every age. Posters for bands I'm surprised he's even heard of, a basketball on his desk with a few signatures, a bowl of red lollipops of all kinds, one of those corner ceiling hammocks filled with stuffed animals, and a framed San Antonio Spurs jersey.

He closes the door behind us, and I think that all the air there is left to breathe in the world is sealed in this room. When it runs out, that'll be it. The death of me in Bo Larson's bedroom.

We sit on pillows on the floor with our books and notes spread out. For a bit, we talk about what might be on the exam, but all I can think is: BO-BO-BO-

BO'S-ROOM-HE-SLEEPS-HERE-BO-
BO-BO-BO-THIS-IS-WHERE-HE-
TAKES-OFF-HIS-CLOTHES.

Beyond Bo's head, hanging on his doorknob, is an oversized ring full of keys.

"What's the deal with the janitor keys?" I ask.

He glances over his shoulder. "Oh. From my dad." He scoots around and leans against the bed. I do the same.

"I started collecting them when I was a kid. My dad would get me to help him clean out his van by telling me I could keep whatever spare keys I found. They're mostly miscuts or old keys people couldn't use anymore."

Our hands sit splayed out on the carpet, our fingers not even an inch apart. "Do you still help him?"

He shakes his head. "Things changed when I started going to Holy Cross. I was always busy with basketball. And friends, I guess. I don't know. Life started feeling too important for his stupid keys. You know how you start getting these big plans for your life and suddenly all the

396

work your parents do feels so meaning-less? And I guess I was embarrassed by him. I got pretty used to seeing all the dads at Holy Cross in their polo shirts and khaki pants that I started to beg my dad not to pick me up in his van." He shakes his head. "I was an asshole. I still am sometimes."

"I think being embarrassed by your parents is as much a part of growing up as getting taller."

He smiles with his lips closed. "I used to love watching him pick locks. Just the way he'd stand there listening to the lock like it was his favorite song. And then it would click."

"I don't know if it matters, but I don't think you're an asshole. For the most part."

"It wasn't my dad," he says. "My ex-girlfriend. Amber. I was horrible to her. She wanted so badly to be there for me. She went to every single one of my games. Even the away games if she could swing it. And all I did to thank her was take her to dark movie theaters to fool around or hang out in her dad's TV room and watch basketball. I thought she was using me as some kind of status symbol, so I figured it didn't matter. But she wasn't getting anything from me she couldn't get anywhere else."

My mouth goes sour. This scenario sounds too familiar. And it's nothing I want to revisit. "What does Loraine do?"

His entire body blushes and he covers his face with his hands so that I can barely see him. "She throws romance parties."

"Wait." I try so hard not to laugh. "I'm sorry. What did you say?"

He throws his head back against the bed. "Romance parties."

"Like, um, sex toys?"

He turns an even deeper shade of red.

"My mom works at a nursing home," I tell him to try to save him even if his blushing may be the most adorable thing ever.

He turns to face me, his color fading. "I thought she was the beauty pageant lady."

"She is. She's the beauty pageant lady who wipes your grandparents' asses by day."

"Wow," he says. "I never would've thought."

I sigh. "The glamorous life."

"So you really entered the pageant?"

"Yeah," I nod. "Why?" Everyone seems to have something to say about me entering and I'm sure Bo is no different.

"Well, I've always thought pageants were dumb, but I thought that about Dolly Parton, too."

I smile. "Right answer."

"What about your aunt?" he asks. "The one that passed away."

I swallow. "She didn't work. She was on disability."

"Oh, so it was kind of expected? I mean, that doesn't make it better. I meant that —"

"No." My voice is soft, but he hears me. "It wasn't expected."

He waits for me speak.

"She was big. Not like me. Like, five hundred pounds big. She had a heart attack. She took care of me, though. Like a second parent."

"I wish there was something better to

say than 'I'm sorry.' "

We sit there for a few minutes watching the shadows created by the blowing tree limbs outside of his plastic blinds.

"I think he was kind of happy when I lost my scholarship."

"Why would he be happy about that?" I ask, knowing without a doubt who "he" is. He crosses his arm and when he does, his hand brushes mine. Every little thing — hands touching and doors sealing — sends a shooting warmth up my spine.

"I don't even mean happy, really. More relieved." He leans his head back again and watches the mini basketballs hanging from the chains of his ceiling fan. I imagine it must be weird to live in this shrine dedicated to a sport he can't play anymore. "I think I was on this path to get out of here. I was good at basketball. Good enough to get noticed by some smaller colleges, and maybe he saw that, too. But I was never supposed to leave Clover City. Before Holy Cross, I was supposed to live here and die here, working with my dad."

Each word is familiar to me. His truth is my truth. There's a version of the future in my head where I stay here forever. I watch my mom work until the day she dies. And then it's just me in that house with its broken front door, full of pageant supplies and Dolly Parton records. Bleak, I know. But, still, there's a bit of comfort that comes with knowing how your life is going to turn out. I've never had a surprise turn out in my favor.

"I don't blame him," he continues. "It's that feeling of people leaving. It's scary."

"Yeah, I know what you mean." I think maybe we're both talking about a different kind of loss. The kind that can't be fixed with a plane ticket.

There's a knock at his door.

"Come in."

"Hey, son." Bo's dad is a shorter version of Bo. Sturdy and broad. He notices me and nods.

"Dad, this is Willowdean. We go to school together. She works at Harpy's, too."

I stand up. "Good to meet you, Mr. Larson."

He waves a hand at me. "Call me Billy." He turns to Bo. "I need your help swapping this tire out on the van real quick."

"Sure." Bo hops up and promises he'll be right back.

I stand there for a moment. In Bo Larson's bedroom. By myself. On his desk, next to the signed basketball, are three frames. The first one is Bo from a few years ago. He's wearing a Holy Cross jersey and has a basketball tucked beneath his arm. He looks younger with his close-cropped hair and his stubble-free face, but the outline of his biceps foreshadows the next few years. A promise of the Bo I know today. The next one is old and kind of grainy, like it might have been taken on a cell phone. It's Bo's dad, Bo, and his brother, Sammy. Bo looks no older than nine. The three of them are on a dingy-looking beach — definitely a Texas beach — with the water at their backs. Bo stands alongside his dad, with his arms crossed and his feet spread wide. Mr. Larson holds Sammy over his head like a dumbbell. The final frame is his parents' wedding photo. And now I see where Bo gets his height from. Mrs. Larson had at least three inches on her husband. She wears a light yellow tea-length dress with gold sandals and her hair loose around her shoulders. It's a candid photo. Mrs. Larson's head is thrown back in laughter, while Mr. Larson wears the grin I've seen on Bo so many times.

"She was beautiful. A total Scorpio, too."

I turn. Loraine stands in the doorway, wearing a quiet smile.

"I'm sorry," I say, but for what I don't really know. "I was waiting for Bo to get back."

"Nothing to be sorry for."

I chew on my lip for a moment before asking, "Did you know her?"

"Only in passing, but, from what I hear, she was a good one to know."

I look at the picture once more.

"Come have some iced tea with me," Loraine says.

Most women in the South take great pride in their iced tea and pass their recipes down from generation to generation. But Loraine is not most women. She mixes her tea with powder from a box. To my mom, powdered iced tea is almost as bad as the possibility of being left behind in the wake of the rapture.

"You want some lemons?" she asks.

"Yeah, that'd be great." I squeeze two lemons before taking a sip. *Delicious.* Like frozen lasagna. Wherever my mom is she's just fainted.

Loraine sits down in front of me with a glass for herself. She's one of those people who could be twenty-five or forty-five and you wouldn't be able to tell the difference. "What's your sign, Willowdean?"

"Pardon?"

"Your star sign? Astrology?"

"I — well, I don't know." According to my mom, astrology is two steps away from demonic possession. "I never really paid attention before."

She shakes her head and tsks. "I'll never understand how it is people navigate their whole lives without knowing their signs. What's your birthday?"

"August twenty-first."

"Ah," she says. "A Leo, but barely."

I lean in. "What's that mean?" I'm learning a whole new language for the first time.

"You, my dear, are a lion." She says it with such great dramatics, but it's lost on me. She sighs. "You're the king of the jungle, baby. Walking confidence."

Yup, this is total bullshit.

She waves a finger at me. "Don't write me off so soon. There's more. You're a fire sign. You love big, but you hurt big, too. But you don't always let the hurt show, because it's a vulnerability. You're the sun. Always there. Even when we can't see you."

She believes this so wholly that it's pretty difficult for me not to buy into it, too. And I like the idea that somehow I am the way I am because it was meant to be.

"But" — here it is, the other shoe is about to drop — "you need approval, too. And that flaw is big enough to stop you. What's important to remember though is that despite our signs, we still make our destiny."

It's hard not to notice how true her

words feel. "How do you know all this stuff?"

"Everyone's got their own religion, right?" She shrugs. "Even if their religion is no religion."

"What are you?"

She grins. "A Sagittarius, but what's really interesting is Bo's sign in relation to yours."

I am hooked. She's got me. And she knows it.

"Bo is an Aquarius. Just like his dad. Detached and brooding, but with a good heart."

It takes me a second to realize I'm nodding.

"According to the stars, you two are quite the pair." She sips her tea and winks at me.

I know that *pair* could mean anything. Friends, cohorts, partners. But that doesn't stop my cheeks from feeling as warm as a sunburn.

She reaches for my knee. "Oh, sweetheart, are you okay?"

I nod a little too fast. "Do you —

Where's the restroom?" My face is on fire.

Her brow wrinkles with concern. "Two doors past Bo's on the left."

I get up, and turn back to her as I stand on the threshold between the kitchen and the dining room. "I liked talking to you," I tell her.

I hear the garage door open.

"You're always welcome to come by for a chat."

In the bathroom, I splash my face a few times. I want to wake up every day, like that old movie *Groundhog Day,* and relive this day over and over again.

Here, though, by myself, it's hard not to wonder if he ever brought Bekah home. Or if Amber got along with his stepmom as much as I feel like we did.

Bo is waiting in his room. He's changed his shirt and has moved our books and notes to his bed. TO. HIS. BED.

But the door's open, and I'm slightly grateful for it, too. Because how do people even function like this? Like, how is it that people can even pump gas or pay bills or tie their shoes when they're in love? Or might be in love. Or are in love. Or are in between the two.

My phone buzzes in my pocket.

MITCH: what are you doing tonight? wanna grab some tacos? watch a movie?

I exit out of my messages.

"Who's that?" asks Bo.

"No one," I say. "Just my mom."

We study for the next few hours until it's time to turn his bedside lamp on. We've both slid from sitting positions and are slumped against pillows in a sea of papers.

When he drives me home, I find myself addicted to the comfort of him. I've spent an entire day being so myself. Not a daughter, or a niece, or a token fat girl. Just Willowdean. The feeling of it makes me miss El. But I'm tired of other people making me feel this way. I'm ready to make myself feel this way.

"I like Loraine," I tell him.

"She has a way of making people do that. Infectious, my dad says. I tried really hard not to like her. But the harder I tried, the more I wanted to like her. She doesn't try to be my mom. Not like some other ladies would. She's something else to me, though. Not a friend, but not a mom. I don't know."

And *that* — right there in those handful of words — is how I feel about Lucy. But there's no real term for it, and I sometimes think that makes the pain of losing her that much harder to reconcile.

He parks in front of my house. "So is that what you normally do on Saturdays? Study at home?" I want to know everything about every minute of his life.

"Yeah," he says. "Unless my dad needs me."

"What about Sundays?" We're off every Sunday, which means it's this one day a week where Bo is a complete mystery to me.

"I go to church. Mass. I go to mass."

"Wait, you're actually Catholic?"

He doodles designs on his steering wheel with his finger. "I don't know."

"How can you not know?"

The streetlight reflects off the silver

chain peeking out from his collar. "Coach used to always have us go to mass during the season, and I guess I got in the habit."

"How punny."

His lips form an uneven smile. "I like the tradition of it."

"Does your family go, too?"

He laughs. "Not a chance."

The quiet of my street seeps in through the cracks of his truck.

"I better go," I whisper.

He leans toward me and hooks his hands behind my ears, pulling me to him. Our lips brush, so light it tickles. But it's not quite a kiss. "I want to kiss you. I want to kiss you very soon." His words spill right into my mouth. "But I'm not going to mess us up this time."

I have so many questions, but I think I've got enough for today.

He drops his hands, letting his fingers trail down my cheeks.

"Come to mass with me tomorrow."

I bite in on my lips. "Okay."

FORTY-EIGHT

The minute I walk inside, reality crashes down around me. Mom is working on my dress and watching some Lifetime movie with the volume turned up too high.

I want more than anything to call El and tell her about every inch of these last two days. Lee Wei, Dale, Bo, Loraine. All of it. I slump down into a chair at the kitchen table and swipe through my phone until I find our last texts from almost two months ago. I hit compose.

ME: I spent the day at Private School Bo's house. He likes me a lot. We talked about everything and nothing. He almost kissed me and it was the most amazing non-kiss ever. I'm trying not to think about Mitch. I've ignored his texts all weekend. How can having such an incredible day make me feel like such a shitty person? I miss Lucy. And I miss you so fucking much. I apologize. I apologize for everything I have ever done wrong. A blanket apology.

I stare at the words, wondering what might happen if I hit send. I press the delete button because the fear of her not responding is too great for me to risk it.

Bo texts me when he arrives, which is perfectly timed because my mom is getting in the shower.

"I'll be back later!" I call to her.

If she asks where I'm going, I don't hear her over the water.

I'm not even trying to hide that I'm going somewhere with Bo. It's that I'm going to a church with Bo, because my mother would rather me not go to church at all than go to a Catholic church. Which makes no sense to me. Catholics, Protestants, Christians, Baptists . . . they all believe in the same things, I think. They just have different ways of saying it. I guess we're Baptist. I mean, my mom goes to Clover City First Baptist, and so do I on holidays.

Bo, in his pressed khaki pants and black polo, is leaning against the passenger door, waiting for me. I feel slightly overdressed in my black dress, the one I wore to Lucy's funeral, but it's the only church-appropriate thing I own.

He holds the door open for me, and we drive the whole way there with our hands on the bench seat between us. Nothing but our pinkies touch, and it feels like a spark on the verge of a flame.

I have never in my life been inside a Catholic church. I imagine they're all these ancient buildings with steeples, stained-glass windows, and those kneeling benches like you see in movies.

Holy Cross is newer though. There are still pews with kneeling benches and stained-glass windows. It's quieter than my mom's church. More peaceful. There are no boisterous greeters or gossipy Sunday school teachers.

It's nice.

At both sides of the altar are candles in

red votives, but not all of them are lit.

"What are those for?" I whisper to Bo after we've found a seat in the middle of the church.

"You're supposed to leave a dollar or something in the collection box and light a candle in memory of someone. And, I guess, say a prayer if you want."

Service starts and after a few announcements and some hymns, the collection plate is passed around. Bo pulls a crumpled ten from his wallet and drops it on the plate before passing it along. Father Mike gives his sermon. I guess I expected it to be in Latin or something, but it's not, it's in English. Each word is measured. The whole thing feels a little bit like a ceremony, like when I was in Girl Scouts and I went from Daisy to Brownie.

After the service, I follow Bo to the candles where a few other people have gathered. He drops a few dollars into the lockbox and gives me a stick to light a candle from a larger candle. We both light a candle. Neither of us says who the candles are for, but we don't have to.

I imagine what it might be like to do

this every Sunday with Bo. Even if I don't know if all of this is something I believe in, it's nice to be a part of something. With him.

We walk outside to the parking lot, where all the socializing is happening. Bo waves to a few people. He points to a man in a navy blazer and khaki pants. "That's my coach." It breaks my heart to hear him talk about this man so firmly in the present, as if he still was his coach.

"Bo!" It takes me a moment to recognize him, but it's Collin. That same guy who came and visited Bo at Harpy's. He jogs toward us.

"Hey," he says, pointing at me. "I recognize you."

I feel myself recoiling.

Bo holds his hand out and the two exchange a firm handshake that looks more like a show of strength. But there's none of that suffocating tension radiating off Bo like there was the last time these two saw each other.

"What's up, man?" asks Collin.

Bo shrugs. "Work. School."

A few other guys from the team are

heading over now. I feel like the elephant in the room — or the parking lot. Literally and figuratively.

He shakes each of their hands.

They ask him about school and his knee and if he's going to try to do some rehab to get back on the court. My shoulders ease a little as I almost start to feel invisible.

Then Collin points to me and says, "And what about this one? She your girlfriend now?"

Bo glances over at me and says, "This is Willowdean." He turns back to his friends. "And I'm working on it." Then he takes my hand. He holds my hand. Right there in front of everyone. I am equal parts thrilled and mortified.

A few of his friends whistle as he says bye and we walk to his truck. Hand in hand.

We sit in his car, waiting in line to turn out of the parking lot. "What was that about?"

He brushes his knuckles over his chin. "I told you I wanna do this the right way. And I'm done keeping you a secret. I didn't even mean for you to feel like a secret in the first place. I was — I don't know. Sometimes good things happen to you at the absolute worst time. You were a good thing, Willowdean."

"What about Bekah?"

"What about her?"

"Aren't you guys dating?"

He scoffs. "Hardly. We went out a few times." He pauses. "Okay. I guess we kind of dated. But I was trying to get over you. Or maybe make you jealous. I don't know. And I didn't expect for you to be all over that jock, so I guess I was the jealous one."

"Mitch. His name's Mitch. He's not that guy. He's my friend."

He doesn't respond for a minute. "Is he anything more than that?"

"No," I say, like I'm shocked by the idea.

I feel his gaze on me.

"I don't know." Oh God. Of course we're more than friends. At least to him we are. And maybe sometimes for me, too. "Technically, we're not anything. But he wants more."

"Do you want more?" he asks. "With him?"

"I — I don't know. Usually, no. But I haven't really said so." I twist a piece of hair around my finger. "But what about you and Bekah?" I shake my head. "It's never going to be the right time for us, Bo."

"I haven't told Bekah we're not dating if that's what you're asking."

"So, what? You were going to leave her hanging?"

"It's not like we're boyfriend and girl-friend."

"Well, neither were we," I tell him.

Jerking the wheel, he turns off into a random alleyway and puts the truck in park.

He unbuckles his seat belt and moves toward me. "I want more," he says. "I want more with you. I want to hold hands in public. I want to drive you home from work and give you a kiss good night. And talk on the phone so late we fall asleep."

I bite down on my bottom lip to stop it

from quivering. There are so many reasons why we are a bad idea. We have a track record — real bona-fide proof. If I were to shake my Magic 8 Ball, I can almost guarantee that it would tell me, *Outlook not so good.*

But Bo is undeterred. "You didn't know me last year, Willowdean. I'm so glad you didn't. I was a dick. All I cared about was getting out of this place. I fucked up with you this summer. I know that. And I'm not letting you go again. I'll talk to Bekah and be one hundred percent clear with her. There won't be any misunderstanding."

"It's not that simple, Bo. Maybe it is for you, but not for me."

He narrows his gaze. "This is what I want: I want you to be my girlfriend. I want to put a label on this. I want everyone to know exactly how I feel about you, Willowdean. I think that sounds pretty simple."

I shouldn't, but I move to kiss him. My nerves hum, and this moment when my body feels both chaotic and determined is what was missing with Mitch.

He pulls back. "I want your answer first."

I break our eye contact, letting my gaze wander everywhere but him. I don't know if I can handle the stares and the whispers. Even if I can get over the total self-revulsion I feel when he touches me — really touches me — I don't think I can deal with people always asking in astonishment, like it's some water-to-wine miracle, how we ended up together.

And now I know exactly how Lucy felt when she decided she couldn't get on that plane to Dollywood. All those years, I thought she was only standing in her own way, and now I know she had no choice. When your options are limited to being miserable in private or being morti-fied in public, there is no choice. I can't get on the plane.

My mom's right. I will never be happy in this body. Not really. I'll never say it out loud, but she's right. I want so badly to prove her wrong that I almost say yes, but instead I chew the skin around my thumb and say, "I need to think about it."

Because I can't bear to tell him no. Not

yet. I want to live with the possibility of what could be. If only for a couple days.

FORTY-NINE

I've only had a serious hangover once.
Ellen and I went to a lock-in at Tim's
mom's church, and Tim, being the good
boyfriend he is, brought us wine coolers
stolen from his dad. Ellen and I poured
them into Sonic cups and kept refilling
them until her mom picked us up the
next morning. We slid into the backseat
of the car and fell asleep slumped up
against each other. Ellen and I slept all
day, and when we woke up, I felt like I'd
been asleep for years. Everything was too
bright, and the only thing I wanted was
to chomp on greasy food before going
back to bed.

On Monday morning, I am hungover
from a weekend spent with Bo. My entire
body is drowsy, and I have to extract
myself from bed in stages. One limb

at a time.

We probably spent eight hours studying for our World History test, but I can barely even remember the review questions, let alone the answers. And my Friday afternoon at the Hideaway feels like a memory tucked deep into the past.

When Mitch walks into second period, I am studying my notes, trying to recall some of what I studied. It's like my brain has decided to purge information to make space for the events of the last two days.

When his huge frame invades the narrow doorway, the memory of him hits me like whiplash. Mitch and I exist in this weird gray area, but I'm thinking it's grayer for me than it is for him.

"Hey," he says. "I texted you a few times this weekend."

"Ah, yeah. I'm sorry. I was drowning in World History notes. It was one of those things like I'd see your text and then say I'd message you when I was done reading, and then I'd forget." I'm doing that crazy babbling thing.

His features are loose, but his eyes are

tense and focused. "The pageant's in, like, two weeks. I was thinking —" He wipes a few beads of sweat from his forehead with the back of his hand. "Maybe I could be your escort. I went to the pageant a few years ago, and I know girls have to get guys to escort them. I could, like, rent a tux. Is that dumb? You were probably supposed to ask me, but you wrote on your face for Sadie Hawkins, and I don't know. What do you think?"

"I . . . I — yes. That would be good. Great." I want to take the words right back. This is more than a friendly gesture. Yet, selfishly, I do need an escort. And Bo didn't technically offer. Besides, if I can't handle the idea of walking down a hallway with him, how will I cope with him escorting me in front of the entire town?

"Okay, cool. Should I get something to match your dress? Like prom or whatever?"

"I think black is good. And you can wear a suit. You don't have to rent a tux."

He shakes his head. "My mom's idea. She's all on board for this."

Oh God. His mom. "Great."

"She really loves that you're doing this. She says it's brave."

I smile. But I don't want it to be brave. I want it to be normal.

After school, Millie tracks me down in the parking lot, which isn't hard since I'm just standing around, hoping to catch Ellen on her own.

Today Millie is a ball of mint green, including her backpack. Her hair is pulled into a ponytail with a matching scrunchie, because Millie might be the only person I know who still wears scrunchies.

"Hey," she says. "So, Friday was pretty great."

"Yeah, it was."

She rocks back and forth on her feet, her hands twisting together. "I'm — my family is kind of religious. Actually, really religious. And my parents. Well, they wouldn't be super happy if they knew where I was. And who we were with."

I feel my shoulders slump. "Okay?"

"I say that because . . . I always thought

people like Lee and Dale were wrong. Like, they were living in sin."

I hate phrases like that. "Jesus vocab," El would call them. Things you learn in church that are hammered into you until they're so normal that you expect everyone else who doesn't go to church to know what you mean.

Millie shakes her head. "My words are coming out all wrong. What I'm trying to say is that I liked Lee and Dale and I had fun that night at the Hideaway. I keep thinking about it and they're good people. I wish everyone could see that." She smiles. "I just wanted to let you know."

Something I can only describe as pride swells against my chest. I grip Millie's shoulder. "I'm glad."

"Pageant piggies!" someone yells from the other side of the parking lot, breaking the moment between us. "Oink! Oink!"

"Eat shit!" I bark back. I turn to Millie. "I'm sorry."

She tucks a stray hair behind her ear and takes a step back. "It's whatever. It's fine."

I knew this was bound to happen eventually. With the pageant two weeks away, the town's attention is all on us. And in our case, that might not be a good thing.

Millie pulls on the straps of her backpack. "I was thinking of having you, Amanda, and Hannah over for a slumber party. Amanda will go, but I don't think Hannah will if you don't. So . . . will you?"

As a rule, I don't do slumber parties, unless you count spending the night at El's. Nothing about sleeping in little more than a T-shirt and underwear on Millie's floor while her parents check in on us every few hours appeals to me. But I don't have it in me to say no to her right now. "Sure," I say. "Yeah, I'll be there."

The next night, after I pick my mom up from work, she says she's made some adjustments to my dress and would I mind trying it on.

She leaves me, again, in her room to change by myself. The top half of the dress is a perfect fit. I can't even imagine how long it must have taken her to get the darts right. But the bottom half is something else altogether. She said she would take it out as far as she could, but it's still snug. I feel fine in it. I'm not embarrassed or anything.

But I see it in her frown.

"The top is good," I say. "Like, perfect."

She presses her palm against my back. "Try standing up a little straighter."

I do.

She makes a tsk noise.

The sound of her disappointment is like needles under my fingernails. "Mom, it's fine, okay? I love it."

"Dumplin'," she says. "It's huggin' on your hips like a straitjacket." She runs her fingers along the seams. "I can't take it any further without risking it splitting."

"Mom, it's good. I only have to wear it for, like, ten minutes."

Her lips twitch.

"What?" I turn around to face her without our reflections standing between us. "Just say it, Mom. Whatever you're thinking, say it."

She waves me off and starts to pack up her sewing box on her dresser. "I thought . . . I just thought you might make an effort to slim down a little for the pageant." She turns back to me. "I mean, are you even taking this seriously? Because you know this isn't a joke. I let you register because I expected you to take this seriously."

Her words send me stumbling. "So the dress doesn't fit because you expected me to lose weight?" I wave my hands up and down the length of my form. "Mom, this is me. This is my body."

She shakes her head. "I knew you'd take that the wrong way. You always see the worst in everything I say. I can't do this anymore. I'm not the bad guy here."

"Then who is?"

She's silent and the words she doesn't say hang there between us like hulking icicles on the verge of breaking. "It's too snug," she finally says. "I'm not going to approve it for the pageant. It's not about you being my daughter. I would do the same with anyone else. It's inappropriate."

"Mom, I feel good." My voice starts out even and calm. "This dress makes me feel like someone I didn't know I could be. I've never owned anything like it. But if when you see this — when you see me — you think it's a pity, that it's a shame I didn't lose a few, then screw you, Mom. Try harder."

There's this still moment as I'm waiting for her to leave. Then I realize it's me standing here in her room. I pick up my dress so as not to trip on the hem, and then I leave her there in that lonely little room that she'll live in for the rest of her life with her sash and her crown and her sea-foam dress.

FIFTY

After work on Friday night, Bo gives me a ride like he has for the last two weeks, but this time he's not taking me home.

We roll to a stop outside Millie's house. Ron let us both off a little early so I could get here before midnight.

I pull my overnight bag into my lap and mentally prepare myself for *bonding time.*

The pageant has become such an afterthought for me. I think I originally signed up because I was so sure I had something to prove. I don't know if it was to myself or my mom or everyone, but with each passing day, I feel more and more like I have nothing left to say.

"So y'all are getting together to practice stuff for the pageant?"

I shake my head. "Not really. More game planning, I think. We gotta stick together."

His brow is heavy with confusion. "So you four all entered the pageant together?"

I nod.

"I'm totally on board with the idea that anyone who wants to should enter this thing, but why does it have to be such a big deal?"

Grinning, I turn to him. "It's kind of like how you keep going to mass even though you don't go to Holy Cross. It's something the team does together, right? But just 'cause you're not on the team doesn't mean you shouldn't go. And just 'cause we don't look like beauty queens doesn't mean we shouldn't enter."

"I guess it would be really cheesy of me to say I think you're ten times hotter and smarter than any beauty queen."

My cheeks burn. "Yeah. Super cheesy."

"I didn't know people still did slumber parties," he says.

"Well, I guess they do. El and I always spent the night at each other's houses, but we never called it a party." In the last few days, I'd told Bo all about El and me and how we weren't really talking. He seemed to think we'd get past it, but I just can't seem to find that same foresight.

I open the door.

He reaches for my hand. "Willowdean? Have you thought any more about what we talked about? You know I wasn't kidding, right?"

It's so impossible for me not to say yes. To tell him that I want to be his girlfriend. "I need a little more time."

He nods. "Okay. Time."

Amanda stands at the door with her jaw dropped so low it melts into her chest. Millie cranes her neck from behind Amanda.

"Oh. My. God," says Amanda. "That was Peachbutt."

I shush her and wave them both inside. The first thing that strikes me about Millie's house is how everything — from the fake flowers to the paint to the throw pillows — matches. Millie is a lavender cotton ball in her matching sweat suit, socks, and headband. It's like she went online and searched "slumber party outfits" and came up with this gem from a Baby-Sitters Club book cover or something.

Amanda is in her soccer shorts and a T-shirt, but she's barefoot. It's the first time I've ever seen her without her platform shoes on, and I don't want to be that jerk who stares, so I keep my eyes on her face instead, which still feels totally obvious.

"Okay, but real talk," she says. "He dropped you off. Here. You were in his car. Tell us everything."

Millie pulls us down the hallway and past the TV room where her parents are watching some PBS series with British people talking in hushed voices about scandalous things like who's going to serve lord and lady their chilled pea soup.

"Wait till you hear about my pageant-dress fiasco. I hope y'all are having better luck," I say.

Millie shakes her head and yanks on my hand, pulling me to her bedroom door, which I know is hers because a wooden heart with her name painted in cursive tells me so.

Amanda covers her mouth, stifling her

own laughter.

"What?" I ask.

Millie's eyes meet mine, and there's a desperation in her I've never seen before. She opens the bedroom door, and on a lavender beanbag in all black is Hannah. She doesn't even look up.

Millie takes my bag and sets it on the foot of her bed. "Okay, sit down."

I do. Right there on the floor.

Millie sits in this crazy wicker throne chair in the corner of her room. It looks like something out of a retirement home, but oddly enough, it suits her. I wish I could take a picture of her in this huge chair with her matching outfit, ringlet curls, and sloped nose. "You can't talk about the pageant in front of my parents."

"Why?" I ask.

"Because they don't know she's in it," says Hannah.

With a huge grin plastered across her face, Amanda slides down onto the floor in front of Millie.

"But what about the parental consent form?" It's more a rhetorical question because I know the answer. I can't imagine Millie being capable of such deception.

She licks her lips. "I forged my mother's signature."

Hannah sits scrolling through her phone, with her lips sealed but smiling.

Millie's round face crumples a little. Her cheeks tinge an even deeper pink than normal. "I asked them. Back when I first found out you were entering the pageant."

I nod along with her, encouraging her to tell me more.

"And my mom took a few days to think about it. But they said no. They said they couldn't have that on their conscience. That I'd get made fun of, and that it didn't seem like a very Christlike way to spend my time."

Hannah scoffs.

I roll my eyes at her. Which doesn't matter because she can't spare a glance away from her phone. "But what are you going to do? The pageant is next weekend. I mean, you're going to be in the paper. And then *everyone* will know."

Sure, we'd been heckled a few times, but once that paper goes to print, there's no turning back. People like Patrick Thomas would have good material on me for the rest of our lives.

"I — I don't know." She chews the skin around her thumbnail, and her eyes search my face, looking for some kind of answer or something. Anything that might tell her it will be okay.

I see it now. I see now what the stakes are for her and how she wants nothing more than to break out of the delicate little box her parents have built for her. "It'll be okay," I say. "It's going to be fine."

"I think it's badass," says Amanda. "I woulda never thought you had something like that in you."

"Oh, I think she's got room in there for plenty," murmurs Hannah.

That's it. I am so over her attitude. "What is it with you?" I spit. "Why are you even here? Can't you just hate on something in your own house?"

"Will," says Millie.

"It's true," I say. "Millie invited you

over here to her home and all you've done since I walked in is stick your face in your phone and brood."

Hannah finally looks up. Her face is all amusement. "Oh, like you even give a shit about these two. You're just here to feel better about yourself. This is some kind of sad circle jerk."

I feel my nostrils flare.

"It's true," she adds. "That's the only reason you're sticking with this little freak show. You were an asshole to your best friend and now all you have is us."

"Stop," says Millie, cutting the cord of tension between us. "Let's talk interview questions. I tracked down some from a few years ago for us to practice with."

"Don't talk to me like you know the whole story," I tell Hannah. "Because you don't." I turn to Millie. "Is there somewhere I can change?"

Millie points me to the bathroom across the hallway. Every little mauve detail matches, including the house-shaped shelf that holds spare toilet paper. Like in Millie's room, there are cheesy inspirational quotes in frames. My personal favorite: *A smile is a curve that sets everything straight.*

Still on her wicker throne, Millie says, "Okay, so like our packets say, there will be an interview session the Thursday before the pageant. The judges will grade us on that, and then combine it with our live interview during the pageant. I think that's one or two questions."

"And we don't know the questions beforehand?" asks Amanda.

"No," I say, letting sleeping memories of my childhood spent backstage resurface. "No, and this is where they like to stump you."

"Interview is the component with the highest point value, so if we —"

Millie's interrupted by a light knock. The door creaks open. Her mom, with hair tall enough to hold a few family secrets, stands with eyes brimming like she might cry or something. "We're heading to bed."

"Okay." Millie bites in on her lips so that they disappear.

"I'll have breakfast ready for you girls tomorrow morning. We're so happy to see Millie have some girlfriends over."

"We're so happy to be here," says Hannah, her voice flat.

Millie's smile is tight. "Good night, Mom."

"Night-night, sugar."

After she shuts the door, we discuss the point value breakdown and how ridiculous it is that swimsuit accounts for more than talent. Once Millie is sure her parents are asleep, we head to the TV room and watch a few videos of former pageants that I stole from my mom's stash.

The more contestants that grace the screen, the more obvious it is how much we do not fit. There's the odd black sheep here and there, but never anything like the four of us. It makes me feel small, like a blip on the history of this little pageant. What about next year? Or the year after that? Soon, we'd be forgotten and what would be the point then?

Millie feverishly takes notes throughout the night, while Amanda asks questions like, "What if we get wedgies during the swimwear part?" or "Do you think there's ever been any major wardrobe disasters, like, a nip slip? Will we get bathroom breaks?"

Hannah looks up from her phone to say, "This is kind of depressing. I mean, this is the actual highlight of these girls' lives. The people on these tapes are moms or even grandmas now and this is probably the best thing they've ever done."

"That's not very fair." Millie's voice is quiet. "Just because maybe these women have stayed here in Clover City or have become stay-at-home moms or cashiers doesn't mean you can deem their entire lives outside of the pageant a waste."

Hannah says nothing, but her lips nearly tremble.

"Listen, Hannah," she adds. "I know people have been cruel to you, but —"

"I'm going to bed." She tucks her pillow beneath her arm and heads back to Millie's room.

After she's gone, I wait for Millie to say something about how horrible Hannah is, but she keeps whatever thoughts she might have to herself.

The three of us stay there for a while longer. Millie tells us how she used the piggy bank she's had since first grade to order a dress from Cindy's.

"I had sleeves added, but at the last minute, decided to have them made with organza instead of satin so it's almost see-through. I'm kind of nervous about how it'll turn out."

"I'm sure you'll look amazing," I tell her.

She smiles and nods. It's dark, so I can't know for sure, but her eyes look watery. I want to wake her parents up and tell them that their daughter is competing in a beauty pageant, and that she's going to win. At least she would if it was up to me.

FIFTY-ONE

I take the couch for the night to give myself some quiet. I slip in and out of sleep the way you do when you're sleeping in a house that isn't your own. Except at El's. I could always sleep.

Maybe it's thirty minutes or two hours, I don't know, but the house creaks as someone walks down the hallway. I turn over so that I can catch a glimpse of whoever it is. Slipping through a sliver of moonlight, Hannah makes her way to the kitchen. Without thinking about it, I pull back my blankets and follow her.

She stands in front of the fridge, the white light turning her into a silhouette.

I flip the overhead light on.

She jumps a little and turns around, but the tension in her shoulders eases when she sees it's me. "I'm looking for a bottle of water."

"Then what's up with the beer?" I ask, pointing to the can of Miller in her fist.

"Found them in the garage fridge. Thought I'd see if there were any more in here." She opens the fridge door wide to show me nothing but bottled water and Diet Dr Pepper. "No one's going to miss these, though." She points to several cans on the counter. "You want one?"

"Yeah," I say, surprising myself. I bet Millie's mom isn't too thrilled by the idea of beer in the house, so technically we're doing Mr. and Mrs. Michalchuk a favor. "Sure."

We sit in the dark on the couch, sipping our beers. The moon shines against the windowpane, casting a shadow on the carpet.

"So what's up with that guy who dropped you off tonight?" asks Hannah.

"What guy?"

"I'm trying to be nice, okay?" It's true. In the dark, she seems like a less hostile version of herself. Like, maybe, she's most comfortable when no one can see her. "I heard Amanda and Millie blabbering about him when they came to bed. Peachbutt, huh?"

"Bo." If she's willing to put the claws away, I can give her a few ounces of truth, I guess. "Bo Larson. We work together. We're, uh, friends."

"Ah." She takes a long slurp from her beer. "Bathroom Boy. I remember now. He's in my study hall. Dude's like an eight. A solid eight. I don't even like guys and I like looking at him."

I search for her in the darkness. Did Hannah just come out to me? I don't know what to say or do, but I do know that I don't really care whether Hannah likes boys or girls. So I decide not to say anything. "Yeah, he's a little too delicious." And a ten, I think. Definitely a ten.

"Friends, huh? Didn't look like friends when I saw you two." I can hear her smiling. "In the girls' bathroom no less."

I shrug. Which is dumb because she can't see me. "Friends who sometimes make out."

She whistles.

My cheeks and chest burn. I hope it's

the beer.

She pops the tab on a second beer. "How'd that happen?"

"It's been on and off, I guess. I don't know. It's starting to become more and he wants to be something official. And it's so stupid because, yes, obviously that is everything I want but . . ."

"But guys like Bo don't date girls like us." The way she says it. It's not mean. Or rude. It's true.

I nod. "Exactly. I don't get why he likes me, but I truly believe that he does. I really do. It's just that I don't think anyone else will understand what he sees in me."

"That's a tough one," she says. "People are shit. Look at people like Patrick Thomas. You dating a guy like Bo would be a field day for him."

It's nice to talk to someone who understands. Hannah may not get what it feels like to wonder if you're going to fit into a chair with armrests or how anytime a floor creaks beneath your weight, everyone looks at you like you're about to break the entire building. She might not get what it's like to walk into a mall and know that 90 percent of the clothes won't fit you or that even thinking about going to a buffet is a bad idea, because a fat person at a buffet is a joke waiting to happen. But she's not patting me on the back, and telling me to do what makes me happy. And there's some relief in that. "I wish that there was some kind of alternate plane we could exist on where he could be my boyfriend." It's the first time I've said the word out loud and it sends a hum all the way through me to my toes. "And no one had to know."

"But isn't that the point of labels like boyfriend and girlfriend? To make things easier for other people?" She slurps her beer. "Isn't that sad? It's like the whole world has to walk around with name tags on so we can all feel more comfortable? I guess things are less scary if you know what to call them."

We drink our beers in silence. Her words sound right, but feel wrong. Yeah, labels make it easier for others to understand you, but I like the safety of knowing. Especially with Bo. That's why I haven't given him an answer yet. I can't bear to tell him no.

"Hannah, I want to ask you a question. It's rude, but I'm not asking to be rude." Although, that doesn't really make it any better.

"Shoot," she says.

"Why haven't you ever gotten your teeth fixed?"

"Why should I have to?" she retorts immediately. Her voice softens as she adds, "Plus it's expensive. Mom's a hairdresser. Dad's a mechanic. Not like we have great insurance or anything."

"You're right," I say. "You shouldn't have to."

She clears her throat. "I don't mean to be such a bitch, you know."

"It's okay."

She laughs. "I wasn't apologizing. But it's hard not to have my claws out all the time. I don't have friends like you do. There's no one there to walk down the hallway with me."

"You have friends. Don't be stupid." But I can close my eyes and see her at school, wearing black from head to toe and with her mouth stretched over her teeth, so that maybe people will just forget.

"I wanted to sabotage this pageant from the inside out. That was the only reason I entered. I wouldn't be the girl with buckteeth. I'd be that girl who ruined the whole pageant." She pauses. "But then my mom found out. She saw the welcome packet. She was so proud of me for entering. And now . . ."

"You're stuck actually doing this thing." It makes sense. If people treated me half as bad as they do Hannah, I would want to ruin this whole thing, too.

"I'm going to bed," she says. "Gimme your empties. I'll throw them out at my place."

I finish the last of my beer. Her hand reaches out and I pass her my two cans. I feel the couch shift as she stands. I don't know where she is or if she's even facing me, but I say, "I'm your friend. Not in a corny way. Not because you said all that about not having friends. But because I like you. I like talking to you."

It's so quiet that, for a moment, I think maybe she's not even in the room. Her voice comes as a whisper. "Okay."

I miss Ellen. I will never stop missing Ellen. But there's a sigh of relief that comes in having another friend who I can talk to about more than this dumb pageant. Even if it's only in the dark.

The next morning when I get home, I find my mom upstairs in Lucy's room. Neither of us has really been in here much since she started the craft room transformation. She's been caught up in pageant stuff, and I've been too wrapped up in myself, so Lucy's room has sort of been sitting here. Briefly, I wonder if, like me, she's snuck in here for moments at a time. Just to see Lucy. To be near her.

But today my mom's got her ridiculous Juicy Couture tracksuit on and has boxes labeled *DONATE.* She's not here to visit Lucy. She's here to get rid of her.

When my mother is frustrated, she cleans. Her cleaning out Lucy's room frustrates me. These two negatives do not equal a positive. She and I are still on eggshells over the dress, and honestly, if she doesn't let me wear it, I'm done for. I have no other options. A fat girl can't just walk into a thrift shop and — POOF — find a decent dress that actually fits.

And that's what really pisses me off about the dress thing. She's the head honcho. The lady calling the shots. All she has to say is yes. I have a hard enough time finding jeans to wiggle over my ass, you think she'd be shooting confetti cannons over me being able to find a not hideous/not stretchy dress that zips. IT ZIPS.

But the room. There she is digging — pawing — through Lucy's things and every little movement feels like I've accidentally touched the coils of a hot stove.

"What are you even doing in here?" My voice is already too loud and too sharp.

She glances back at me. "I didn't hear you come in." She turns back. "This stuff can't sit here forever. You know, I hope that when I die, you don't let my belongings gather dust for months like this."

"These are Lucy's *things,* Mom. This stuff belongs to her."

"Baby," she says. "*Belonged.* These things belonged to her. We're coming up on a year in December. I'm not lettin' all this sit here like some kind of shrine."

I shake my head. Tears spill out onto my cheeks. A year. A whole year. "Stop," I say. "Please stop."

She turns to me now. Panic flashes across her face. I think that maybe I will forever judge her based on what she does and says at this very moment. We don't have this kind of relationship. I don't cry on my mother's shoulder. We dance around each other, but never intersect.

Her house shoes slap against the floor as she takes the few steps toward me.

I lean forward, expecting her to hug me. And I don't mean her wrapping her arms around my waist, and commenting on how her fingers nearly touch. I mean a real hug. One I can sink into. "I'm taking all this stuff to the shelter this weekend. If there's anything you want, now's the time to pull it out." She pats my shoulder. "I'm going to go put together some lunch before you have to go to work."

The door closes behind her, and I sink down onto Lucy's bed. The memory of the last few weeks washes over me.

I have no dress. A not-really-maybe

boyfriend who I can't bear to be seen with in public, because I feel that repulsive when I think of us standing side by side. Mitch, who I've been horrible to. My mom. Ellen. And no Lucy.

I need Lucy. She should be here to tell me what to do. Some solution that would never even occur to me without her.

I consider the things I can change.

The dress.

I could eat lettuce until the pageant and maybe then it will fit like how my mom had imagined. But then what? It's that vicious dieting cycle, like when I was younger. I would lose the weight to wear the dress, and then what? I start eating food that's not lettuce and gain it all back. Maybe even some extra.

All the pageant season diets my mom and I have done flip through my head like index cards. Protein bars in fourth grade. Weight Watchers in fifth. Salads in second. And none of it ever worked.

She wins. My mom wins. I didn't even know this was some kind of competition with her until this moment. But I'm losing. I have no dress. Barely any talent.

And an escort whose heart I'm breaking without him even knowing it.

If I do this pageant, I'll make a point — that's for sure. It just won't be one I want to be remembered for.

FIFTY-TWO

Sitting in the break room later that night, I use a compact mirror to examine the green ring around my neck in the reflection. I snap the mirror shut like a clam, and take the fake gold necklace off and lay it out on the table. The gold chain is that twisty type of chain they sell at mall kiosks, and the charm says *Dolly* in a bubbly cursive script.

I ended up fitting as much of Lucy's stuff as I could in my closet. I tried my best to get all her Dolly collectibles, including a pair of glitter-encrusted shoes Dolly wore to a show in Vegas. The soles are signed in her big loopy signature, proving their authenticity.

Bo plops down in the chair next to me. "What's that?"

I drag the chain around with my index

finger so that he can see it. "It was my aunt's."

He nods.

"My mom's cleaning out her room. Again. It's happened in small spurts in the last few months. But I think she's serious this time."

"I'm sorry." He drags his finger along the chain. "When my mom was dying, she kinda cleaned out her room for us. Like, as soon as she found out it was bad, she started inviting people over and no one ever left empty-handed. By the time she was gone, all that was left were a few nightgowns and some shoes." He concentrates on the necklace, his jaw twitching. "I was kind of mad at her for doing that. But I don't think I could have done it myself anyway. If it'd been up to my dad, we'd still be using her perfume as air freshener."

Bo watches me for a moment before yanking on the leg of my chair and pulling me closer to him. He wraps his arm around me and I ease into his frame. My breathing hitches a little, but that voice in my head that begs me not to let him touch me is nothing more than a murmur. His lips press against my hair, sending calming vibrations through me.

"Am I interrupting something?" Mitch stands in the doorway with a brown grocery bag clenched in his fist.

I pick my head up so quickly that I hit Bo's jaw. "I'm sorry," I say, but to which of them I'm not sure. Panic sinks all the way down to my toes, holding me in place. "Hi," I say to Mitch. "Hey. What are you doing here?"

Bo stands, rubbing the spot where my head collided with his. "I better get back to work." His voice is rigid.

The tension between them buzzes like an electric fence.

Mitch doesn't move out of his way, so Bo squeezes past him. He watches Bo go before stepping through the doorway. "The guy at the front told me you were back here." He drops the bag on the table, and whatever's inside rattles for a second. "I got you some magic supplies. For your talent."

I try too hard to keep my voice light. "Sit down."

He doesn't. "Who was that guy?"

"Bo. We work together."

His two brows crinkle into one. "Do you like him?"

"What? We were talking, Mitch." I sound defensive because I am. So we kissed once. We hold hands sometimes. That doesn't make us anything. And yet maybe it does. It's not like he caught me making out with Bo or in a state of undress, but I feel just as guilty.

"Do you?" he asks again.

I tuck my hair behind my ears and take a long moment before I answer. "I do."

He shakes his head and pulls down on the bill of his baseball cap. "Good luck with the pageant, Will." He turns on his heel and exits through the nearest door, which happens to be the employee exit.

My heart aches from losing one of my precious few friends, knowing all too well that if this is anyone's fault it's mine.

That night, Bo drives me home in silence.

I'm halfway up the driveway when I hear his door slam shut as he says, "I wish you would give me an answer." He circles around the front of his truck.

"What?" I walk back toward him. "We have to do this tonight?"

"I want to be with you," he says. "But I can't if you won't let me."

"Why?" I drop my bag in the driveway. "Why do you want to be with this?" I wave my arm up and down the length of my body. Immediately, I hate myself for this. The only person making this about my body is me.

"Because I like you. I think I might feel a lot more than that for you, Willowdean. How is that so hard to believe? When I can't fall asleep at night it's not because of work or school or Amber or Bekah. It's you. You're the one that drives me crazy."

I shake my head because it makes no sense. "Have you ever thought about what people will think? What they'll say when they see us together holding hands?"

"You never struck me as the type to give a shit what everyone else thinks." His jaw twitches for a moment before he lowers his voice and says, "I want to go everywhere with you. I want to show you off. I want to wear a cheap suit and be your escort for that ridiculous pageant."

My teeth chatter. I'm trying so, so hard not to cry. Because it's all there. I like him. He likes me. But there's so much more. I can't believe it even matters to me, but I'm not going to be skinny anytime soon, and I shouldn't care. I'm pissed that I didn't just throw myself at him right here in my driveway.

But I refuse to hate him for being another reason_for people to whisper about me. "I can't. That might make me a coward, but . . ." The tears are more than a threat now.

He meets me where I am, and because of the downward tilt of the driveway, we are toe to toe, nose to nose. "Willowdean Opal Dickson, you are beautiful. Fuck anyone who's ever made you feel anything less." His chest heaves. "When I close my eyes, I see you. I can talk to you. In a way I never have with anyone else."

Beautiful, he says. Fat, I think. But can't I be both at the same time? I lift my hand to his cheek, and the tension bubbling beneath his skin eases. I kiss him once more on the lips. I linger there for a moment, remembering all the details of everything I shouldn't be allowed to have. "I can't," I whisper, knowing that I'm talking about so much more than just me and Bo.

I turn around and pick up my bag.

He stands in the driveway until I switch my bedroom light off, turning my house into a dark shell.

FIFTY-THREE

On Monday, as I'm walking out of class, Mitch reaches for my elbow. Mr. Krispin has already run off for the teachers' lounge, and everyone's cleared out. It's just us.

"I wanted to say that I don't think I should be your escort for the pageant."

I look up at him, but he only lets our eyes meet for a second before looking away. "I'm not doing the pageant anyway." I hadn't said it out loud until this very moment, but I made my decision on Saturday night, standing in my driveway with Bo.

I can see his thoughts moving across his features. Thoughts of him trying to convince me. Telling me about the bright side. But he says nothing.

"And I'm sorry," I add much too late.

"I didn't mean for you to get hurt."

"But you like him?"

I nod.

" 'I'm sorry' doesn't make it better," he says. "I would've been really good to you."

"More than I deserve."

I want to tell him how close he'd come, and that had I never met Bo, he'd be it. But I met Bo, and now I know what it feels like for one person's name to wreck you.

He stuffs his hands into the pockets of his jacket and walks out.

I give him a few seconds' head start before I leave for my class on the other side of campus.

I take my time. I'd rather be late than out of breath. No one likes to see a fat girl huffing and puffing. The last bell rings and the halls clear.

And then Ellen slips out of the last classroom on the right.

At first, she doesn't see me. She wipes her eyes. She's crying. It could be about anything. But whatever it is, I don't know about it.

She glances back and sees me trailing a few feet behind her. She stops, not bothering to wipe her face free of the tears streaming down her cheeks. Maybe she and Tim broke up. Maybe she got in a fight with her new friends. Maybe she failed a test. I don't know. This is my moment to step up. To ask her how she's doing, and apologize for everything.

But she turns and rushes into the bathroom. The moment is gone.

I don't stay for any of my other classes. This day has already gone wrong in too many ways for me to risk sticking around. When I get home, there's a text from Millie asking if we should all get together to practice our talents. The pageant. It doesn't even matter anymore. When I entered, I did it for Lucy. And with Ellen by my side. But Lucy's dead and Ellen is further away than ever.

I text Millie, Hannah, and Amanda:

ME: I can't do the pageant. It's short notice. I know. But I'm backing out. Y'all are going to be amazing. You

464

deserve to be there. I'll be cheering you on from the audience.

After calling into work sick for the night, I turn my phone off and decide to keep it that way for the entire evening.

FIFTY-FOUR

I spend Tuesday and Wednesday faking a fever and nursing a bag of mini chocolate chips I found in the pantry from a few holidays ago. We're not the type of household that just has sweets on hand (surprise!), especially with my mom still on Operation Squeeze into Pageant Gown.

When I tell my mom I'm not feeling well, she closes my bedroom door without any questions. "Sorry, sweetheart," she says. "Can't risk getting sick. You take the day off."

For Mom, every single moment not spent on an elliptical at the YMCA or at work is a crafting 911. Our house is a war zone of fabric, props, and sequins, but the chaos of it actually gives me some quiet.

I want — no, need — a few days to be

a total slob. I haven't showered since Sunday, and it's oddly comforting to know that I look almost as disgusting as I feel. When Ron gave me the week of the pageant off work, I don't think this is what he had in mind.

By Wednesday night the freedom is fading, and I find myself lying facedown on my bed listening to one of Lucy's records, which turns out to basically be the worst of Dolly Parton. The songs I like to forget she ever did. Like, "Me and Little Andy." I mean, what the hell with that song, Dolly? It's about a little girl and her dog dying. Who even wants to hear that?

The front doorbell rings, interrupting my inner rant. I smile into my comforter. I couldn't answer it even if I wanted to.

It rings again. My mother must not be home. And again and again.

I push myself off my bed and take my time going down the stairs. Standing on my toes, I look through the peephole. *Sigh.* I bang my head against the door.

"What do you want?" I yell.

"Let me in," says Hannah. "Come on." She rings the doorbell over and over again. Nine, maybe ten times.

"Come around back," I finally yell.

She doesn't even ask why.

I stand with the back door open, and she brushes right past me. Riot sniffs her out for a second before running off.

"I've called you, like, eighty-five times this weekend," says Hannah. "I don't even like talking on the phone." She hands me a Tupperware full of stew. "My mom wanted me to bring you some of her sancocho."

"Your mom?" I open the fridge and wedge the container between a carton of milk and a jug of orange juice. "I've never even met your mom."

"Well, you're like her favorite person ever because of this stupid pageant, so I hope you're pleased with yourself." She plops down into my mom's seat at the kitchen table. Hannah's the type of person who can be comfortable in anyone's home, I think. There's none of that extra care most people have when they're in a new place for the first time. She leans forward on the table with both elbows. "You can't quit the pag— Wait, are you listening to Dolly Parton?"

I shrug.

She glances up at me, and takes note of my current state. "There is so much wrong with this picture."

I pour a cold cup of coffee and pop it in the microwave. "I guess if by wrong, you mean right, then yeah."

"When's the last time you showered?"

The microwave dings. "Showers are so subjective." I shrug. "Let's go upstairs."

"Only if you turn off that horrible music."

Upstairs, I pick the needle up from the record as Hannah spreads out on my bed. She takes the Magic 8 Ball from my nightstand and shakes it. "Has Will lost her shit totally?" She reads the answer. "You may rely on it."

I sit down at the foot of the bed and lay across the length of it on my back. Maybe this will be easier if I can stare at the ceiling the whole time.

"Okay, so something happened with Bathroom Boy, I'm guessing?"

"Boys. There were two. And I don't

even know why I wanted to do this in the first place." I stretch my arms out and let them hang off the edge of the bed. "Maybe I thought I deserved all the same things all those other girls do. I don't know? But I'm different from other girls, and even if I do deserve the same things they do, that doesn't mean I'll get them. Me getting up there and competing against them would only prove that."

"Nope," says Hannah. "I call bullshit. You don't deserve to win anything or be in any pageant until you make the effort and do the work. Maybe fat girls or girls with limps or girls with big teeth don't usually win beauty pageants. Maybe that's not the norm. But the only way to change that is to be present. We can't expect the same things these other girls do until we demand it. Because no one's lining up to give us shit, Will."

"That's easy for you to say. I walk into a room and the first thing anyone notices is how fucking huge I am in comparison. But for you, all you have to do is keep your mouth shut, and no one knows the difference."

"Whoa," she says. "Low blow. Yeah, I

can keep my mouth shut. Until I have something to say. You try being the half Dominican lesbian with buckteeth in this town, okay?"

I shake my head. "I'm sorry. I'm a mess and —"

"And you're projecting whatever. This is still bullshit. If you're not going to do this for you, do it for Amanda and Millie." She chews her lip and stares past me into the mirror in front of my bed. "And me too, I guess."

"You guys'll be fine without me."

"No, actually, we won't. Millie can't compete unless you do."

I sit up. "What are you talking about?"

"Her parents found out about the pageant," she says with nonchalance. "Millie begged and begged. She told them about how your mom runs the thing, so they said if you were competing, then so could she." She pauses for effect. "Then you dropped out."

Guilt settles in my chest. I lick my chapped lips. Slowly, I'm becoming aware of how gross I feel after going the whole weekend without a shower. "Listen, that sucks really bad, but —"

"But what? Please tell me you're not that selfish."

She's right. This isn't a joke for Millie. This is about idolizing and studying these pageant contestants her whole life, and finally allowing herself to be one. My leg bounces up and down as I think. I don't know that this would earn me any good karma. I might be too much in the negative for that, but I owe this to Millie. If I'm not going to go out there and grab life by the balls like she is, I should at least offer the courtesy of not standing in her way.

Hannah reaches over to my leg, stilling me.

I turn to her. "This is going to be a total disaster," I tell her.

She smiles with her mouth barely open. "I'm kind of counting on it."

FIFTY-FIVE

Boys get out of school to travel to football games, so I guess it shouldn't be that much of a surprise that every contestant is given the Friday before the pageant off from school. The extra day is spent in interviews and grueling dress rehearsals. We're talking blisters, double-stick tape, and tears all over the place. This isn't some low-budget high-school musical. This is Clover City's Miss Teen Blue Bonnet Pageant.

Last night, Hannah drove me to the community theater where my mom was setting up so that I could have my entire wardrobe approved. Seeing as I couldn't wear my formal, I had to go for a sequined black mother-of-the-bride looking thing I found in one of Mom's donation piles in Lucy's room. It was wrinkled, but new with tags. My mom, Mallory Buckley, and Mrs. Clawson all made me promise to steam it before Saturday. As for a swimsuit, my options were limited to my black one-piece and the red and white polka dot one I bought last summer but hadn't had the balls to wear. I chose the red. Go big or go home. Plus the black swimsuit has little lint balls all over the butt.

My talent costume was another thing. I dug through my room until I found the flapper headband I'd worn on Halloween. I had the black dress from Lucy's funeral, and my mom agreed to lend me her black satin gloves if I returned them before she had to wear them for the formal wear segment.

On Thursday morning, as I'm getting ready, Mom comes in to see what I'm wearing for my interview. "I like that skirt," she says. "But maybe add the teal blazer I got you for your birthday." I look in the mirror, considering her suggestion, and nod.

We drive to the Silver Dollar Banquet Hall where the interviews and luncheon will take place today. The air-conditioning buzzes above the twang of the radio. With Thanksgiving next week, it's getting pretty cool, but Mom's got the air blastin' because she's got the "flashes."

We park and she wriggles into her dusty-rose suit jacket. "Dumplin', I love you. And I'm hoping you'll make me proud."

My stomach does somersaults. I don't want to embarrass her. I really don't.

"But," she adds, "I can't have anyone thinking I'm giving you special treatment, so we're all business until Saturday night after the pageant."

"Right," I mutter. "All business."

Okay, so this place really is all business. They've got us contestants lined up outside of the banquet hall. No one is allowed to talk to each other until after the interviews are completed, which really makes no sense because this doesn't strike me as the type of thing you could cheat on. I mean, they pull questions from one huge list, and no one gets the same combination.

After the interviews is the luncheon, and after that is when contestants are allowed to set up their dressing room spaces. And that's when shit really starts to get real. Tomorrow is dress rehearsals; Saturday morning is reserved for a light run-through before the show, which starts promptly at seven p.m.

All of us look so ridiculous. Like, we're here for a job interview and the one requirement is that you wear one of your mom's polyester suits.

I watch as girls with last names starting with A, B, and C file in and out of their interview. Some come out with broad smiles. A few are shell-shocked. And a handful in tears. It sounds horrible, I know, but a small part of me sees the girls in tears as eliminated competition. I don't even want to win, but I think there's this survival instinct inside all of us that clicks on when we see other people failing. It makes me feel gross and incredibly human.

Since we're in alphabetical order, Ellen and I — Dickson and Dryver — are sitting right next to each other. Every time our shoulders so much as touch, she moves an obnoxious distance away from me, like she's been electrocuted.

"Dickson? Willowdean Dickson?"

I startle a little, and instinctively look to El. Our eyes meet for a second, and I see a slow smile linger on her lips before she catches herself and glances away.

I am going to bomb.

Mallory holds the door open for me. "Remember," she whispers. "You never get a second chance at a first impression."

"Well, that's encouraging," I murmur.

The four judges — who until now were anonymous — sit in a row at the front of the room behind a long buffet table.

They each introduce themselves. But I know exactly who they are.

Tabitha Herrera — owner of not one, but two beauty shops in Clover City: Tabitha's and the cleverly titled Tabitha's #2. Tabitha does everything from highlights to perms. She's the type of hairdresser with mind-control abilities. You can sit down in her chair and swear that you came for bangs, but leave with a bob. And because it's part of her charm, Tabitha lets you think the whole thing was your idea. She's got huge boobs and the hair to match. When people up north think of Texas, it's Tabitha they think of.

Dr. Mendez — I know little about him except that he's the only orthodontist in town. He's from Philadelphia or Boston or one of those places where people are always yelling, and he always looks a little jarred by everything. I mean, I guess if I move to this small-ass town from Philadoston, I'd be a little on edge, too.

Burgundy McCall — I shit you not. That is her real name. No, she is not a porn star or the leading lady of a soap opera. Her parents are Texas A&M graduates (technically, their colors are maroon and white, but I guess "Burgundy" had a better ring to it), and she's a Miss Teen Blue Bonnet turned kindergarten teacher. She made it all the way to the statewide Miss Teen Blue Bonnet Pageant, and came in as second runner-up. My mom — who only ever competed in the local pageant because she had me — has never outright said she resents Burgundy, but whenever she says her name, it sounds like she's eaten something too hot and is about to spit it out.

Clay Dooley — Clay Dooley Ford. He is probably the richest person in Clover City. His hair is always perfectly coiffed and his jeans are a smidge tighter than a tourniquet. His belt buckles are huge and gold and probably cost more than our mortgage. Clay Dooley is all Texas. He is the stereotype Dr. Mendez's Bostadelphian parents warned him about. He's so rich, in fact, that he has time to judge stuff like this because he doesn't make the money. He has people to do that for him.

I sit down in front of them, and no one looks up except Dr. Mendez. The other three shuffle papers back and forth and murmur something about the previous contestant dodging questions.

Burgundy finally glances up and upon seeing me, one of her perfectly groomed eyebrows raises. Clay and Tabitha both have the same kind of reactions, but are more successful at masking them. It is then that I realize that I am the first of the . . . I'll call us the unlikely suspects.

I think of all the good advice I've ever gotten in my life. Most of it is from Lucy.

But nothing clicks. Nothing prepares me for this moment. So I channel my mother. If my mother were standing here in this room right now, what would she say? If she weren't running this whole show, and she was just my mom, what would she tell me to do?

Smile, she would say. *And don't you dare sigh.*

I smile. So hard my cheeks hurt. And I do my best not to sigh.

"Willowdean Dickson?" asks Tabitha.

I nod. I smile. I. Don't. Stop. Smiling.

"Dickson," says Burgundy. "You're not Rosie's daughter, are you?"

"Yes," I say. I hear my mother: *manners.* "Ma'am," I add. "Yes, ma'am."

Clay clears his throat. "Okay, let's get this show rollin'. Willowdean," he says, holding up a crisp dollar bill. "If I were to give you this dollar, what would you do with it?"

This is a trick question. Still smiling. A dollar. What could I do with his dollar? Okay, I could give it to a homeless guy. I could buy a donut. Yes, sir, please, I would love to buy a donut with your dollar.

No, no. I've got to think bigger. Charity feels too obvious. "I would go to the dollar store and buy a box of pencils. Then on the morning of the SATs, I would roam the halls, selling them to the slackers — I mean, the students who forgot their pencils. For three bucks apiece."

It's quiet for a moment, and then Clay lets out a hoot of laughter.

Beside him, Burgundy purses her lips. "And what would you do with the money?"

"Buy more pencils," I say. She begins to scratch something down on her score sheet. "And then, once I had a nice chunk, I'd donate it to charity. Or use it to buy a holiday meal for a family in need." Creativity? Check. Savvy? Check. Selflessness? Check.

Tabitha smiles to herself, and I think maybe she even winks at me.

Once the judges finish writing down their comments, Tabitha looks up. "We have one other question for you. Define loyalty."

The adrenaline is sucked from my body like a vacuum. I am not smiling. "Loyalty." I take my time with each letter, trying to stretch out how long I have before I've got to give an answer. "Loyalty is . . . loyalty is being there for someone. It's selfless. It's about standing by someone's side even when you don't want to." Ellen. All I see is Ellen. "Because you love them."

That night when we lay in her bed, talking about the first time she had sex. It was so hard. I felt like there were nails in my stomach, but I stayed there with her. I listened to every detail because that's what you do for your best friend. I can feel her out in that hallway, thinking of me. For as angry as she is with me, I know she's sitting out there wondering how I'm doing in front of these judges.

"Loyalty isn't blind." Even when I wish it was. "Loyalty is telling someone they're wrong when no one else will." It embarrasses me to know that I told El she couldn't enter the pageant. Like us competing alongside each other would somehow ruin the point I was trying to make. When, really, with her, I am only stronger. I am the best possible me.

I think that my whole world has cracked into all these little pieces, and the only way I can go about fixing it is one shard at a time. For me, the first piece is always Ellen.

FIFTY-SIX

They serve us barbecue for lunch. I think that maybe lunch is some secret component of our final score because there is no higher achievement for a southern woman than the ability to eat barbecue and walk away stain free. After lunch we all have to sit through a keynote from Ruth Perkins, a seventy-eight-year-old former Miss Teen Blue Bonnet, who decides not to use the microphone because it gives her feedback in her hearing aid. Which means we're all left smiling and nodding as she talks at a secret-telling level of volume.

After a while, there's this awkward moment where she's waiting for applause and none of us can tell if she's done talking. We eventually clap and Mrs. Clawson takes the stage to thank her and offer her a bouquet of flowers.

"All right, ladies," she says into the mic. "None of you can leave until you've had your picture made for the paper. There are chairs along the wall, so sit in the same alphabetical order you were in today. You've got five minutes to touch up your faces."

I turn to Hannah, who sits next to me, and bare my teeth. "Anything in my teeth?" I ask.

She shakes her head. "Me?"

"Nope."

We part ways and go to our respective chairs as everyone else storms the bathrooms. I wait for El to sit down beside me. I can't make my brain concentrate on what I might say, but I'm going to talk to her. I have to.

She plops down in the chair next to me, and licks her thumb as she tries to rub off a barbecue stain on the lapel of her blazer.

"I bet they can take it so the stain's out of frame," I say. "Or Photoshop it."

She keeps on with the stain, diligently

making it worse and worse, but says nothing.

They begin to call us one by one and we scoot up a chair each time they do.

With two girls ahead of me, I say, "I don't want us to be mad at each other anymore."

I wait for her response. We move up a seat.

"I was wrong." We move up one more seat. "I was really wrong, and I can't do this anymore. I can't not talk to you every day. Please don't be angry with me."

"Willowdean?" calls Mallory.

I glance back to Ellen before standing up. She'll crack soon. She has to.

"Willowdean?"

"It's not that easy." El's voice scratches, like she hasn't spoken in days. "We're turning into different people."

"That doesn't mean we're not good for each other." I think the parts of me that are built on memories made with Ellen are some of my favorite parts of myself. "I'm sorry," I tell her. "I was stubborn."

I sit down on the small stool in front of

the backdrop. My mom stands behind the photographer. She motions with both her pointer fingers like she's pulling a smile across her face.

I pull in one deep breath and beg myself to smile. Smile. Smile. Smile.

Ellen sits there against the wall, still rubbing her barbecue stain in circles.

I don't smile.

After photos, we're released to set up our backstage dressing areas. The community theater downtown was designed with the pageant in mind, which means the women's dressing room is four times the size of the men's.

Each seat is labeled. I find my name on a piece of paper taped to a small stretch of mirror. Except over my name in black marker in all caps is DUMPLIN'. Scrawled in a hurry like someone had to say my name and couldn't resist. I look right and then left to see if I can spot the culprit.

Ellen plops all her stuff down next to mine. I see her name taped to the mirror. We're in alphabetical order again.

In the reflection, her gaze catches mine. She digs through her purse for a minute before coming up with a pen. Stretching over me, she reaches for the paper with my name on it. I watch as she scribbles my name sans *Dumplin'* on the back, tears the piece of tape off and reapplies it before sticking the sign back on the mirror.

"Thanks," I say.

She sits down on the stool next to me. "It's just a word. Doesn't mean anything unless you let it." She turns to me. Her eyes don't quite meet mine. "But if it hurts you, it hurts me."

My whole body relaxes, but my chin trembles. "I'm so sorry."

"I'm sorry," she says.

I shake my head. "No. No, I am."

She looks up then, notices my quivering chin, and takes my hand.

The room begins to swell as more girls file in.

"Come on," she says.

I follow her, and she holds my hand and leads me to a beat-up leather love seat a few feet from the stage manager's desk.

We sink into the sofa and without making a big deal of it, El swings her legs over mine. "Okay, talk."

"Okay. I got mad at you for entering the pageant. And then you got mad at me for being mad at you. And then I stayed mad at you. And then you stayed mad at me." I shake my head. "I know this was a long time coming. We've been drifting."

She nods. "It scares me. I don't want to feel apart from you. But maybe we're not supposed to do everything together? Maybe we're supposed to have some space."

"It's hard to accept." I look for all the right words. "I want to see you be happy. And make new friends. Even if they're people like Callie. I want to not be jealous of you." I've never said it out loud. I think I've even been scared to let myself think it, but I know it's true the second it leaves my mouth. "I don't mean jealous in a weird stalkery way, but sometimes I think our lives are moving at different speeds and it's hard not to feel like you're gonna lap me."

She laughs, and it sounds like a hiccup. "I'm not lapping you anytime soon. And if this is about sex . . . I love Tim, okay? But know that there's been a learning curve." Her shoulders bounce as she adds, "Maybe I'm jealous of you sometimes, too. You don't care about people like Callie or any of the girls I work with. But I need them to like me. It's the kind of thing that keeps me up at night. I don't even think they're that cool. My mind keeps this kind of tally of how many people like me and I care. I don't want to."

I smile, and the knot in my chest unwinds a little. "You're my best friend. Even over these last two months, it's always been you. And you never treat me any different. Not like other people do sometimes. And I know I'm good at being who I am. I'm good at saying, 'This is me. Back me up or back the fuck out.' Ya know? But —" Oh Christ. There's so much I haven't told her. I start at the beginning. "But I met a boy over the summer. Bo. Private School Boy. At work. And we kissed."

490

"You didn't tell me?" She smacks my arm. "The hell, Will?"

I shake my head. "I know. I'm sorry. But we kissed some more. And then it just kept going."

"Oh my God. You had sex with him. Was it amazing? I'm still mad at you for not telling me."

I laugh. "No. No. We didn't. Have sex. But I liked the way being with him made me feel." My head feels like a spool of thread unwinding. "But then . . . did you ever get freaked out when Tim would touch you? Like, at first?"

She drops her head against my shoulder. "Shit. Yeah, I did. He'd touch my waist or a spot of acne on my chin or something and I'd clam up like a total psycho."

The warm relief of recognition spreads through me. "That's what happened when Bo touched me. Like, I felt straight-up drunk when we would kiss. But then he'd touch my backfat or my hips and I would totally shut down."

"I can't believe you hid this from me." Her voice is soft. "I should be so pissed at you."

"I know, I know. I'm sorry. But, like, all of this was happening, right? And you'd told me that you and Tim were going to start having sex, and it made me feel like I might explode. It wasn't all jealousy. It was more that I felt young and inexperienced. And I couldn't — and kind of still can't — imagine myself letting someone else see me like that."

"Oh, Will."

"And that pissed me off. It was like I was losing you. But I felt so gross about myself at the same time. It all made me so mad because I didn't want to be one of those girls who felt bad about themselves because of some guy."

She sits up and I lay my head in her lap as she pulls her fingers through my hair. I tell her about every little thing. About Bo at the mall, and how he didn't tell me he was changing schools. And Mitch. And the dance. Halloween. Going back to Harpy's. Bo. I tell her all about Bo. And how she'd like him so much. And how he wants to be my boyfriend.

"He wants to put this label on us," I tell her. "And you know we won't even

492

make it one day at school without being ridiculed. He doesn't get that."

"Listen," she says. "Lots of people are assholes, okay? I won't lie to you there, but look at Tim and me. He's way shorter than me. You think people don't laugh at us? They do."

It's true, but until this moment, it's not anything I've even heard El mention.

"But you don't always get to choose who your heart wants. And even if we always did get to choose, I'd choose Tim. I'd choose him every time. So you gotta think: a relationship is between two people. All those assholes at school are bored spectators. You and Bo behind the Dumpster at Harpy's. That was y'all's hearts talking. But you and Bo dating. Being exclusive. That's your head. Your heart is all in, but that doesn't mean you don't get to choose. From what it sounds like, he's already made his choice."

It's so easy, I think, to say so in my head. Even out loud. But doing. Taking his hand and saying *I deserve this. We deserve this.* That's terrifying. "I was scared y'all broke up," I say. "You and Tim. I saw you crying in the hall the other day."

Her hand stops for a minute. She sniffs. "My parents are fighting again. My dad went and spent the night on Uncle Jared's couch. He's back. But I don't know. This feels like it might be it."

"God. El, I am so sorry."

"I wanted to tell you so bad. But I was being stubborn. And dumb."

"No, I should've gone up to you when I saw you there."

"It's okay," she says. "This isn't the first time. Some things just can't be fixed. Not forever."

The thought makes my heart flinch. I sit up and we stay put for a little while, entwined like a set of cats.

FIFTY-SEVEN

I end up hanging out with Ellen and Tim for the rest of the afternoon. As we drive up to my house, I see that Bo's truck is parked out front. "Um, is that who I think it is?" asks El.

He stands outside my front door with a huge metal toolbox at his feet.

Tim pulls into my driveway, and El hops out so I can drag myself out of the backseat of the Jeep.

I walk across the yard, and can feel Ellen at my heels. I turn abruptly. "What are you doing?" I ask her.

"I want to see this."

"No. Nope. You're going home."

"Call me," she says. "DO. NOT. FORGET."

"Okay."

She hugs me, and I hold on for a second too long, hoping that part of her will seep into my skin.

I wait for Tim to pull away before I take the last few steps to Bo. "Is this a home invasion or something?"

He whips around like he hadn't heard Tim drop me off. A brown leather tool belt hangs low on his waist. "I swear this isn't as creepy as it looks."

"It looks pretty creepy."

His smile is steady, yet nervous. "I was out with my dad, helping him with a few jobs when we ran into your mom at the gas station. I guess they went on a few dates in high school."

I laugh. "So not surprised."

"She mentioned your front door again, and my dad . . . well, actually, I volunteered to come fix it. I hope that's not weird."

I sit down on the stoop and he does the same. "Kinda weird."

Unspoken words that I don't know how to say weigh against my chest. "Did you get it fixed?"

"It was a really easy fix actually. I kind

of can't believe you guys left it like that for so long."

I pull my knees into my chest. "You don't have to answer a broken front door."

He reaches back behind me and turns the knob. The door swings wide open. "No excuse now."

"Yeah." I point to his neck. "What's up with the necklace?"

He pulls the chain out from under his T-shirt to reveal a small medallion. "Saint Anthony," he says. "Supposed to help you find lost things."

"What are you looking for?"

"I don't know." He tucks the necklace back behind his collar. "I think maybe I found it. But then some days I think it found me."

I nod. There's some kind of peace that comes with knowing that for every person who is waiting to be found, there's someone out there searching.

"Willowdean?"

"Yeah?"

He stands and reaches for his toolbox. "You look like an insurance adjuster."

FIFTY-EIGHT

I wake up to find that Mom has slid a copy of the paper beneath my door. I unfold it and find my face there, right in the middle of the crease. The headline reads: CLOVER CITY'S MISS TEEN BLUE BONNET: PUTTING NAMES WITH FACES. The entire front page is tiled with our head shots from the previous day. Beneath our pictures are our names, ages, favorite foods, and our definitions of Clover City in one word.

I'm guessing my mom wasn't given a first look at this before it went to print. But, either way, there I am. My not-smiling face.

At rehearsal, we all sit in the auditorium for a long time while waiting for the lighting to be perfected. Miranda Solomon, God's gift to Clover City community theater, turns around in her seat and explains to me, El, Hannah, Amanda, and Millie that half of final rehearsals is always spent sitting around, waiting for the techies to get it right. She shrugs. "That's the biz."

When she stands to go to the bathroom, El turns to me with her shoulders hunched up and her voice high. "That's the biz."

Callie sits a few rows behind us with another girl I recognize from Sweet 16. I'm actively trying not to look smug, but it's not easy.

Other than that, things are alarmingly quiet. Pageants are the perfect recipe for drama. You have to look perfect. You have to be perfect. And on top of being perfect, you have to be the best at being perfect. The nerves here are almost palpable. Especially Millie's. She bounces her legs so hard that I can feel the vibrations three seats down.

Ellen turns into me. "So are you really doing those magic tricks? I love you, but those were pretty sketch."

"Well, it's not like I really have an option now."

"I don't know," she says. "I guess if you cared about getting DQ'd, you don't."

The thought of doing something completely different hadn't even occurred to me. "I don't even really have anything I *could* do."

She sits for a minute, lost in thought, as she chews on her hair. Then she gasps, and whispers in my ear. It only takes three words for the idea to take me. She leans back, waiting for my response.

I can picture it so perfectly. There's so no way I'm winning this thing, so I might as well go out in a blaze of glory. "I could even —"

"Millie Ranea Michalchuk!" a voice from the back of the theater crows.

The vibrations I've felt for the last half hour stop as Millie's entire body freezes.

I crane my neck to see her mom storming at the top of the aisle. Her dad isn't far behind.

I whip around and elbow Hannah in the gut. "What is going on?" I whisper-yell at her.

Millie squeezes past each of us to meet her mom in the aisle. She holds her chin out straight, inhaling and exhaling measured breaths.

It takes a second for Hannah's eyes to adjust. "Oh," she says, and sort of laughs into her fist.

"Oh *what*?"

"I lied," she says. "I definitely lied."

Everyone's watching now. Including the tech guys.

"Are you kidding me?" I ask.

"Millicent," says Mrs. Michalchuk. "You lied to us. To our faces." Tears brim at the edges of her eyes, and it becomes very obvious that she is not wearing waterproof mascara. Millie's dad settles behind his wife, his arms crossed. "You went behind our backs after we decided not to sign the release form. Why — why would you do that?"

"Is this true?" My mom stands onstage with a clipboard tucked beneath her arm.

With her fists curled at her sides, Millie turns to my mom and says, "I forged my mother's signature." Her face crumbles for a second like she might cry. She looks back to her parents. "But you were wrong." Her voice softens. "I know you

want to protect me. I know that. But —
but sometimes I just need you to support
me."

My mom frowns. "Let's take this out
into the foyer."

I watch as Millie makes the trek up the
aisle with my mother close behind her.
Standing up, I climb over El's long legs.

"Where are you going?" she asks.

"I have to help her," I say.

I jog up the aisle and push the door
open wide enough for the entire auditorium to hear my mother say, "I'm sorry,
but we cannot allow you to compete
without parental consent."

The door swings shut behind me. "Millie has to compete." Millie's parents turn.
"She's worked so hard," I tell them. "And
she's not fragile. She isn't. She's got this
thick skin you don't even expect. Everyone in this room, even the girls with the
long legs and the silky hair, knows what
it is to be teased. Millie and I know.
Amanda and Hannah. Ellen." I motion
to my mom. "Even my mom knows. But
we can't walk around scared all the time.
That's no way to do things."

Millie reaches for my hand and squeezes tight. "I really want this," she says. "I've dreamed of being in this pageant for as long as I can remember. There's nothing in the rules that says fatties need not apply." Her mother flinches at the word, and discreetly wipes away a tear. "The only thing keeping me from this, Mom, is you."

Mrs. Michalchuk looks to the huge pageant banner hanging above the auditorium doors and then to my mom, who offers a faint grin. Her husband takes her hand. She turns to Millie and nods.

Side by side, we walk back into the auditorium where all the other girls have so obviously been eavesdropping. A few contestants turn to give Millie smiles of encouragement as we take our seats. Ellen takes my hand, and then Millie's, who then laces her fingers with Amanda's. I turn to my other side to face Hannah, palm up. She takes a deep breath before taking my hand.

A bond bigger than any crown pulses through the five of us, and, for the first time since the start of this pageant, I know it's me who has the upper hand.

■ ■ ■ ■

When we finally do rehearse, it's a mess. None of us do our talents. There isn't time. Callie slips on the ramp during the opening number. All our cues are off. There are spills. And tears. And even some blood. In the end, it is exactly what I expected.

At home, my mom is sunk deep into the couch with a bottle of cheap champagne just like she is every year. At this point, there's nothing left to be done, and if there is anything, it's too late to make the effort. All she can do is *let the glitter fall where it may.* (Her words, not mine.)

I sit at the kitchen table with a huge cardboard box, a few bottles of craft paint, and scissors. Somehow I've got to create a prop for the opening number.

I've barely given any thought to my assigned landmark, Cadillac Ranch, since that day at dance rehearsal. Normally I'd just blow off this kind of thing as dumb pageant fluff, but it's actually kinda cool. Sure, Texas has all the famous landmarks that everyone's heard of, but we have all these unknown gems, too. Like, the

Marfa lights or Jacob's Well or Dinosaur Valley or even the Prada sculpture a few hours from here. I guess Cadillac Ranch falls into that oddball category. It's so perfectly Texas, and yet, completely beyond the stereotype.

Cadillac Ranch is this public art installation up in Amarillo. All these old Caddies are half buried nose first in a row off the side of the highway. Their paint jobs have long since faded, and visitors are encouraged to spray paint the cars. So, yeah. I have no idea how to make a decent prop that says "I am so obviously Cadillac Ranch."

My mom wanders in for some ice — yes, she drinks her champagne with ice. "Is this for some school project? You've got to get some beauty sleep tonight, Dumplin'."

She's going to kill me for not having done this sooner. "It's for my, uh, opening number prop."

She sits down beside me. "Oh dear."

I nod.

"Okay," she says. "Okay, we can do this." She glances at the paper with my assignment. "Cadillac Ranch." I watch as she stands and grabs a plastic tumbler from the cabinet. She pours a few sips of champagne and hands it to me.

I take the cup, but say nothing. I don't want her to change her mind for some reason.

"You think your waist can fit in that box?"

I eye it for a second, and take a sip of champagne. It bubbles in my chest. "Yeah."

"Run out to the garage for me and grab a spool of that wide elastic, the glue gun, and my box of spray paints."

I come back with the requested items, and she's already at work on the box, slicing through it with an X-ACTO knife. "Dumplin', you're going to have the best damn prop in that opening number."

My whole body buzzes with satisfaction as I take another sip.

A few hours and one bottle of champagne later, I say, "Mom?"

"Yeah, Dumplin'?"

"That was good of you to let Millie

compete. Even though she lied."

She finishes off her glass. "She's a good girl. A sweet one. With a good smile."

I wait for her to say something about her size, and how she's at a disadvantage, but she only opens another bottle.

We paint a white base coat in silence, and when it's almost dry, something cool splats against my cheek. I drag my finger against my skin. Paint. "Oh no, you didn't," I say, and flick what's on my fingers onto her nose.

We laugh. Hysterically. Like, the kind of laughing you can't stop. The kind that hurts. I think I'm drunk. I know my mom is. But I feel good, and who needs beauty sleep when you've got champagne?

When we're finally done at one in the morning, we leave the kitchen with the table covered in randomly spray painted newspaper pages, and stray pieces of cardboard. Riot hops up onto the table and sniffs out our finished project. His tail whips and licks against our little cardboard Cadillac covered in spray paint.

I try it on. It sits suspended from my

shoulders with elastic and hangs right around my waist. It's so damn ridiculous. It's so damn perfect.

Before we go to bed, I open the front door. The street is quiet and dark. Standing here from this exact vantage point, my entire house feels new with possibilities.

My mom flicks the hallway light off behind me. I close the door and lock the dead bolt.

In bed, I text Ellen a list of all the things I'll need for my talent tomorrow.

MAGNIFICENT, she replies.

The champagne still streaming through my veins lulls me to sleep. Magnificent indeed.

FIFTY-NINE

ELLEN: It is the day of the show, y'all. IT IS THE DAY OF THE SHOW.

El's text message is the first thing to make me smile. But I wake up with this bout of uncertainty. Did last night really happen? I look down at my hands and see the speckled flakes of dry paint there.

We have a few hours before we have to leave, so I take my time scrubbing my whole body and pushing bobby pins into my hair until I've fashioned some sort of updo with my bangs swept across my forehead. Carefully, I paint my nails a deep purple.

I open my closet to make sure there's nothing else I need. Hanging there front and center is the red dress my mom bought me. I push the plastic cover up and hold the dress out by its hem, studying the sheen of the fabric.

My mom knocks on my door before letting herself in.

I slam the closet door shut.

She's all made up, ready to play glamorous hostess for a day. "Time to go. I'll be in the car," she says. Her head tilts to the side. "Your hair. It looks good." She closes the door before I can say thank you.

Perching on the edge of my bed for a moment, I reach for the Magic 8 Ball and shake it hard.

It is decidedly so.

I open the closet door.

The dressing room is a haze of hair spray. Like, seriously, I have to breathe through my nose or risk swallowing fumes. The counters are full with makeup, flowers, teddy bears, Vaseline, and energy drinks.

Girls run through their talents. Singing to themselves as they apply lipstick. Counting out their dance routines as they spray their hair. Reciting monologues as they coat their lashes with mascara.

I barely even have time to absorb anything. I spot Millie toward the back of the dressing room. Her hair. It is huge. Huge enough to have its own solar system. Seriously, she's got at least an extra five inches on her, not including heels. She smiles and waves.

Sitting in front of my mirror is a small bouquet of sunflowers wrapped in tissue paper and twine, a single red rose, and a bottle of sparkling cider.

I reach for the card stuffed inside the bouquet first.

Break a leg! — Bo & Loraine.

And stuck to the stem of the rose is a Post-it note that reads:

xoxo Mom

Lastly, I open the envelope taped to the bottle of cider.

I wanted to get you the real stuff, but Dale said no. Party pooper. Knock 'em dead. Love, Lee (& Dale)

I wish Lucy were here. Not to see me compete, but to see *this.* Because this moment feels as much hers as it is mine.

I've only put on my makeup when Mrs. Clawson swings the door open and calls,

"Ten minutes, ladies!"

Ellen sits down next to me, her phone in her hand. Two perfect circles color each of her cheeks and her too-bright lipstick is smeared across her front tooth. "Tim," she says. "That fucker has food poisoning. Will, I don't have an escort."

The whole pageant seemed like such a lost cause that it didn't even occur to me to be concerned by the fact that I didn't have an escort. I shake my head. "I don't have one either."

She's breathing too quickly. I forgot how anxious stuff like this makes her.

"Okay," I tell her. "Listen, don't worry about the escorts, okay?" And then lower, I add, "We can escort each other. That's how it should be anyway, right?"

She chews on her bottom lip for a moment before nodding.

"Five minutes!" calls Mrs. Clawson. "Time to line up, ladies."

If there's a God up there, I'm pretty sure she picked Ellen and me out from a lineup of embryos and said, *Them.* Dickson. Dryver. It could not be more perfect.

We stand backstage in alphabetical order, waiting for our cues. El got the Dallas Cowboys, so she's carrying a set of blue and silver pom-poms and wearing a matching cowboy hat. I've got my Cadillac on. Our hands are clasped so tight that they're drained of blood.

I try to make myself remember the dance we've rehearsed over and over again, but I can't seem to imagine it. My mind is a maze and I'm chasing a shadow.

Bekah Cotter passes El a tub of Vaseline. "Put it on your teeth and gums," she says. "Helps you smile."

We both glance at each other and shrug before dipping our fingers in and smearing the Vaseline across our smiles. It tastes disgusting.

"Thanks," I tell Bekah.

Mallory stands a few feet in front of us with a black headset on. "Go, go, go."

We rush out past her, and the minute the lights hit my skin, my memory comes back to me. We rotate in circles so that everyone has two and a half seconds to say their names.

The song finishes and the lights cut

out. I can't even process how quickly this is moving. It feels like life on triple fast forward, where everyone's voices sound like chipmunks.

Next is the swimwear competition.

It hadn't occurred to me that I would have no privacy when changing into my swimwear. But here we are, and privacy there is not. I strip down as strategically as I can, with my swimsuit half hiked up over my thighs and my skirt bunched up around my waist. For a moment, I allow myself a glance around the room. I find that I am the only person not minding my own damn business. I'm gonna be perfectly honest here and say that there are boobies everywhere and no one even cares.

I bite the bullet and rip off my shirt. After shimmying the rest of the way into my swimsuit, I tuck the red heart-shaped sunglasses Bo gave me all those months ago into my hair. I hadn't even thought twice about them until I was cleaning stuff out of my closet last week.

We file into the wings and Mrs. Clawson runs up and down the lines, spraying our asses with Aqua Net. "Can't have those swimsuits ridin' up," she says.

I watch as Ellen walks out onstage. She's freaking out on the inside, I know it. But she's all confidence in her green two-piece and espadrilles.

I know I shouldn't, but I glance down at my black sandals and my red suit stretched over my round belly. But that's not even the thing that bothers me.

Everyone has one thing they absolutely hate about themselves. I could be lame and say that I hate my whole body, but what it all comes down to is my thighs. Thunder thighs. Cottage cheese. Crater legs. Ham hocks. Mud flaps. Whatever you want to call them. My legs don't even look like legs. I'm pretty forgiving of the pudge, but in the rare moments spent in front of a mirror in nothing but my skin, all I see are two pillars of cellulite that carry me from place to place and rub together, creating one hellish case of chub rub. (Chub rub, by the way, is fat-girl talk for the most miserable inner thigh chafing of all time.)

Mrs. Clawson taps my shoulder, letting me know it's my turn.

I pull in a deep breath, and smile. *Smile,*

Dumplin', I hear my mother say.

I may be uncomfortable, but I refuse to be ashamed.

Maybe it's because I can't see the audience. Or maybe it's because no one is yelling for me to get off the stage, but my thighs survive their moment in the spotlight. I don't scurry away like I did that day at the pool. No one boos. The world doesn't end. The audience doesn't go blind.

There's something about swimsuits that make you think you've got to earn the right to wear them. And that's wrong. Really, the criteria is simple. Do you have a body? Put a swimsuit on it.

Amanda waits for me at the other end. "You looked super fine out there!"

I squeeze her arm. "Thanks. You ready for your soccer showcase?"

She nods. Her cheeks turn light pink. "I joined the soccer team," she says.

"Did you really?"

Amanda grins. "I figured if I could survive this, I could limp my way onto the soccer team."

"That's amazing," I tell Amanda as Ellen comes to stand beside us.

From the wings, we watch as Millie takes the stage in her skirted gingham swimsuit and matching wedges. She wears huge white sunglasses and bright red lipstick, and even carries a beach ball tucked beneath her arm.

"God," says Ellen. "She was born for this. There's a beauty queen in that cute, little fat girl."

A slow, satisfied smile melts across my face. "No," I say. "That cute, little fat girl is a beauty queen."

SIXTY

"Oh, sweet bastard damn!" My brain feels like it's been pushed through a food processor. "Do all wig caps hurt this bad?"

"This might be a size too small," says Ellen. "I don't know. I took whatever my mom had in her dressing room."

We've commandeered the one-stall backstage bathroom to prepare for my talent. Ellen's hair is divided into two braids and she's managed to squeeze into her clogging costume from seventh grade. (Though her mom had to sew an elastic band into the waist.) "Okay, okay." I breathe in through my nose, trying to ease some of the tension in my huge-ass head, and close my eyes. "Put the wig on."

Ellen tugs the blond wig on over my

head. "Okay," she says after pushing in the last bobby pin. "You're set. Take a look."

I lift my head. Staring back at me is Dolly Parton. A fat teenage Dolly Parton.

"Oh my God," says El. "I want to kiss your face."

I wait offstage. She's clogging a few beats behind the music and keeps rolling her eyes. If I weren't so nervous, I'd be laughing my ass off.

We were careful to sneak me around backstage so that no one saw me. Especially my mom, Mrs. Clawson, or Mallory.

El's music ends a few seconds before she's actually done clogging, but she finishes and curtsies before running offstage.

"Okay," she says. "You got this."

We paid the sound guy twenty bucks to go along with us. "Cool," he said. "Beer money."

My mom steps out from the wing closest to the audience on the other side of the stage. "That was lovely, Ellen. And what a workout I bet that is!" The audience rumbles with quiet laughter. "Next up we have Willowdean Dickson performing a few magic tricks for us."

Yeah, getting that wig cap over my head was a pretty impressive magic trick.

I walk out onstage into the spotlight, my boots clicking against the floor. My suede-fringed poncho-shaped shadow stretches out past the pool of light.

My mom stands at the edge of the stage with her microphone dangling from her fingers. Her eyes are wide and her body is wound with tension.

The music starts. It's those first couple chords that every person in this auditorium knows so well. I can see the judges whispering back and forth at their table with their desk lights glowing.

I turn back to my mom and hold the toy microphone to my lips. Dolly's voice sings "Jolene, Jolene, Jolene, Jolene, I'm begging of you, please don't take my man." I synch my lips to each word.

I close my eyes and see every moment I've heard this song. Driving down the highway with my mom, Lucy, and Gram. The windows down. All four of us dragging our hands through the wind. Sitting in Lucy's room with her as "Jolene" pipes out from her record player. Laying on the cool tiles of El's kitchen as her mom hums and makes spaghetti. At Lucy's funeral. In Bo's truck. At the Hideaway, watching Lee perform. Right here on this stage.

I sing "Jolene," and maybe it's my imagination, but I hear a few voices out in the audience singing it back to me. It's the kind of iconic song that is bigger than geography or languages or religion. *It's "Jolene."*

The song ends, and the audience applauds. For a second, I think I hear an *oink!,* but it is soon drowned out by the cheers.

The second I'm offstage, my mom yanks me by the arm. "What was that?" But she doesn't give me enough time to answer because she's already rushing out to announce the next contestant. "Well, wasn't that a surprise?" her voice rings.

I pass Callie on my way to the fitting room. "You know they're going to DQ you for not doing your approved talent, right?"

"It was worth it," I say without bothering to stop.

In the dressing room, I slump down beside Ellen. We've got some downtime while the talents finish up.

Hannah walks past me on her way out. She holds her hand up for a high five without saying a word.

After the talents wrap, there's an intermission before the formals. I help Ellen into her gown — a coral halter dress with rhinestones. She fluffs my hair back up after the wig cap had its way with me.

Mrs. Clawson peeks her head in and says, "So far so good, ladies! Ten minutes! And, Willowdean, your mother needs to speak with you."

Blush spreads to my cheeks. A few girls *ooooo* as I follow Mrs. Clawson to my mom's private dressing room.

I knock, and before I've pulled my fist away, my mom swings the door open.

She shakes her head. "I knew you had some trick up your sleeve."

"No, Mom, that wasn't it. I didn't plan

it or anything." Well, not until yesterday at least.

She holds her unzipped Miss Teen dress up around her chest. "You're disqualified," she says. "We can't let you finish the pageant. It wouldn't be fair."

"It's not like I'm going to win the thing," I tell her. "Why can't I just get up there and walk?"

"You broke the rules. It's the same standard I would hold anyone else to. I'm sorry, but this is as far as you get to go."

I know it's stupid. It is so dumb. But part of me is so torn up over the fact that I won't be finishing. After everything that's happened, and I'm less than an hour from completing this thing. I'm not surprised. I shouldn't be at least. I knew that what I was doing was a disqualifiable offense, but somehow I thought she might take mercy on me.

She turns around. "Zip me up, would you?"

The zipper doesn't strain nearly as much as it did the last time, but it's just not — "Mom, this is as far as I can get it," I say with finality. There's still a good four inches to go, and I can pull as hard as I want. But that zipper is not moving up any further. It's science.

She whips around and looks over her shoulder in the mirror. "That's not possible. No, no. I tried it on earlier this week. I've been doing my Pee-lates and spin classes." I think she's about to fall apart, and if my mother falls apart, so will this whole pageant.

"Okay," I tell her. "Listen, we're going to make this work."

"Two minutes!" calls Mrs. Clawson on the other side of the door.

Sweat prickles at my mom's temples.

"Stay here." I run. I haul *ass* through the backstage and to the woodshop where they make the sets.

Saws. Drills. Nails. Hammers. Screws. Stepladders. Wrenches. Pliers. I fill my arms with anything that looks like it might help.

When I race back into the dressing room, my mom is near hysterics. "Dumplin', I have to get myself into this dress. I've worn it every year since I won. People are expecting me in this dress.

It's tradition."

"Turn around." I drop everything on the counter.

"Everyone'll know." She's on the verge of sobbing.

"No," I tell her. "No. No crying. You are not fitting into this dress, okay? It's not going to happen."

She whimpers.

"But that doesn't mean we can't make it look like you do."

I grab two giant alligator clamps that I've seen the tech guys wearing on their shorts, kinda like hairdressers with their hair clips. They use 'em for oddball stuff, like holding back wires or keeping wood together while it's being glued.

"Listen, Mom. You can't turn around up there, okay? You gotta stay in one place."

She nods.

I slide a clamp behind her strapless bra and tuck the dress beneath it. I do the same with the other side.

Her breathing eases for a moment as she notices the difference in the mirror.

"See? It looks fine."

She takes a deep breath, and pushes her crown into her perfectly styled hair. "Okay, Dumplin'." She turns to me, her expression hesitant. "You hate that nickname, don't you?"

I smile. "Not as much as I used to."

"I can stop calling —"

"No," I tell her. "I think I've sort of embraced it." Sometimes figuring out who you are means understanding that we are a mosaic of experiences. I'm Dumplin'. And Will and Willowdean. I'm fat. I'm happy. I'm insecure. I'm bold.

"Curtain!" calls Mrs. Clawson.

Mom turns back to the mirror once more. "Thank you. Thank you. Thank you. I love you, Willowdean." She presses her red lips to my forehead. "My sweet Dumplin'." She races out the door, and as she announces the first few contestants and their escorts, I run to the dressing room.

Beneath the counter is my duffel bag, and rolled up inside of it is the red gown my mom bought me. I apply a second coat of lipstick and slip the dress on over my head. I step into my heels and pull the straps over the back of my foot. Trying to zip the dress as I go, I run to where Ellen is in line with Bekah Cotter ahead of her.

"Zip me," I breathe.

She does without hesitation. "You look amazing."

I smile, still trying to catch my breath. "I know."

"Ellen," says Mallory as she double-checks her clipboard. "Where is your escort?" She turns to me. "And Will, you've been dis—"

"I'm her escort."

"Ellen Dryver," my mother calls from onstage.

Mallory's eyes go wide as I loop Ellen's arm through mine and walk her across the stage.

"And escorting her is Timothy —"

We sashay down the ramp to the front of the stage. I walk with one foot perfectly in front of the other, like Lee taught us.

My mom's mouth hangs agape, but then curves into a faint smile. "And escorting her is Willowdean Dickson."

I let go of Ellen's arm to let her take a circle at the edge of the stage, and then we walk backstage again.

We watch together as everyone takes her turn. Amanda with her older brother. The laces in her clunky shoes match her dress — Millie's idea, of course. Malik is a perfect gentleman as he crosses the stage with Millie on his arm. And, of course, Hannah. Hannah with Courtney Gans. Courtney is one of those great names that could be a guy's name, but in the case of Hannah, it is not. Her escort, Courtney, who I'm guessing is from out of town because I've never seen her before, wears her blond hair slicked back into a neat bun. It complements her fitted tux nicely. And best of all, Hannah, in her black slip dress, combat boots, and no makeup, isn't breaking a single rule.

We all sashay, the toes of our heels leading our hips side to side, just like Lee taught us.

Hannah exits stage right where all of us wait for her. Courtney kisses her cheek before saying, "I'll meet you outside later."

Once Courtney's out of earshot, Ellen guffaws and slaps Hannah on the back. "You are the goddamn devil."

It's dark, so I can't be sure, but I'm nearly positive that Hannah blushes.

I stand on the sidelines, watching the rest of the pageant. I watch the Q&A session as some girls surprise me with almost profound answers, while others stumble over their words. Amanda tells a horrible knock-knock joke that has the judges rolling. Millie is cute and sweet with her infectious giggle. Hannah is dry as always, but leaves the audience deep in thought.

Donna Lufkin has left her gardening clogs at home. She wears a plum-colored pantsuit and waits in the wings across from me, guarding the crowns.

My mom stands there in her little spotlight, not moving, like she's got a stiff neck or something. She looks beautiful. And not just from the front. Even with all the hardware holding her dress together in the back, she is lovely.

This moment. It is the truest representation of my mom I have ever seen. I guess sometimes the perfection we perceive in others is made up of a whole bunch of tiny imperfections, because some days the damn dress just won't zip.

Sixty-One

I stick around long enough to hear that Millie — our little Millicent! — is second runner-up. She holds her bouquet of roses and gives the perfect beauty queen wave. I don't stay for the crowning of the winner. I don't need to.

As I'm walking out to the lobby with the bottle of sparkling cider from Lee and Dale clutched in my fist, I see Mitch standing around with a bunch of guys from the team. They won their game last week, so they're going to state on Thanksgiving Day.

It's Patrick Thomas who notices me first. "Back for more?" he asks. "Couldn't handle getting dumped?"

Mitch shakes his head, his expression resigned. "She's not the one who —"

I lift my hand to stop him. "No one

thinks you're funny, Patrick," I tell him. "Don't you get that? No one is laughing. Not even your friends."

Patrick frowns for a second then shrugs before turning back around.

Mitch nods once. I linger for a moment, offering a faint smile.

The audience inside the theater erupts with applause as I turn to leave.

I walk the three blocks in my dress and heels. I love this dress. I want to always look at it, hanging in my closet, and remember this night in November when I stepped into my own light. Wind pushes against me, sending the fabric in ripples as I move down the streets of my little town.

The bell rings above my head as I push the door open to find Harpy's busy with all ten people in Clover City who didn't attend the pageant.

"Whoa," says Marcus as he hands a customer their receipt. "Lookin' fresh, Will."

At the sound of my name, Bo rounds the corner with a red sucker dangling from his cherry-stained lips.

I set the sparkling cider down on the counter.

He pulls his apron down from around his neck so that it hangs from his waist. His lips split into a broad grin. "Willowdean," he says.

I sigh.

ACKNOWLEDGMENTS

I am so lucky. I get to wake up every day and do the job I love — one I believe in. I wouldn't be in this position today without the support and guidance of some pretty incredible people.

Alessandra Balzer, you are the type of editor writers dream of working with, and I am thankful every day that working with you has been my reality. Thank you for investing in Willowdean and for knowing what I meant to say before I quite knew how to say it.

Molly Jaffa, I actually think you would move a mountain for me if you could. Thank you for keeping the wheels of my life spinning, and for that extra push with this book when I was feeling a little desperate. You are my agent and my friend, and for both I am thankful.

Caroline Sun, you are the wizard behind the curtain. Thank you for everything you do.

The School & Library marketing crew (Patty Rosati and Molly Motch!), I am forever grateful to have you all on my team.

Aurora Parlagreco and Alison Donalty, I could not have asked for a more perfect cover. My love for your design is bigger than words. Ruiko Tokunaga, for making that cover perfectly tactile.

There are so many people at Balzer + Bray/HarperCollins/Epic Reads/HCC Frenzy to whom I owe a world of gratitude. Susan Katz, Kate Jackson, Andrea Pappenheimer, Kerry Moynagh, Heather Doss, Donna Bray, Kelsey Murphy, Nellie Kurtzman, Booki Vivat, Margot Wood, Alexei Esikoff, Suman Seewat, Aubry Parks-Fried, Jennifer Sheridan, Kathy Faber, and anyone else I might have missed (because I'm sure I have!), your kindness and faith in my work have been invaluable. I am so humbled to be working with such dedicated human beings.

Jessica Taylor, for always reading and letting me be my most bare, horrible self.

There will never be enough cupcakes.

Jeramey Kraatz, thank you for always being my partner in crime and for crossing state lines with me to see Dolly Parton — a day I will never forget.

Natalie Parker, I am of course grateful for your honesty and fairness, but most of all for your friendship and for always letting me tag along.

Corey Whaley, thank you for all the hours spent reading over Skype and for all the hours spent talking about everything and nothing at all.

Tessa Gratton, for pulling me out of the book-two black hole and for spending two weeks with me in a car and still loving me in the end.

Kristin Treviño (and everyone at Irving Public Library!), all that you do is incredible, and I am so thankful for every opportunity I've had to take part.

Jenny Martin, my hometown sweetheart. Thank you for always rooting for me.

Like Joe Cocker said, "I get by with a little help from my friends." Katie Cotugno, Adam Silvera, Bethany Hagen,

Jennifer Mathieu, Kristin Rae, Sarah Combs, Christa Desir, Michelle Krys, Amy Tintera, Kari Olson, Jen Bigheart, Caron Ervin, Preeti Chhibber, Stef Hoffman, Courtney Stevens, Ashley Meredith, John Stickney, Hayley Harris, Jeffrey Komaromi, and Asher Richardson. Every blogger, librarian, teacher, and reader. My Lone Star community, One-Four KidLit, #Luf kin6, the Fourteenery, and the Hanging Garden. Thank you all.

Mom, Dad, and Jill, thank you for always being my home and for believing in me and all my wild dreams.

Dolly Parton, for never apologizing for yourself and for every last song. Your music was the grease this book needed.

Ian, for loving me always.

The fat kids, the skinny kids, the tall ones, the short ones, and everybody in between: I am so thankful that not a single one of us is the exact same. What a boring world that would be.

ABOUT THE AUTHOR

Julie Murphy is the #1 *New York Times* bestselling author of *Dumplin', Puddin', Ramona Blue,* and *Side Effects May Vary.* She lives in North Texas with her husband who loves her, her dog who adores her, and her cats who tolerate her. When she's not writing, she can be found reading, traveling, or hunting down the perfect slice of pizza. Before writing full time, she held numerous jobs, such as wedding dress consultant, failed barista, and, ultimately, librarian. Learn more about her at www.juliemurphywrites .com.